Stone of Lust

by

Margaret Izard

Stones of Iona, Book Three

The Wild Rose Press, Inc.
PO Box 708
Adams Basin, NY 14410-0708
Visit us at www.thewildrosepress.com

Publishing History
First Edition, 2024
Trade Paperback ISBN 978-1-5092-5753-9
Digital ISBN 978-1-5092-5754-6

Stones of Iona, Book Three
Published in the United States of America

Dedication

To my husband for loving the fighter in me and encouraging me to pursue my dreams. To my kids, thank you for your continued support and for allowing me the time to chase a dream. You are my inspiration on hard days, as you are to many.

Chapter 1

The evil of man, why they are a surging, seething, murmuring crowd of beings that are human only in name, for to the eye and ear, they seem naught but savage creatures, animated by vile passions and by the lust of vengeance and hate.

It was what her da always said about the evil in men. He often spoke of it after he or her ma told her the Fae fable story about the Viking warrior, her favorite bedtime story. Her da, she missed him so. Thinking of him always brought her favorite memory up.

A young Ainslie held her wooden sword at her front, ready to combat any Viking foe. The blade was nearly as tall as her, but she kept it as her hands trembled. Standing in the yard at Dunstaffnage Castle, one of her family's three castles the MacDougalls owned, Ainslie was determined to learn to fight with a sword. She wanted to practice with her brother, but Colin never allowed her to join, saying sword fighting wasn't for measly little girls. As she tried to hold up the sword, her arms faltered. The tip dropped to the ground. But her seven-year-old self scolded, *Stay strong, and ye will defeat those marauders.*

She raised the sword as her arms shook. She swiped down left, then right, only to throw herself off balance, twist, and fall on her rear. The sword dropped to her side, and she rubbed her arm where she'd twisted it.

Laughter erupted in the yard, and she looked up. Peeking around the stone ruin archway was her older brother, Colin MacDougall, the future laird of the clan. Colin had the confidence and arrogance of a dozen teenage boys wrapped into one smug ten-year-old, which annoyed her to no end.

"Ah, Ainslie, won't ye ever learn. Fighting is for men, not girls." Colin approached, with John MacArthur trailing behind. John was the son of Dunstaffnage's Captain of the Castle, and, while friendlier than Colin, he annoyed her just as much.

Ainslie picked herself up and dusted herself off, feeling like the failure Colin saw her as. On her butt with her sword on the ground.

"Leave off, ye bugger. Girls are just as strong as boys and can fight." She would prove it to him one day. She just needed to learn, practice, and she would show him.

Colin laughed out loud. "Doubtful, Ainslie."

Their father, Laird Ronald MacDougall, rounded the corner. His booming voice bounced off the castle walls as Colin and John jumped. "Colin, leave yer sister be. John and ye need to be off now."

Ainslie jumped and dropped her sword again.

Colin stood tall and replied. "Aye, Da." The boys took off and ran for the castle entrance.

Her da muttered, "Boys, not men, bah!"

Ronald turned to his youngest and grinned. "Ainslie, ye practicing at swords again?"

Ainslie stood with her sword behind her back as she frowned at his feet. No one ever caught her practicing swords. She wasn't permitted to, and it seemed her father caught her red-handed.

"Ye know, if ye want to be good, all ye need is a bit of practice." Ronald swung his wooden practice sword from behind his back and surprised Ainslie with a swipe at her middle. She barely dodged getting smacked in the stomach.

She glanced up at her da. He swung at her, his daughter!

He stood laughing.

"Da!" Ainslie gasped.

Her father grinned and came for her again, swiping at her head. She barely had time to raise her sword for a block. But block it, she did. His hit wasn't hard. This attack was only part of his full strength. If he had used his full force, he would have knocked her unconscious on the ground.

She glanced above her head as his practice sword slid off her block. He pushed so hard that she nearly dropped her sword. Her earlier exercise weakened her arms.

Her da pulled back, nodding at her.

Ainslie glanced at her da, worried he might laugh at her—the measly little girl who tried to be brave with a sword.

He stood there grinning from ear to ear. "Aye, better. Now yer first lesson is defense." Her da's voice boomed over the courtyard as he began her first instruction in medieval warfare. She worked hard that day, never wanting it to end. The following day, her arms hurt so much that she needed help eating since she couldn't lift anything.

The memory faded as tears streaked down Ainslie's cheeks. She wished her da were here to see her. This year was her turn to fight in the Viking reenactment event. All those years of practice with her da led to her hobby, Viking fighting. She wiped her tears and safely tucked her memory in her heart.

Her da had continued working with her until his death a few years ago when her parents died in a car accident. The accident convinced Colin that an evil Fae searched for the magic Iona Stones. The Fae had charged the MacDougall family with keeping them hidden and safe. Colin was sure an evil Fae killed their parents, but Ainslie wasn't so easily convinced.

She glanced out her window early in the morning at her favorite view. The sun barely peeked over the mountains, framing Loch Etive as the sky changed from night into day in hues of red and blue—fire from the sun and ice from the clouds. The sight was pure magic.

Finally, at twenty-six years old and an accomplished special-needs teacher obsessed with Viking warfare, she would get her chance. Ainslie shook herself, anticipating the Historical Reenactment event. This year was her year to shine.

She dressed for her morning jog and made her way down the hall, past the portraits of the MacDougall ancestors, not bothering to look at one. Mrs. Abernathy, the housekeeper and the person who ran the castle's day-to-day life, had already made tea in the kitchen. The twins, Evie and Ewan, Colin and Bree's kids, sat at the table, bleary-eyed, over breakfast.

Mrs. Abernathy, or Mrs. A as everyone called her, handed Ainslie a cup of tea as she spoke. "Somehow, I knew ye'd be up early, dearie. Tea, as usual. Yer brother, the laird, is up bright and early as well."

As Ainslie mixed in her creamer, she smiled at the

twins. "Good morning, bugs. Ready for a fun-filled day?"

The six-year-old twins, usually an endless bundle of energy, seemed like they would fall asleep on top of their rowies, savory Scottish rolls known for their flaky texture and buttery taste. Bree, their mom and an American, called it a smashed croissant.

Ewan grunted, much like his father, Colin.

Evie stared past Ainslie, blinking her eyes.

Ainslie smirked, "It's day one of preparing for the Viking invasion. Aren't ye kids excited?" Silence met her comment.

John MacArthur strode into the kitchen. "Ready for our jog, Ainslie? After our workout, we can review the final plans for the reenactment battle." John was the castle captain, and his hereditary duty was to prepare the property for the laird and his family. John had a hand in everything the castle planned. Well, he and Mrs. Abernathy.

John turned to Mrs. Abernathy as she handed him some water. "Marie will be down with Douglas soon." The MacArthurs lived in Ardchattan Priory, which Marie, his wife, remodeled. Part of the sanctuary now was their home. With the reenactment event coming up, they stayed at the castle so John could spend his time planning the big event. Douglas was John and Marie's pride and joy, a son they named after John's da. Marie, an expert on historical buildings, was part of the chapel renovation project with Bree and the recent dig for artifacts on the castle grounds. The priory renovation, her last project, was her dream project she started after falling in love with John.

Ewan piped up. "Doug is here?"

John smirked. "Aye, and ye'll all get to play later, after breakfast." Ewan sat up taller and beamed as Evie rolled her eyes.

John looked at Ainslie. "Ready to go?"

Ainslie finished her tea. "Aye, but we must stop by and tease Colin. It's his first time he allowed Bree to go to the States without him. Can't pass this opportunity up."

John chuckled and shook his head.

****

Colin sat in the study, reviewing some documents about the plans for the reenactment event. This year's theme, Vikings, Ainslie's favorite. He and John would be required to lead the Viking raid, duplicating the attack in the twelfth century when his ancestor Dubgall mac Somairle, now fashioned MacDougall, Lord of the Isles, first settled at Dunstaffnage, which was before his ancestors built the castle. Another descendant, Duncan MacDougall, developed and added to the castle in the early thirteenth century. Ainslie would join them as a lead this year, but she would lead the offensive against him and John. He smiled as a memory of them practicing swords came to mind. He recalled she liked to turn on him and whack him with her sword.

He looked over the agenda for the event when his cell phone rang. He glanced at the caller's I.D. and saw the head of the security detail he hired for his wife's first trip "across the pond" without him.

He punched the red dot. "MacDougall here."

Mr. Smith's business monotone voice greeted him. "Check-in time. All's good, sir."

Colin grunted a reply. He still felt uncomfortable with Bree back in Houston, Texas, her hometown. She was on her museum tour of the artifacts and information regarding Dunstaffnage and the chapel renovation. Marie and John MacArthur's historical wedding, duplicating a thirteenth-century ceremony, a recent addition to the exhibit, made it the star attraction.

Mr. Smith's voice came through clearly. "She's happy, sir, and in her element. Professor Mac and her brother are here. All is well."

Colin pinched the bridge of his nose. "Aye, see that it stays that way. Till next check-in." He ended the call with a touch of the red dot.

Professor Mac, her professor and mentor, stayed with Bree. Dominic, her Navy pilot brother, remained there, and with the security team, she stayed safe. Her damned ex, Tony Stiles, couldn't get near her. Colin still boiled every time he thought of him.

When he first met Bree, the ex-jerk remained in jail for a while. But the courts in the States, being what they are, freed him soon after. Colin obtained a restraining order, which kept Tony away from Bree, but that hadn't worked the last time she visited the States. And good thing Colin traveled with her. It felt good when he beat the crap out of the guy before he called the police to have him hauled away.

His eyes traveled to the Brooch of Lorne, an artifact Marie uncovered in the most recent dig on the castle site. The brooch remained an emblem of the MacDougall family for generations. It was supposed to go on the museum tour with Bree, but shortly before the trip began, she suffered a nightmare. He recalled that night vividly.

Bree whispered in his ear, "Colin?"

He mumbled a half-asleep reply. "Um, mm."

"Colin, I want you to keep the pin, the Brooch of Lorne. I want you to keep it with you wherever you go."

Colin's eyes snapped open; he was wide awake now. The Brooch of Lorne remained a MacDougall trinket lost after the Battle of Dalrigh in thirteen hundred and six. John of Argyll, chief of the Clan MacDougall, ambushed Robert the Bruce of Scotland, where he ripped Bruce's cloak off and kept the brooch for the family. Colin recalled the story well, and the family believed they'd lost the badge until Marie dug it up weeks ago. Designed to carry two magic stones, one atop another, the pin held powers, or so his ancestors claimed.

Colin's heart dropped. "Why would I be needing the brooch, Bree?"

She sighed. "A feeling I have. You must keep it nearby. Promise me."

Colin's brow frowned. "Aye, if keeping one of yer old things will make ye happy. Aye, I promise." He tried to make light of her worry, but her request sent chills though him.

Bree sighed and curled up in his arms. But the sense of doom didn't leave Colin.

Looking at it now, it strangely brought him peace as if the piece cast a cloak of safety. The damn thing felt bulky, but Colin kept it close to appease Bree.

His sister's voice interrupted his musings, the sarcasm clear in her tone. Something she had perfected over the years, still annoying him to this day. "Ye think he's lost his mind pining away like that for his wife." Ainslie was the first to poke fun at her brother.

He glanced up as Ainslie and John entered the

study, dressed for their morning jog.

He rolled his eyes and sighed.

John smirked. "Got it bad he does. I'll be glad when Bree gets back. I can't get him to focus on a damn thing."

Colin growled, "Don't ye two have something more important to do than rile me?"

Ainslie and John laughed and made their way to the door.

John stopped and added over his shoulder, "Aye, we are off for a run around the grounds. I'll make sure and stop off at the chapel. If I run into yer Fae, Brigid, I'll let her know ye miss her."

The click of the door shut filled the room.

Colin threw a book, and it hit the closed door. "If ye see Brigid, tell her, go to hell!"

****

Ainslie followed John as he stepped out of the castle. "Our usual trek? Uphill first, then back down to the dock and back up the hill to end at the Chapel in the Woods?"

Ainslie nodded, and they began a light jog in their typical silence.

Ainslie relaxed at her usual pace, allowing her mind to wander. There was no activity from the Fae in years. The last occurred when John traveled back in time to rescue his love, Marie, whom a fanatical priest kidnapped and forced Marie to search for one of The Stones of Iona. Of all the things to happen on that trip, John ran into his da, who went missing years before, only to turn up in the sixteenth century from a bargain with the Fae. After that, the castle became silent of Fae activity for years.

That is, until last night. Ainslie didn't want to alarm anyone, not yet at least. She thought back over her dream the night before. She needed to figure out what it all meant and how it all came together with the Fae and a Stone of Iona.

She stood in a Viking village, something she liked to daydream about. This time it wasn't her typical daydream, a pleasant stroll through an imaginary fantasy. This time was more real, too real. She fought amid a battle—her adrenaline high, her fear palpable. The weight of her sword stayed heavy in her hands, tiring her limbs. The stench of blood wafted from the wounded and turned her stomach. The burning fires stung her nose. The roars of the warriors echoed across the field. Everything moved in a blur. She attacked at the forefront of combat alongside a large man. Someone she felt very familiar with.

The sensations felt odd. Ainslie had casual boyfriends over the years but never sensed a spark, unlike her brother and Bree or John and Marie, where both couples claim earth-shattering feelings of true love. She hadn't experienced it—yet.

But in this dream, Ainslie sensed many things about this one man. First came hatred, then competition, and when they fought side by side, camaraderie or, more so, an equality. When he turned and looked into her eyes, that spark shot through her. His eyes caught hers, the light blue, almost white, with a blue ring around the edges. The emotion behind them as he gazed at her, a sense of lightning struck her heart.

Her dream shifted, like a film skipping in a movie. She sat on a rock island, stranded, as she called for her true love. Begging to be rescued, she prayed for faith.

Faith to keep her alive, faith to keep her sane, and faith that her love would save her. That was when she saw it—a glowing deep-blue diamond-shaped gem rested within the rocks of the shoreline. She reached to pick it up, and when she held it, a voice murmured, "Faith."

She woke so abruptly that she lost her breath and grabbed at her chest to breathe again. When she glanced up, the Green Lady of Dunstaffnage, the castle's ghost, floated at the foot of her bed. Ainslie had never seen the Green Lady before. She'd heard many stories of her appearance and knew the ghost had appeared before her parents' death years back. Ainslie studied her, curious about why the spirit visited her. Glowing green in medieval clothing, the apparition floated at the foot of her bed as she slowly rose and lowered in her ethereal drift.

So stunned by the ghost's appearance, Ainslie didn't notice her expression. But she looked now. She had to; the ghost's expressions foretold the future of the MacDougall family members. If the spirit smiled, good came for the person the apparition appeared before.

But now, the ghost cried. The spirit didn't weep, but bawled in hard rocks that racked her body with heaving sobs that echoed in Ainslie's mind—a wail she never wanted to hear again. If the ghost appeared in Ainslie's presence, her crying meant only one thing. Something horrible was about to happen, and Ainslie became truly frightened for the first time in her life.

Chapter 2

The *Fae Fable Book* thumped from its case by the window. Colin ignored it. Brigid, his Fae, usually wouldn't permit him to read the damn thing. It thumped again, and Colin cursed Brigid under his breath.

The kids laughed in the Great Hall. Ewan and Doug played pirates, likely with their wooden swords.

Ewan's bright voice said, "Argh, matey, hand over yer plunder."

Doug's deeper reply, "Over my dead body."

Mrs. Abernathy scolded them. "Now, boys, ye be careful."

He closed his eyes and pictured the scene. The boys chased each other around the couch as Evie read a book. Evie stayed so introverted, but Bree said their kids would turn out as God intended. Possibly Evie would be a scholar like her mother and Ewan a fighter like his da. He grinned as the sounds drew his thoughts to Bree and his family.

Someone tugged on his arm, and he opened his eyes to find his daughter, Evie, at his side. So engrossed in his thoughts, he hadn't heard her enter. This was the second time his thoughts distracted him today, which was rare.

From the forlorn look on Evie's six-year-old face, Colin immediately picked her up and held her in his lap. "Aw, sweet girl, why the frown? Today ye should be excited. We are preparing for a party."

Evie held her da and rested her head on his shoulders. "I know, Da, but Brigid's trying to talk. Ye aren't hearing." Colin's heart dropped. His children never spoke of the Fae, any Fae, or even his own. He carefully pried Evie from his shoulder and held her, so he looked into her face. He took a deep breath as he wished Bree were here. She was much better at dealing with their eccentric daughter than he.

"Evie, what is it Brigid wants to say?" Colin hoped Evie saw this as a game. But deep down, he knew it wasn't. Evie was special. She possessed a unique presence that seemed otherworldly and, frankly, sometimes scared Colin. He loved his family and wanted to protect them.

"Mommy needs ye. She needs ye now!" The *Fae Fable Book* flew across the room and landed on the floor, open. It was not the book flying across the room or even his daughter's odd declaration that concerned him most. It was the fact he saw the writing in the book. His Fae, Brigid, typically refused his attempts to read from the *Fae Fable Book* to tease him.

There was no teasing today. Brigid needed Colin to read the book. The fables told the fates of the magic Fae stones, the Stones of Iona. Each tale shown signaled the Fae required a member of the family to search for a stone. When he read the book this time, what would he find?

Evie glanced at the book and back at him. "See, now ye can read it. All will be okay. Brigid said so." She kissed him on the cheek, climbed down from his lap, and skipped out of the room, leaving Colin staring after his daughter. He blinked, unsure whether what she said was reality or a dream.

Shaking himself, he stood and strode around the desk. As he reached for the book, apprehension seized him. What story would the Fae show this time? Who would have to go after a stone, and what toll would the task take?

He bent and picked up the *Fae Fable Book*. It was open to the Fae fable story, "The Stone of Lust." He returned to his desk as his heart hammered in his chest. Each time the *Fae Fable Book* demanded they read it, the book exposed a story leading to a Stone of Iona. The stories were fables harmlessly written, but what unfolded in reality was far from any childhood story and usually preceded tough times for him and his family.

He swallowed the lump in his throat and read. At first, reading seemed a little awkward. The last time he read from the book, the Fae wouldn't allow him to read anything but portions at a time. This time, he flipped through the pages before reading the story to ensure he got the whole tale. Only a few pages showed, and it showed the entire story. So, he read.

When he hit the second sentence, his cell phone rang. He glanced at it to check the caller's I.D., not wanting to answer. When he noticed Mr. Smith, the head of the security detail for his wife, his heart nearly stopped.

He grabbed the phone and answered. "Aye," his voice boomed.

The voice on the other end spoke rapidly and out of breath. "Laird MacDougall, thank goodness, I got you. We tried to get to her, but he was crafty this time."

Colin growled, and red flashed before his eyes.

Smith's deep sigh punctuated his concern. "He's got her. Brielle, she's gone. Tony grabbed her while we exited the museum. He had it planned. We chased him down an alley, and you will not believe this, but both vanished in a flash of light."

Colin stood. "What do ye mean, vanished?"

"We have the police on the way. I have the security detail doing a perimeter search, sir. They couldn't go far. We'll find her, sir. I'll keep in touch."

"Ye do that." Colin nearly flung the phone across the room.

There was a commotion from the study door.

John burst into the room. "They were here, Colin. I swear I saw them with me own eyes."

Marie, John's wife, followed him into the room, concern etched on her face.

Colin took a deep breath. "Saw who, John?" Damn, he knew what would come next, and he might come unhinged. Bree feared this exact thing for the past year. His eye caught the Brooch of Lorne on the corner of his desk as it sat in the morning light and winked at him.

John spoke between breaths. "He was there—she was there—he dragged her. We stood there, joking about the fake Viking raid. Ainslie saw them first. Damn, yer sister can run fast, even when she's tired. Blinding white light flashed—they all ran." John panted as his words tumbled over one another as they spewed from his mouth.

Colin rounded the desk and grabbed John by the shoulders.

He shook him as he asked, "Who, John? Who ran?"

John stopped at Colin's touch, and he gaped at him.

His mouth went slack as his eyes bulged. "Bree and a man I've not seen before."

Marie gasped as John glanced at her. "They appeared outside the chapel in a flash of light, like the portal light, but brighter and in the middle of the yard. No doorway, nothing, just a flash, and there they were."

Colin gripped John's shoulders to the point John had to pry him off. "Careful, Colin, ye're hurting me."

Colin dropped his arms and strode to the mantel. He gripped his hands at his sides and faced John, ready for what would come next. "What happened next, John? And leave no detail out."

John shook his shoulders and glanced at Marie, who nodded at him as she slid into the chair in front of the desk.

John ran his hands through his hair and took a deep breath. "Ye know, before, I wouldn't have believed it. That was before we had run-ins with the Fae. But now, it almost seems—typical." John stopped as his gaze landed on the book on the desk. He glanced at the *Fae Fable Book* enclosure and then at the tome on the desk.

He eyed Colin, who glared coolly back. "What happened, John? I am quickly losing my patience."

John moved to the table behind the desk, poured a whisky, drank it in one gulp, then poured another. He turned to face Colin and paused.

Colin stared at his best friend's face and saw his panic reflected there. All the trials they had gone through tumbled through his mind—his parents' deaths, the duty to the Fae, the magical Stones of Iona, his trip back in time to restore his ancestor, and him saving Bree. The time a fanatical priest kidnapped Marie and dragged her back in time, chasing an Iona Stone, John followed her to rescue her.

What could it be this time? What the hell did the damn Fae have in store for him now?

John took a sip before he spoke. "Ainslie ran before I could even think. She's damned fast, ye know."

Colin growled. "She's my sister. I know. Go on."

"The man dragged Bree toward the chapel. That's when it dawned on me what he was about. Ainslie was there before I could even move. He didn't even have to chant to open the portal. Just waved his hand." John waved his hand before his face and blinked bug-eyed at it. "That was when I knew our time was up, and things would become difficult again. I knew when he turned and glowered at me across the way, and I saw his eyes. They were all black. Like what Bree described when a Fae possessed Constance Ross in the eighteenth century."

Colin's knuckles cracked when he gripped them. "Fuck and damn it!"

Marie covered her gasp with her hand.

John gulped his whisky. "He took her, Colin. A Fae took Bree through the portal. And before I could stop her, Ainslie grabbed Bree's hand and screamed, 'I got ye.' In a flash of light, she disappeared with them."

Colin jolted. Bree was gone. The Fae took Bree and his sister through the portal.

Everyone in the room stilled. The silence became deafening. Colin stood rigid for a moment and a moment more. First Bree was taken by her ex-boyfriend in Houston, then arrived here in mere seconds. He knew of only one capable of such travel, travel without a portal. Colin had to make sure. He had to know. Had an evil Fae possessed a psychopath?

He strode to his desk, opened a drawer, and pulled out an unmarked manila envelope. He held it momentarily. The image inside flashed across his mind as the hate for the man built inside him. All the hurt the bastard had caused her, and he had her now. *Please let John say he doesn't recognize the man in the picture.*

He opened it and pulled out the picture. Colin glared at the psychopath's face, and his expression darkened. Rage and anger poured through him as he glared at that face. He hated the photo, yet the image was seared into his memory. A bleary-eyed, narrow face with a few days' growth of beard frowned back. The man in the picture held a sarcastic smirk on his long-drawn face. His greasy hair hung over his face, and his beady eyes seemed in a constant slit, like a snake.

He flipped it around showing it to John. "Was this the man, John?"

John approached the desk and peered at the criminal's headshot.

John squinted at it and nodded. "Aye, that's him."

Colin crumpled the picture. Fury flowed through him, anger at the Fae who made Bree part of his duty. His rage blinded him—the Fae needed to answer for this. An evil Fae took his true love.

John took a deep breath. "Is that who I think it is? Is that Bree's ex?"

Colin bellowed, "Brigid!" as he stormed from the study.

****

John and Marie stared at each other.

Marie was the first to speak. "Oh, no."

John set his glass down and started for the door.

"Keep the children here and safe, away from the chapel. And don't tell Evie and Ewan about their ma. Let Colin do that."

He glanced out the window and saw Colin as he ran toward the chapel. "I'll have to go after him. It may be a while."

John walked through the hall and out the castle doors as he moved slowly to the Chapel in the Woods. He figured Colin needed time alone to reconcile all that had happened. John needed time to resolve what he witnessed that morning as well. The Fae remained inactive for years. Why now and without warning? They usually gave some sign that the Fae needed the MacDougalls—the *Fae Fable Book*—the Greene Lady—something. But nothing this time.

The *Fae Fable Book,* damn. It sat out on Colin's desk, but it seemed Colin hadn't read it. He'd known nothing about a fable or any stone it spoke of. John ran his hand through his hair.

He needed to get Colin from the chapel, read the *Fae Fable Book*, see what stone the Fae needed them to find, and form a plan. As captain of the castle, John's duty was to keep them all safe. He was required to protect the family and the Iona Stones.

He neared the Chapel in the Woods. All appeared almost too quiet. He approached the building, knowing Colin was inside, concerned about what he would find when he entered.

At the open doors, he stood and examined them. Colin had ripped them from the hinges. No small feat—they were solid oak. He walked into the nave and his gaze traveled the room. The wind blew in a few leaves, and they came to rest on the scattered pews.

While Bree and Colin were in the eighteenth century, a possessed Fae sealed Bree in the crypt. He figured that was where he'd find Colin, in the tomb, looking for Bree. But he found him someplace else. Colin kneeled in the center. His shirt was ripped in multiple places with dirt smudged here and there, a testament to Colin's tormented moment when he didn't find Bree or his Fae, Brigid, here.

Now, Colin calmly kneeled.

John approached and kneeled next to Colin in support of his friend.

****

Colin sensed when John entered the chapel, and he didn't care. His thoughts were only on Bree. How could he make a mistake this costly to her safety—again? Every step of the way, it seemed like fate worked against him. Now his sister had become mixed up in this mess with the Stones and the Fae. Oddly, he wasn't concerned much about Ainslie. She always handled trouble well for as long as he could remember. The memory came to him so fast he gasped.

"Aye, Colin, that's it. Shift yer weight to parry left, then right." His da's voice echoed in the yard as they sparred during sword practice. His father insisted they kept fighting and trained as a weekly activity, even on holiday. He and John took turns sparring with his da, Laird Ronald MacDougall.

Ainslie approached with her sword in hand.

Colin was the first to comment. "What are ye doing here, Ainslie? Swords are for men."

Ainslie opened her mouth, but her da spoke. "I invited her, Colin. It's time she practices as well."

Colin lowered his wooden practice sword and

20

laughed out loud. "Come on, Da. She's a girl. She can't best me. I'm better than her."

Ainslie's face turned bright red as she gripped her wooden sword tighter. She glanced at her da, who nodded toward Colin as he smiled. Ainslie charged with her sword raised and caught him unprepared. She swiped and connected with his middle, causing him to double over as pain radiated out. Before he raised his sword, she spun and whacked him on the shoulder. Pain shot down his arm, numbing it.

Colin dropped his sword and grabbed his arm. "Ouch, Ainslie, that hurt." Damn, his sister bested him with a sword. His wee sister!

Her father laughed out loud. "Aye, my boy, and I am certain she has more to dish out than ye are willing to receive." He nodded to Ainslie, who smirked at her older brother.

His da's voice boomed over the yard. "Colin, get yerself together. Ye will now spar with yer sister. Let's hope she doesn't wipe yer face in the ground today."

The memory faded as quickly as it came. No, Colin wouldn't worry about Ainslie, but Bree. Thinking about what her ex might do to her now nearly ripped his heart out. He'd failed to keep her safe. He didn't know if she would ever forgive him or if he would ever forgive himself.

It was some time before Colin considered moving or saying anything. John seemed to wait him out. His tantrum flashed in his mind, partially remembering for the first time what he'd done moments before while he searched for Bree.

He yelled as he tore the doors from the hinges. "Bree!" He chanted part of the portal chant. "I bathe thee in blood. Open, damn ye! Glow!" Nothing happened.

He stormed through the nave, upending pews as he went. "Brigid! Damn it, Fae, where are ye when I need ye?" When he arrived at the altar, he vaulted over it, landing on the sealed opening to the crypt.

He beat the cement with his bare hands. "Bree, Bree, are ye there? Call for me!" Nothing. No sound. He crumpled into a ball. "Please, Brigid, please come. He's taken her, and I know not when or where." Tears streamed down his face as he imagined Bree in the hands of a madman.

Colin rose and ran around the altar, stood in the center of the chapel, and yelled as loud as he could. He did so again until his breath ran out and he fell to his knees. He shouted again, this time hoarse, and stayed on his knees praying for a miracle to save his true love.

Coming back to his senses, he glanced around him at the beauty of Bree's work that he partially ripped apart, like his heart, torn to shreds.

Colin spoke in a raspy voice. "Ye know, I never thought much about this chapel. Not my whole life until Bree came. Then, it became the most important thing because it was important to her."

Colin drew a deep breath. "I've gone through time for her. Saved her from purgatory." His laugh became bitter. "Hell, I went to purgatory to save her, my true love." His head bowed as he whispered, "Now, what do the Fae do? Take her from me."

He threw his head back, yelling at the top of his lungs. "Ye fucking took her! Why?" His breath hitched, and a sob escaped him in a growling moan.

John glanced around. Colin followed his eye,

thinking this would be a good time for the Fae sisters to appear, but no one was there. It figured. They always damn well did what they liked, regardless of the consequences to anyone.

John sighed. "Have ye read the *Fae Fable Book*?"

Colin shook his head as he replied in a rasp, his voice long gone. "Didn't have time. Got to the second sentence, and all hell broke loose."

John rose from his knees and put his hand out to Colin. "Come on, my laird. We've got work to do. We'll be getting them both back. But first, the *Fae Fable Book*."

Colin took John's hand and rose as he wiped tears from his eyes.

John led him out of the chapel. As they passed through the doorway, Colin stopped and glanced back inside. "I'm coming for ye, Bree. Ainslie, my wee warrior, look after Bree as I know ye can. But I'm coming and bringing hell with me when I do."

Chapter 3

A few days earlier, The Houston Museum of Fine Arts, Houston, Texas

Tony stood in the back of the museum, partially hidden behind a pillar. He hated these places, stuffy and boring, filled with over-educated oafs that blabbed on about nothing. Tony spied on her at the speaking podium. If he stood in the right spot, he saw her entire face, body, all of her. She belonged to him, always had, and always will. She carried on about some old church in Scotland. Fuck Scotland. Her place was here, serving him.

His eyes moved over her. *Brielle*. She'd changed quite a bit. Her hairstyle appeared different. She put on weight and wore stylish clothing. Probably provided by her rich husband, that's what it had to be. He bought her from him. Brielle was his.

His eyes traveled over the people on the stage. That stupid professor stood with her, the old Scot. God, he hated him, always kept his woman away from him as they examined old crap. Another man stood on her other side. It couldn't be the highlander husband. He'd looked the guy up online and met the bastard in person the previous year. He hated the man. This man possessed medium brown hair, the same color as Brielle. He huffed; must be her brother. He never met the loser since Brielle hadn't spoken to him in years. He despised them all, everyone who kept her from him. Brielle was his. *They would all get what's coming to them, all of them.*

Someone tapped his shoulder. "Sir, will you come with me, please?"

Tony turned and came face to face with a large black man in a black suit who wore an earpiece. "Buzz off, asshole."

The man's gaze shifted over Tony's shoulder.

He turned, and another large man in a black suit stood to his left. "I don't think you understand. He asked. I'm demanding. Mr. Stiles, your presence here is unwelcome. You can leave peacefully or not. The choice is yours."

Tony stepped back. "I don't have to go anywhere."

Both men smirked at each other. The one on the left spoke into a mic on his wrist. "The snake has refused the offer. Send backup and close in the perimeter."

Tony's gaze jumped to Brielle on the stage, and two men in black suits shifted behind her as she continued to speak. They pissed him off. She was his, always had been, and always would be. He moved toward the stage.

Both men grabbed his arms as one spoke. "That's not the way to the exit, Mr. Stiles. Let us show you the way." They hauled him by his arms toward the exit.

Tony yelled, "You can't make me leave! I have a right to be here, just like anyone else!"

At the scuffle, Brielle stopped speaking and gasped into the microphone.

Tony turned his head, and their eyes connected. "You're mine, Brielle! You belong to me!" The security detail shoved him through the doors. Outside, both men held on to Tony as they dragged him off the museum property, where they dumped him in a trash can.

His head popped up. "That's abuse. You can't do that."

Both men strolled away.

One spoke over his shoulder, "Looks like we just did, and stay away from *Mrs.* MacDougall." The emphasis on Mrs. made Tony furious.

The other guard spoke as they continued to walk away. "If you don't, I'll happily send Laird MacDougall's regards with my fists." Both men laughed as they strolled back into the museum.

****

During the reception, Professor Mac approached Brielle. "Grand job, my dear. Always good to hear about the work at Dunstaffnage. The university and museum are right pleased with yer work."

Brielle sipped her champagne. "Thank you, Professor Mac. I'm honored to present our work. I wish Marie were here to share it with us."

Professor Mac put his arm around her and gave her a brief hug. "Aww, Marie is in spirit and will be in person soon enough."

Professor Mac dropped his arm and turned to her brother. "Hello, Dominic. What did ye think of yer wee sister?"

Her brother stood by her side. "That was truly impressive, Brielle. I didn't know how much went into your work. I can tell you truly love it."

She blushed and took a sip of her champagne. Her brother, Dominic DeVolt, smiled, put his arm around her, and gave her a light squeeze. He possessed the same brown hair as Brielle but a tall, muscular body. Their mother's death brought them together again and they recently mended their relationship. Dominic was an Air Force pilot flying top-of-the-line fighter jets. Dom—she smirked at her old nickname for him. She called him an adrenaline junkie. He seemed always busy flying off somewhere where he did something important. Most times he was prohibited from discussing his missions, and he rarely sat still.

He and Professor Mac stood and spoke of planes while Brielle glanced around the museum. The security team Colin had hired remained positioned around the room. On her first trip to the States without him, Tony was here. She couldn't believe it when his yelling interrupted her speech, making a scene.

"Will he ever leave me alone?" She shivered as a chill spread down her spine.

Professor Mac leaned over and whispered in her ear, "He's gone, and the brute squad yer husband hired did a fine job of getting rid of him. The last ye'll be seeing of that trash."

Brielle nodded weakly and studied the room again. *He is gone. It will be okay.*

Her cell phone rang.

She glanced at the caller's I.D. and set down her glass to answer it.

"Hello, husband," she said sweetly.

Her husband's Scots accent came through the phone, easing her. "Bree, are ye okay? I got the report from security. Damn, I should have come on this trip."

She stepped away from the crowd and shifted down a hallway to speak privately. She glanced up.

Margaret Izard

Two lights were out.

"Colin, I'm fine, and no, you didn't have to come with me. He's gone, and it's okay. Now, how are my wee bugs?" Bree spoke with a fake cheer, hoping Colin wouldn't hear it.

His voice came through, the concern clear. "Bree, I can hear the fear in yer voice. And don't change the subject even if it is to my pride and joy, our kids."

Bree sighed and leaned against the wall. She scanned up and down the hallway—alone.

She spoke freely. "It was awful, Colin. He created a scene. I felt like such an idiot." Tears gathered in her eyes. She hated that her ex-boyfriend still affected her this way after so many years. Would she ever be free of him?

Colin spoke over the sound of shuffling papers. "Ye are no idiot. If anyone's the idiot, it's him. Don't worry. I upped security, and they will remain on duty twenty-four-seven till ye get home. Hell, I may even fly out tomorrow. Aye, that's it. I'll be on my way, so ye don't have to worry."

"Nonsense, Colin. It's only a couple more days for the tour. Then I'll be home and in your arms." The murmur of voices and the clinking of glasses came from the main room. She needed to get back to work. Then she wouldn't worry; she'd keep busy until she returned to her true love's arms.

"I have to go. The reception is still going on. Kiss my wee bugs for me. I love and miss you all."

His firm voice came to her. "My wee Bree, I love ye too." Colin hung up, and Bree stood and looked at her phone. A tear escaped, and she wiped it away. *No use getting upset.* She pocketed her phone and turned to go into the main hall.

Someone stood in her path. "Hello, Brielle."

She glanced up, and a chill ran down her spine. That face—he's here. When she recognized who stood before her, a rock dropped into her stomach. Tony Stiles, her ex-boyfriend, and they were alone in a dark hallway. She froze. He stood between her and the exit.

He's here, and he wants me. Good God, I—I can't.

He leaned against the wall as he folded his arms. "Why, you come to town and don't come to see me, your love?"

No, he doesn't own me anymore. Not now and never again.

Brielle fisted her hands. Anger at him built in her. Would he ever leave her alone?

"I am not your love. I am married. Married to someone else."

Tony softly laughed. "Marriage won't stop me, and it won't stop you."

Tony took a step toward her.

She took a step back.

The detail. I have to alert them. Brielle reached for her phone.

Tony shifted his jacket and revealed a knife. Not just any knife. A knife she knew all too well. The six-inch hunting knife. The one he kept on hand and had shoved in her face many times before.

Tony hissed, "I wouldn't be touching your cell phone or anything else, little Brie."

"Don't call me that."

Brielle took another step back as Tony followed. "You left, Brie. You left me. We had it all—a happy life, you by my side where you belonged. And you left

29

for that awful country."

Brielle stepped to the side to go around him.

Tony grabbed her arm and brought her against him. His stale beer breath blew in her face. Brielle turned aside as bile rose in her throat.

He grabbed her face, forcing her eyes to his. He kissed her hard, his lips wet and the brush of his stubble rough against her skin.

No! Not ever again! She spat in his face.

Tony slapped her, making her head snap to the side as her hair fell across her face.

He grabbed her shoulders and shook her as he spoke. "You left, you bitch. I lost my job, and my apartment flooded. I got tossed in jail. All because of you. I lost my friends. My family disowned me because they said I was being unreasonable."

Tony yelled in her face as his spittle flew on her. "You did this, all of this! It's your fault!" Whispering, he tilted her head as his hands tightened painfully. "You should never have left. You are mine and always will be. Not some dirty Scot's." He was there one moment, and the next, he wasn't. He dropped her to the floor in a heap. Movement happened all around her. There were shouts—a crack as someone punched a face, loud like a broken bone.

Dragged from the hallway, she found herself on the floor as she stared at the friendly face of the head of her security detail, Mr. Smith. It was funny how they all used such unassuming names, Smith or Jones. She figured they were aliases. Dizzy, she blinked and shook her head.

Another black suit passed a water bottle to him. "Mrs. MacDougall, are you okay?"

She glanced up, and two black suits stood beside each other. After a while, they all appeared the same. Mr. Smith opened the bottle and handed it to her. She took it and a sip, the cool water soothing her throat as she dried her tears with her sleeve.

He glared at her and sighed. "You didn't call out or anything. We could have responded earlier."

Brielle sat up farther, adjusting herself, and moaned at the aches and pains in her body. Her face felt on fire. She touched it, she could already tell it swelled. She would be sore in the morning.

She snapped at the man, "Sorry, I'm not used to being attacked. I'll work on my response next time." He didn't seem to mind as he glanced over his shoulder at the commotion as they hauled Tony away.

Mr. Smith turned and leveled his eyes at her. "There won't be a next time. We're placing a guard on you that will stay with you always. That would be in the hotel room, everywhere, within short reach. This Tony is too crafty." She rolled her eyes. The brute squad, cute at first, quickly became annoying.

Mr. Smith helped her up as Professor Mac approached and hugged her.

Dominic stood beside him. "God, Brielle. I didn't know. That was the ex?"

Professor Mac nodded.

Dominic stepped closer to her. "I think I should stay with you in the hotel." He glanced at Mr. Smith, who nodded as if they had already discussed it.

"Yes, Mr. DeVolt's a good choice. That way, you will have a trained guard you can feel comfortable with. I'd feel secure not placing one of my guards at your side, giving you some privacy."

Dominic and Mr. Smith exchanged a look as Mr. Smith spoke. "I doubt we'll see much of that asshole tonight. I suspect he'll be too busy in jail this evening."

Brielle nodded. Maybe being with family was what she needed. Considering his training, her naval officer brother could likely serve on the security team. Over Dom's shoulder, the security team hauled Tony away. As they dragged Tony out, he made eye contact with her. A shiver passed over her body. This wasn't over. Not by a long shot.

****

Late the next night, Tony returned to his apartment. He struggled with the key in the lock and slammed his fists against the door.

The neighbor yelled, "Keep it down, loser."

Once he opened the door, his dark, lonely apartment greeted him. God, he hated her more now than ever. The security team took him to the alley, beat him to a pulp, and, to pour salt on the wound, called the police since he violated the restraining order. The lying jerks claimed he fought them, but they held him down and took turns hitting him, reminding him Brielle had married that damned Scot. After a day in jail and a bail bond he couldn't afford later, he was finally home.

He went straight for the fridge and grabbed a beer. On the way past the bar, he snatched the whisky bottle and sat on the couch in the dark. He opened the beer and chugged it in one tilt. Tony crushed the can in his hand, tossed it aside, and reached for the whisky bottle. He opened it and tilted it back for a long draw. Gulping twice, he lowered the bottle and sat, panting to catch his breath. He rocked the bottle back to his mouth, drank again, and sat on the couch with the bottle between his legs. The familiar warmth spread through him as he closed his eyes and rested his head back on the sofa.

"Ye know, there are easier ways to escape than liquor."

Tony sat up at the voice. He was alone in his apartment. He searched for the man the Scots accent belonged to and found him sitting at his bar. The man sat in shadow, the small stove light illuminating him from behind. He made out some of his face, chiseled and strong, like the rest of his body. When he turned his head, his short beard was shaped in sharp patterns, not typical for men. He grinned, and his white teeth glowed in the dark. Pure evil oozed from him in waves. Tony had met no one that chilled him like this man.

Tony slowly set the whisky bottle on the coffee table and reached under the couch for his revolver. The .44 magnum with hollow-point bullets, perfect defense, would blow a hole through the man at this short range.

The man's smirk disappeared. "Yer wee gun won't harm me, but go ahead. Shoot it if it makes ye feel any better. Ye'll only shoot up yer nice place."

Tony held the gun but didn't cock or point it at the man. "Who are you, and how did you get into my place?"

The man laughed. "At least ye are direct. Stupid, but direct."

Tony stood and drifted closer to get a better look at the man who smugly sat at his bar.

His teeth flashed white as he spoke. "I am Balor, and I can come and go as I please. We have something in common, Mr. Stiles. I can help ye, and ye can help me."

Tony stopped as he studied the man. He seemed

normal, but the Scots accent made him not trust him.

"Why should I trust you, a dirty Scot?"

The man laughed. "Not all Scots are dirty. I *am* powerful. I can give ye everything ye want and more."

Tony grabbed the whisky bottle and upended it, gulping twice but not taking his eyes away from the stranger as he kept his gun in hand.

Tony replied between whisky gulps, "All I want, eh? You don't even know all I want."

Balor sneered and focused directly into Tony's eyes as a sensation traveled over him.

The man crawled through his mind as he spoke. "Ye want Brielle." Tony felt the man shift in his mind, dig deeper into his desires, dreams.

"Ye want to fuck her. Ye want her success to be yers instead of hers." The sensation shifted and his soul filled with satisfaction.

"Ye want to get rid of her husband. Did I miss anything? Oh, and ye want to be rich without working for it."

Tony laughed. "You must be a daydream brought on by a bad day."

Balor grabbed Tony by the throat, and the gun and whisky disappeared from Tony's grasp. "I am no dream. I am real, and ye want what I offer."

Balor reached into his pocket and withdrew a deep-black rectangular gem. He offered it to Tony. The temptation to grab the stone came strong. The desire for power, for control, overcame him. So mesmerized by the rock, Tony took it and held it up to the light from the kitchen. The black gem winked at him, and his will to dominate all around him consumed him. *I can do it. I can conquer the world.*

"Lust. It's lust ye seek, Tony. It's good because we want the same thing—Brielle."

Tony stared into the gem. It glowed. Lust echoed in his mind. The room tilted, and a buzzing rang in his ear and grew louder. Dizzy. He was dizzy, and the dark stone held him immobile, unable to take his eyes away.

The man's voice spoke from in his head. *~Lust, Tony. We lust after her. We've wanted her for a long time, ye and me. Together, we will have her and more. ~*

Tony blinked and focused on the mirror in the hall. His reflection glowered back. His eyes appeared solid black. The man had disappeared, but Tony felt strong. He took a deep breath, and the aches and pains from the day fled his body. Tony sensed power in an other-worldly sense. The voice in his head directed him what to do, what he needed, and how he would use the power of the Fae. The power of Balor, King of the Fomoire Fae, who wanted the Stones of Iona and to destroy the MacDougalls one by pathetic one.

The voice spoke in Tony's head. *~Tomorrow, she will be ours. ~*

Tony leered. *Yes, Brielle. I want her, and I will have her.*

Chapter 4

Dunstaffnage Castle

"I don't get it," John said as he glanced over Colin's shoulder. They both stared at the *Fae Fable Book*.

Marie sat in the chair before the desk, quietly waiting for them to figure out the newest fable.

Colin growled, stood, and strode to the mantel. "That's what they want. The Fae don't want us to understand a damn thing." He ran his hand through his hair and leaned on the fireplace. "One of these days, the Fae fable will tell the story, the true story, and we won't believe it because the damned fairies have spent too much time teasing us with lies."

John shook his head. "There is something we're missing. In the first part of the story, the Fae came to the man and gave him The Stone of Lust, so he could gain all he desired. I get the first part. The part about the man with greed is Bree's ex-boyfriend, or at least a symbol of him, but the rest makes little sense."

John sighed. "I thought the Fae fable, The Stone of Love, was Colin and Bree's story. I didn't think there would be another story about ye."

Colin growled again, "Damn Fae. If this one is about Bree, I'll kill them all."

Marie waved toward John. "John, reread the part about the island again. Maybe that is where we are missing something."

Marie sat forward as John read aloud. Colin stood by the fireplace staring into the flames as John's voice filled the room.

He sat upon his island surrounded by all that he had amassed and was happy for once in his life. He had the wealth he desired and the woman he loved. But she ignored him and refused his affections. He took his frustration out on her and beat her, for he wanted her to desire him as he desired her.

Colin growled from the fireplace, "He will die if that is what he is doing to my Bree."

Marie shushed him and nodded at John to continue reading.

" '*Eventually, the weight of the world's wealth was too much for the tiny island, and he soon sank the island, taking his wealth and his life with it.*

As he descended into the murky depths, he held on to The Stone of Lust, for he felt it would save him. Ultimately, all he had was his lust for greed, and The Stone of Lust sank with him lost to the Fae.

As the island sank, the woman called out for her true love, the man he'd stole her from. She prayed and prayed, hoping he would come and save her.

When the island was almost sunk, and there remained only a small plot for her to sit on, she stared upon the rocks she sat on. A beautiful blue gem winked at her in the setting sunlight. It was The Stone of Faith. She grabbed the stone and held it to her heart, praying for her true love, and her true love sailed to her rescue.

When lust is conceived, it brings forth sin. Sin, when finished, brings death.

Marie sat back, rubbing her forehead. "Are ye sure

that's all the story says, John?"

John turned the page over and thumbed the rest, all of which were blank.

Marie chewed her nail. "Well, the book has concealed part of a story before until it was time for us to see it."

John nodded. "Aye, it has also given us a story that wasn't about anyone here. Maybe the woman isn't Bree, but someone else? Ainslie maybe? She went back with Bree."

Colin paced in front of the fireplace. He responded, slashing his hand out. "It's not Ainslie. She has no previous love or serious boyfriend, no one she is pining for. It must be Bree and that son-of-a-bitch ex of hers. It all matches."

Colin ran his hands through his hair again and slightly pulled on it. His Bree was in the hands of a madman. And his sister traveled through the portal with them. He had to do something soon, or he would go crazy.

Marie turned to him. "Colin, ye spoke with the twins, didn't ye?"

Colin stopped and turned as he focused on Marie. The worry was evident on her face—his wee bugs, his pride and joy in life, the twins. Their mother went missing, and their father was nearly insane with worry. He bent the truth, but their solemn expressions, even at a young age, spoke of understanding.

Especially Evie. Her response chilled him. "It's okay, Da. Fight hard like a Viking! As Auntie says, be strong."

He took a deep breath. "Aye, I told the wee bugs that their ma got delayed in the States and left it at that."

He frowned at John. He hadn't told John and Marie what else he'd said to the twins. "I also told them I was going away to join her. I told the twins I would bring their ma home."

John and Marie gaped at Colin, wearing similar expressions, mouths open and frozen.

John was the first to break the silence. "Well, I suppose one of us will have to go back in time to retrieve them, but we don't know what date."

Marie sat for a moment.

She gasped as her gaze shot at Colin. "Isn't Ainslie obsessed with Viking life? Isn't it something she has studied extensively?"

John nodded. "Aye, she is obsessed with it."

Colin waved them off. "Ye said yerself the Fae was inside the madman. I doubt Ainslie could guide them through the portal, and I am certain the evil Fae in Tony had a plan." Colin growled at having to say the bastard's name. "He likely has The Stone of Lust, and a Fae is now in his head controlling his thoughts and moves."

Marie put her hand up. "Wait, but the Fae fable story is partially true. What if his lust, combined with the power of The Stone of Lust, became so overwhelming he didn't care where or when he landed?"

John and Marie continued discussing the Fae fable, sharing plausible theories. The time for thinking was over. Colin wanted to act. The longer he stood here talking the more he lost precious time. Bree could be in danger or hurt at the hands of a madman and an evil Fae. An evil Fae tried to kill her once in their search for the magic Fae stones. Damn it if they tried again.

Colin crossed to his desk. The Brooch of Lorne still sat on the corner. He picked it up and held it in the sunlight from the window. Colin sensed the brooch had something to do with this, but the Fae fable offered no answers, and his Fae, Brigid, was nowhere to be found. Bree had sensed some danger when she insisted that he kept the piece instead of her taking it on the museum tour. He just needed to figure out how all this tied together, so he could save his sister and his true love.

Committed to his plan, Colin interrupted John and Marie's banter. "Marie, please look after the twins. John, guard them all with yer life. I need to know they are safe. And by all that is holy, don't let them near the *Fae Fable Book*."

Colin nodded. "I'm going back in time. I'll do it and bring them both home." He turned to John. "Ask the lads from the wharf to repair the chapel doors. Tomorrow at dusk I'll open the portal."

Chapter 5

The other side of the portal in the past

Brielle fell on the forest floor as three bodies tangled in a heap of arms and legs. Ainslie was the first to break free. Ainslie grabbed her hand and pulled as Bree stood up on wobbly legs.

Whack! The sound echoed as Ainslie froze, then fell over, knocked out.

Tony grabbed Brielle, and she struggled against him, trying to break free, but his grip was as firm as it had always been.

She screamed, and Tony dealt her a blow that left her head spinning so badly she couldn't tell which way was up or down. She stumbled and fell. Tony hefted her over his shoulder and ran. He bounced Brielle's stomach on his shoulder to the point of nausea. She swallowed back bile as she tried not to pass out. She needed to stay awake and alert so she could escape.

When she first saw Tony's face, Brielle knew she was in real trouble. In his eyes, she spotted a Fae. They were all black, and his voice sounded deeper as he spoke with a different cadence. She'd seen the portal in the chapel doorway open before, but when Tony waved his hand in the alley beside the museum and opened a portal out of thin air, she knew this was no ordinary Fae. It seemed an evil Fae took over the mind of a man who was already insane. This Fae was not only evil but powerful. Real fear now chilled her, for whoever was in Tony's head would not stop.

Tony set her on her feet but kept a firm hold of her hands while she stared down at a dock.

She tried to steady herself as Tony hailed a crewman on a boat. "*Stad, Thu!*" *You, stop!*

She blinked as her eyes traveled up the large vessel. A massive ship with a dragon's head sat in the water. Bree gasped and stood transfixed, frozen in place. Before her was a Viking longship. Her eyes traveled over it as she stood amazed at the sheer size and craftsmanship. Very few remained recovered and preserved. She'd only seen a replica once. That one was tiny compared to what floated before her.

Tony spoke Gaelic with the crew members. Since when did Tony speak Gaelic? She picked up "your master." And "my ship now." Before she could react, two crew members tied her hands and feet and hauled her into the boat. She struggled, but it was too late. They placed her in the front area and strode away.

Tony, or the Fae in his head, took control of the entire crew. No one stopped to question him as all did his bidding like zombies. She wondered what Fae took over Tony's mind and what power he held. Tony had never learned Gaelic or any other language besides English. He spoke that more like a sailor than an educated man.

His gaze snapped in her direction. Had he read her mind? He moved toward her, the sway of his step hinting at the other in his mind. He bent down and brushed her hair off her face.

His voice wasn't Tony as he rasped like another's, sending chills down her spine. "Brielle, my sweet, sit and enjoy the ride. We will be in the village soon enough. Ye will be my thrall, my slave, and see to my every desire." He bent, brushing his lips across hers. The beer taste of his breath soured her already upset stomach. The firmness of his kiss hinted at the one inside her ex.

She spat in his face.

He smirked as he wiped the spit and licked it off his finger. "All is going as I planned. I will have a human lover again, and the power shall be mine."

She struggled against the ropes, not caring that they rubbed her skin raw and brought tears to her eyes. She would do anything to escape him.

Tony glared at her with a sneer resembling the man she knew. "I have ye where I've always wanted ye, Brielle. Tied up to do my bidding." He rose and sauntered away without glancing back.

Her gaze took in the ship as crew members filed into the boat and set to rigging the lines. The crew pushed the ship away from the dock in synchronized precision that took years to perfect. One large square sail unfurled and flapped, filling with the wind. It reminded Brielle of her sailing trip with Colin. A tear escaped and trailed down her cheek. This would be no leisurely trip. She was on a Viking warship with hardened warriors headed to hell.

As the boat sailed away, yelling came from the shoreline. Brielle wished she could sit up and see.

It was Gaelic and she picked up "My ship."

Tony stole an entire longship with the whole crew.

She glanced back at Tony, seated at the stern beside the man holding the rudder. His hand glowed black as he held it to his chest, the light reflecting off his white shirt. He closed his eyes, took a deep breath, and waited momentarily. He leaned over and directed the crewman which direction to sail. Brielle knew he held a Stone of Iona but didn't know which one.

She closed her eyes and prayed for Ainslie. She prayed for Colin and her wee bugs, the twins. But mostly, she prayed for rescue.

****

Water hit her face. Ainslie sputtered and came to. God, her head hurt something fierce. Her lips tasted of blood. She opened her eyes, but all she saw was dirt.

"*Uachdaran dùisg phrìosanaich.*" *Prisoner's awake, jarl.*

Lying on her side, Ainslie couldn't move. They'd bound her feet and hands, and she hurt all over. Someone picked her up, and they held her standing between two enormous men. She glanced from side to side. Both were taller than her, which was rare, as she stood almost six feet.

Each possessed sandy-blond hair with a full beard. Long hair styled more like an eighties hair band than a man. Shaved on one side, with varying thickness of braids dangling from the back with metal rings and beads weaved through them. At first glance they could be twins. She studied the one on the right, and he had a more prominent nose. She examined their clothing, furs, and leather. She recognized them in a heartbeat, Viking. Head down, she took a deep breath and closed her eyes. The Fae, the Stones of Iona…damn if she hadn't followed Bree through the portal in the Chapel in the Woods and landed in the time of the Vikings. Vikings she knew well. This would be the twelfth century.

Someone slapped her hard, and she whipped her head to the warrior on her right. "*Thugaibh urram dot-sròl, agus freagair air son na luinge a ghoid do charaid.*" *Pay yer respects to the jarl, wench, and answer for the longship your friend stole.*

Ainslie gaped at him as she replied in rough Gaelic. "My friend stole a boat? What friend?" Tugging on Bree's hand was the last thing she remembered. Then it all went black.

She turned and focused on the man before her. Her breath left in a whoosh. It was the man from her dream, the man she dreamt of as her true love. He stood tall with black hair, almost as deep a black as hers. He also wore his hair styled with the left side shaved and the right side cut short with patterns shaved into the short hair. He had more braids in his mohawk, and the beads winked in the light of the room. His hawk nose appeared regal. A sharp jawline covered with a beard accentuated his handsome looks. But it was his blue-white eyes that she remembered. To her, they seemed like a Fae's eyes. She locked eyes with him for a moment. Breaking contact, his gaze traveled up and down her body as though she was the worst thing he'd set his eyes upon.

"Jarl?" Ainslie asked. The man before her smiled as if she made a joke.

The one to her left shook her. "Aye, this is Rannick MacRaghnaill, jarl of these lands, who serves Dougal MacDougall, Lord of the Isles, and ye need to answer for yer friend's crimes."

It took a moment, but it registered they spoke Gaelic or a rude form of it. She hadn't spoken it before, but this easily rolled off her tongue yet remained

45

English in her mind. Did he say *crime*?

She snapped at the man, her voice rasping from her dry throat. "What crime?" She coughed. "He kidnapped my sister-in-law." She gagged from her dry throat. "I followed—need to find her—in danger."

The man beside her yanked back her ponytail as he forced her eyes to meet his. "The longship yer friend stole. Too bad he left ye behind. Now ye will pay for his crime."

She spat in the man's face, the result coming out more air than saliva.

He slapped her again.

Dizzy from the blow, her head fell forward, rocking from side to side.

"Enough!" Rannick spoke for the first time. Her lengthy hair fell from her ponytail as she peered at him through the black strands. He studied her for a moment and eyed her up and down. Her clothing certainly had to be a shock to him. She doubted women in the twelfth century wore sweats or running sneakers. She smirked. Given the direction of his look, he probably hadn't seen the shape of a woman's leg or a woman's apex in snug clothing before.

Rannick's eyes traveled from her lower area to her face as he leered. "Sit her down. She can barely stand. I doubt she's any real danger to me tied up as she is." He waved. "Bring mead and let us learn what the woman's story is. Then I will decide the truth of what she speaks."

The warriors set her down, not very gently. Someone pressed a horn into her tied hands. She had to struggle to drink it, but she did, gulping it down, relieved at being able to revive herself. Honey mead soothed her parched throat. She held the horn between her legs as she flung her long hair out of her face.

Rannick took a long drink from his horn as he kept his eyes on her the entire time. Instinct told her he wasn't a very trusting man. If he was a jarl, he probably didn't have many he could trust.

Wait, he said the Lord of the Isles was Dougal MacDougall. She sat across from a man who served one of her ancestors. She squinted at the dirt floor as she tried to recall her family history. Dougal's son or grandson built Dunstaffnage castle and, eventually, the Chapel in the Woods.

Rannick spoke, and her eyes went to his. "What is 'sister-in-law'? I do not understand what yer sister has to do with the law?"

Ainslie sighed. History was not her strongest subject. Brielle could navigate this better than her. She needed to stay on her toes. One mistake, one wrong word, could get her in a lot of trouble. She glanced at her tied hands and feet. Well, more trouble than she was in now.

She took a deep breath and tried to tell her tale as best she could. "A man, the one who stole yer ship, kidnapped my brother's wife. I chased them, and he knocked me out. I tried to free her."

Rannick nodded. "Where is yer brother now? Why has he sent his *sister* to do a man's job?"

Ainslie wasn't certain how to answer that. She couldn't just come out and say, *Oh, he's in the twenty-first century, and I just came back in time.* Or could she? If these were the first people to settle the land, then this was around the first time the Fae approached The MacDougall and gave him the duty to protect the

47

Stones of Iona. It was one reason the Fae chose this land—that, and its strategic position at the point of the firth for a fighting sea base.

She must have spent too much time thinking since the man beside her kicked her. "The jarl has asked a question. Ye will respond."

She glanced at the man, then around the room. It was the first time she stopped to take in her surroundings. She should know better, assess the situation, and then form a plan. She needed any edge she could get.

They were in a large open room, with multiple areas, a cooking area, and a bed in the corner with a curtain. Ainslie sat on the floor facing Rannick, who sat on a platform. Many warriors were seated around them, with women serving them. She'd need to be careful. She was a woman in a man's world, something she didn't like—a world where the odds stacked against her only due to her sex. Her face settled on Rannick, who waited for her response.

Ainslie said everything carefully and slowly as if she spoke to a child. "My brother cannot be here. I am here and need to go after his wife, Brielle. She is in danger. I need to save her."

Rannick glared at her. His eyes examined her face, then her clothing. His stare settled on her breasts in her form-fitted workout tee. His gaze moved to her sneakers and tilted as if he tried to solve a puzzle. His scrutiny traveled up her legs, stopping at the juncture of her legs. She moved, bending her knees, and his eyes snapped to her face. She raised an eyebrow, knowing she caught him staring at her woman's parts.

Rannick commanded quietly, "Leave us."

The warrior beside her spoke. "But she's a prisoner."

Rannick waved his hand. "Who is bound. My captain stays. Everyone else, leave us now." The man at Rannick's side leaned over and whispered something, but Rannick shook his head. He must be his captain, large like Rannick but blond with braids and very muscular. He glared at Ainslie like she might jump up and attack him at any moment. Untied, she might if alone.

Once everyone left, his captain spoke. "Who are ye? What is yer name?"

Ainslie smirked. "Who are ye?"

The captain took a breath, but Rannick set his hand on the captain's arm, stopping him.

Rannick grinned at her. "Aye, introductions first. Ye know who I am." He waved to the man beside him. "This is Erik MacSomerlie, my first and captain."

Rannick leveled his eyes on her. "Who are ye?"

It was time, do or die. Her da always said to stick to the truth, even if it sounded false. His voice rang in her memory. *The truth shall always prevail.*

Ainslie shifted her seat and sat taller. "I am Ainslie Fiona MacDougall. I am from the future. I came through a Fae portal. Laird Colin Roderick MacDougall is my brother, and a Fae has kidnapped his wife, Brielle." She shrugged her shoulders. "Well, a man possessed by a Fae."

Rannick tilted his head to the side. "I do not know of any MacDougall relations by the name Ainslie or Colin." He nodded. "Ye lie."

Erik snorted next to him.

Ainslie took a long drink from her horn. It was now

or never.

She took a deep breath and thought, he who hesitates is lost. "I do not lie. I am who I say. A Fae kidnapped my brother's wife, and I must follow them to save her."

Erik shook his head and turned to Rannick. "She's a witch. Ye cannot trust her."

Ainslie gasped. "It is I who should not trust ye. My dearest friend, my sister-in-law, is in grave danger, and I need help. She needs help."

Erik grunted and kicked his feet out, shoving dirt on her.

She shook it off and replied hotly, "I know why ye are here. Ye settle this land for Laird MacDougall. His son, Duncan, will build a grand castle here. It will be called Dunstaffnage. Tell me I lie now. Tell me I am a witch. I don't care. All I want is to get to Brielle and save her from a madman."

Erik turned to Rannick. "Ye cannot believe her. We do not know if she is from the evil Fae."

Ainslie yelled at Erik, "I am not evil! I am from the future!"

Rannick shouted, "Stop!"

Ainslie and Erik glared at each other, panting.

Rannick spoke as he stared at Ainslie. "I have made my decision."

Ainslie turned to him and blinked.

Rannick smirked. "From the future or the Fae, we will see who and what ye are, Ainslie."

His head tilted down, and his eyes shifted, his expression threatening. "We will take her to The MacDougall. He will know if she is truly his relation."

Erik nodded. "I'll sail in the morning."

Turning to Erik, Rannick placed his hand on his arm. "No, I shall go." He glanced at Ainslie with a smirk. "And our guest shall accompany me."

Erik gasped, and Rannick took his arm. "I need ye here. Continue the work in the village and raise the army. The builders will complete the next longship soon, and we will need all the men ready."

Rannick glanced at her. "Ye will be my honored guest, always kept with a guard." He smirked. "For yer protection."

Erik barked. "Guest? She'll likely kill us all in our sleep."

Rannick waved his hand at her. "Untie her. Take her to the women to properly clothe her. I can't stand her dress. It's a distraction. If the warriors see her, they'll take her for a whore and attack her."

Ainslie gasped as Erik cut her ties away and pulled her to stand.

Rannick glared at Ainslie. "Ensure the men know she is under my protection and a guest. She is to remain untouched and unharmed."

Erik nodded, and Ainslie tugged her hands out of his grasp and turned to Rannick. "My brother Colin will soon follow; I'm certain of it. He will come for his wife. Please help him find us. He's a warrior and can help."

Rannick nodded, not taking his eyes off her.

Erik waved her to proceed with him out of the room.

Head held high and unable to hide her excitement, Ainslie preceded him into the world of the Vikings.

****

Rannick sat and contemplated all that had

developed in the last hour. This woman, Ainslie, knew they were there to settle the land for the MacDougalls. But she could have heard that information anywhere. It was common knowledge.

Her clothing was what threw him. He'd never seen the like. How it hugged her form, accentuated every crevice and curve. He saw it all and looked again. He shifted in his seat, adjusting himself, and growled.

She was forthright for a woman, too outspoken. Could she truly be from the future? He knew the Fae approached the MacDougall about a duty, which was one reason he settled the land. But the talk of Dougal's son puzzled him. Dougal married but hadn't given birth to an heir. Rannick drank from his horn and sighed. He needed to be on guard with the witch from the future.

Chapter 6

Dunstaffnage Castle, present day

Colin sat at his desk, staring at the *Fae Fable Book*. He reread the story multiple times and couldn't figure out how he would open the portal to travel in time. He slammed the book closed.

John appeared in the doorway, crossed, and sat in a chair before the desk. "The boys finished repairing the chapel and the doors." He shook his head. "I still don't know how ye ripped them off the hinges, but they replaced them, and the doors now close."

Colin nodded as John continued, the familiar routine soothing Colin. "Marie and Mrs. A took the kids out today. They will return before ye leave, so we have the day to prepare."

John glanced at the Fae book on the desk. "Still nothing from the story?"

Colin shook his head. The story ate at him every time he read it. Beating her. Was Tony beating her? Ainslie—somehow, he knew she was safe, sensed it in his soul. She was a warrior; she'd be all right anywhere.

John rubbed his chin. "Ye hear from Brigid yet?"

Colin shook his head and ran his hands through his hair. Of all the times he needed his Fae, this was it. He mentally called for her all morning. He begged her to come and show him how to save his true love. She didn't come, and the story didn't reveal anything. No one would help. He felt lost, and he feared Bree was lost to him. The Fae betrayed him. Anger built in him. Bree, at the hands of her ex, taken to God knows when, and what he might do to her...

He stood abruptly, scooping up the *Fae Fable Book*, and strode to the fireplace. He held the book before him as he looked into the fire.

John rose and walked toward him. "Colin, we'll figure it out. We always have."

Colin gripped the book tightly as he rested his head on it. In a roar, he threw it in the fire's flames.

John gasped and tried to reach into the fire.

Colin blinked. The book vanished.

Both men stood and watched the flames. Together, they turned to the shelf that held the *Fae Fable Book* to find it safe in its glass case.

Colin grabbed the mantel and roared again. "She's gone, and there's nothing I can do! A madman has her, an evil Fae is with them, and God only knows if she's safe! I didn't keep her safe! I promised to love, honor, and cherish her in this life and the next! It's killing me, John!"

John went to the table behind the desk and poured each a generous whisky. John sighed, returned to the fireplace, and handed Colin the drink.

Colin gulped the glass in one swallow and leaned on the mantel as he glared into the flames.

John sipped his whisky and regarded the fire as well.

A glass clinked, and the sound of liquid gurgled. A loud sip vibrated in the air. A long sigh from a man followed.

Colin and John turned to each other, then glanced

over their shoulders to find a man sitting at Colin's desk.

He sat and held the glass up. "Do ye know how long it has been since I had a good tot of whisky?"

Colin and John exchanged glances and turned as they gaped at the man. "Hello, Colin. Ye ought to treat my book better. Yer da did nothing like that, and he'd whip yer ass if he knew what ye had done." The man took another loud sip of the whisky and moaned.

Colin was the first to recover. "Who are ye, and how do ye know my da?"

The man gazed at Colin. His hair appeared pure white, so white it almost glowed. It fell long and straight down his back, looking like silk. When he shifted, his hair parted, and the point of his ear peeked through. He possessed bright white eyes. His skin shone light-colored, and he had the muscular body of a warrior. His suit was all white, but not of this world. The fabric glittered as he shifted his body, looking like satin, like something else not from earth. He was good-looking, gorgeous for a man. A shiver of awareness trickled down Colin's back. This man was Fae, pure Fae.

Colin took a step toward him but stopped. Something clicked in his mind, but it didn't seem to register. *The dream? Could this be the King of the Fae from his dream?*

John spoke from behind Colin. "Ye're Dagda, Morrigan's father. Ye're the King of the good Fae."

Dagda took another sip of his whisky and closed his eyes, obviously savoring the taste as he swallowed it slowly.

He frowned at Colin, then at John. "Sit, lads. We

have a lot to discuss."

Colin set his glass on the desk and paced. "No, thank ye. I'd rather stand."

He rounded on Dagda, placed his hands on the desk, and leaned toward him. "Where the hell have ye Fae been? Bring my *wife back!*" He roared the last in Dagda's face.

Dagda glared into Colin's eyes. "Ye always were such a hothead, Colin. Ye really need to control that anger. The evil Fae feed on it and will use it against ye."

Colin snatched his hands off the desk and resumed pacing.

John crossed to the desk and sat in a chair. He turned to Colin. "Colin, he's here to explain. We need to listen. I have a feeling he will tell us where and when Bree and Ainslie are."

Colin growled and continued pacing. "Speak, ye damn fairy, and don't leave out any details."

Dagda shook his head, glanced at the ceiling, and breathed deeply. "Colin, some details ye're better off not knowing."

Colin stopped and stared at Dagda, who returned his gaze solemnly.

Colin found it hard to speak. "Bree, God, is she even alive?"

Dagda lowered his head, took a deep breath, then looked into Colin's eyes. Dagda's expression shot fear straight into Colin's heart. He took a step to the chair and sat, not taking his eyes from Dagda. Colin choked on a sob. No, not his wee Bree. Could his chance to save her already be lost?

Dagda set his glass down. "They both are alive, but

not together."

Colin breathed deeply and placed his elbows on his knees. Dizzy. He was dizzy. Taking a few deep breaths, he repeated in his head, *She's alive. She's alive.*

Dagda's somber voice came to him. "We made a mistake. A grave mistake."

Colin's head snapped up to Dagda, who shook his head. "Imprisoned in our world was a Fae, the King of the Fomoire, the evil Fae. He committed crimes against our realm. His crimes used humans as weapons when he made them into changelings to hunt the Iona stones. Damn, he even used his sons, making them more monster than Fae or even human."

Colin whispered, recalling his Fae dream, "Balor."

Dagda took a sip of his whisky. "He escaped from prison, and we still don't know how. We thought Balor was secure. He is the one who took Brielle. Ainslie wasn't in his plan, but fate pulled her to another time with them. They landed in the twelfth century, when the Fae first approached Dougal MacDougall, Lord of Lorne, asking him to keep the Stones of Iona. They ended up where it all began."

John shook his head. "Wait. I saw the man. It was Bree's ex-boyfriend. I saw him clear as I see ye."

Dagda nodded, "Aye, ye saw Tony Stiles, that's for certain. But do ye remember the eyes?"

John nodded. "Black, all black. Possessed by the Fae, then. So, it wasn't Tony but this Balor ye mention."

Dagda shrugged. "Yes and no." He looked out the window. "It's complicated; possessions are. Sometimes the human mind rejects the Fae, and sometimes the mind match is so perfect, it's dangerous."

Colin leveled his eyes on Dagda. "So Tony and Balor took Bree?"

Dagda nodded. "Aye, the mind of the evilest Fae to exist mixed with a madman. Both are obsessed with Brielle. The minds have joined and work together."

John rubbed his chin. "How do ye know? The minds, that is, working together?"

Dagda laughed. "We are Fae. We see all and know all." He glanced between both men as Colin glared at him. "Well, most of the time."

Colin grunted. "So, the twelfth century. I'm going after my wife and my sister. How are ye getting me there?"

Dagda smiled and waved his hand. From the corner of the desk, The Brooch of Lorne floated in the air. He twirled his finger, and the brooch spun.

As Colin watched the piece spin, John spoke. "Ye know, a few years ago, that would have shocked me. But now I feel like it needs a showier display to impress me."

Dagda laughed and twirled his hand, and the brooch spun faster. A flash of light burst from the trinket. It slowed as it came to rest on the desk before Colin.

Dagda turned to John. "Showy enough for ye?"

John gasped, and Colin jolted when he examined the brooch. There were two stones in the settings—one with a red heart, and over it a purple oval stone.

Colin reached for the brooch and picked it up. He had to use his whole arm, for the piece alone was heavy. Weighted with both stones, it was substantial. "The Stone of Love and The Stone of Fear. Bree was right."

Dagda stood, crossed to the table, and refilled his glass to the brim.

Colin held the brooch and sighed. "She knew, didn't she? Bree knew something would happen. She insisted I keep this instead of taking it on tour."

Dagda sat back down behind the desk and took a long sip of the whisky, swishing it around his mouth before swallowing. He placed both elbows on the desk, wrapping both hands around the glass. "Aye, Balor visited her dreams. He became obsessed with her when she followed ye back in time. He saw her through the Fae that possessed Constance Ross. That's what makes this so dangerous. Balor is working off Tony's mind. Balor has had The Stone of Lust for centuries. While The Stone of Lust's power hunts The Stone of Faith, Balor's and Tony's minds are so gone, the lust has overtaken their minds. All they see is Brielle."

He sipped his whisky again, held the mouthful for a moment before swallowing. "We aren't sure if the stone chose the twelfth century because it might be where The Stone of Faith is or was at that time. Was it a place Balor picked? After all, that's where we started this journey with the Stones of Iona."

John gasped. "...or if it was where Ainslie wanted to go because she is obsessed with Vikings."

Dagda nodded. "Aye, but Balor and Tony have Bree. Ainslie is with a jarl. She is safe for now."

Colin growled, "I'll kill them. I'll kill them both, Balor and Tony."

Dagda set the glass down and held both hands up. "Not before ye cast Balor out of Tony then into purgatory. 'Tis why we have given ye both stones. Ye'll need that much power. If ye kill Tony before we capture Balor, he will escape. Ye must harness the stones' power to send him to purgatory. If not, he will forever haunt yer family."

Dagda waved his hand. In a tinkling laugh and a cloud puff, Brigid's small form appeared as she sat on the mantel.

Her tinkling laughter filled the room.

Colin growled, staring at the mantel. "What fresh hell is this, ye damn sprite?"

She shrugged. "So testy, Colin. I thought ye'd be happy to see me?"

Dagda groaned. "Daughter, stop teasing him and give him the book."

Colin turned to Dagda. "Did ye know she's been speaking to my daughter? Ye tell her to leave Evie alone."

Dagda spit out his whisky. "Brigid, ye will stop playing with the humans. Leave the poor child be."

Brigid flew to Colin and dropped a book in his lap. It landed heavily for a small book, causing Colin to groan and bend forward.

She whispered to Colin, "Blessed they are, yer wee bugs. Blessed by the Fae. She has such potential."

As Colin sat up, he swiped at her, missing as she flew back to the mantel and laughed in her tinkling way.

Dagda groaned, "Enough, Brigid. The spell in the book. Memorize it."

Colin glanced at his lap, and Bree's book of *Poems and Sonnets* sat there. Memories of their nights together came crashing into his mind stabbing painfully at his heart. He held the book and sighed. He opened it and turned the pages, looking for the poem they had read that night of the storm. It wasn't there. Only one page held writing, and he read it to himself.

I bathe them in blood; I place fear in your heart,
That the truest love may ne'er depart!
Nor other women will go thy way,
Nor deal with you, be it as it may.
But all these things together thrown,
His heart and soul that he be torn,
He may perish and forever be,
Only not in my company.

This was a spell to send a Fae to purgatory.

He glanced at Dagda. "If I speak this now, can I send Brigid to purgatory?"

Dagda laughed as Brigid disappeared. "Let's not try it."

Colin slammed the book closed.

Dagda focused on Colin as he spoke; his intent flowed through Colin deeply. "Colin, to harness the power of the stones, ye must concentrate very hard on Balor to send him away. It will take all yer energy. Ye cannot falter. Once he is gone, do what ye will with the human. It is of no consequence to the Fae."

Colin grumbled, "How will I know Balor is gone?"

Dagda peered at him. "Trust me, ye will feel it. Ye will know."

Colin glanced at John. "The twelfth century. That was before they built the castle, No bolt hole."

John shook his head. "Ye'll do fine."

Colin nodded and peered at Dagda, who chugged his whisky. "How do I return?"

Dagda slammed the glass on the desk. "The book. The page will appear when the time is right."

Dagda faded from sight.

Colin and John stood up and gazed around the room.

John spoke, the first to break the silence. "God, I hate it when they do that."

Colin looked at the Brooch of Lorne. "Dusk. I'll go at dusk."

John nodded. "Wait, he didn't tell us how to open the portal."

Colin looked at the book in his hand. "Yes, he did—the book. The chant will appear."

Colin gripped the brooch and closed his eyes. He focused all his thoughts on Bree.

He opened his heart and his mind as he thought only of her. "Hear me, Bree. Hear me, my love. I am coming, and I'm bringing hell with me."

****

The boat rocked as the air grew colder. Brielle huddled down in the boat's front. The crew rowed now as it came closer to dusk and the wind had died down. The ship still moved at a fast pace. A crew member gave her a long strip of fabric, like a tartan, but darker; she couldn't make out the pattern. It was dirty and smelled of sour body odor, but wrapped inside it, she was warm.

She hadn't seen Tony in some time and was content with that. They left her tied hand and foot, but she found a comfortable position on top of some rope. She shifted her hands to her neck and found her Iona stone necklace. When she touched it, the stone brought her closer to Colin. The stone was an identical half that matched Colin's stone. The halves belonged to his parents and, when brought together, made a heart. She held his mother's half and Colin his father's. True love was what it represented.

Brielle gripped it tight, closed her eyes, and whispered, "I put God between us." It was a chant from a Fae fable Hamish MacLean told her when he first gave her the stone, a *rosad*, a Gaelic spell. She used it before and hoped it would banish the evil Fae as in Hamish's story. She kept mumbling it over and over.

Someone ripped the stone from her grasp. The chain pulled at her neck and broke before she could react.

Tony stood over her and held the stone, the broken chain dangling from his fingers.

He sneered as he glared at her and spoke. "No chant or charm will keep me from ye, my Brie." He squinted at the stone, then at her. He smirked and threw the stone into the ocean without taking his eyes off her.

Brielle cried out as Tony laughed. Tears fell down her cheeks. Her stone, the half to Colin's—the stone they made their wedding vows with—lost in the sea. Brielle curled into a ball as silent tears fell down her cheeks.

Tony bent down and grabbed her chin hard, his voice raspy again, not Tony's. "I've waited for this day, Brielle. I watched and waited. I've found a human to possess so I can touch ye, possess ye. No matter if Colin comes for ye, ye will either be mine or die." He stood over her, his hand above her as he chanted something in Gaelic she didn't understand.

He glared at her, and a slow, evil grin spread. "Ye're now cursed, Brielle. If ye go through the portal back to the future, ye will die. If Colin saves ye, ye will die." He laughed hard and strode away.

Die? She would die? So tired; everything hurt.

Brielle wished for Colin. She concentrated hard on Colin, thinking only of him, and his voice carried in her mind.

"Hear me, Bree. Hear me, my love. I am coming, and I'm bringing Hell with me."

Chapter 7

Ainslie stood on the port side overlooking the land at dusk as it slowly progressed past in the distance. The boat clipped through the waves quickly as they headed to Oban, Scotland. That morning, she almost cheered when they led her to the dock, and before her was a large longship with a curved dragon head bow. She dreamed of sailing on one for years, and now she was on a real one.

Ainslie had waited on the ship for Rannick's men to finish loading the boat. She wore an overtunic, a dress of sorts, and a fur wrap pinned at the shoulder to keep her warm. The woman who attended her braided the sides of her hair and captured it in the back, allowing the long tresses to flow free but out of her face. Ainslie preferred the ponytail, but she was happy if the style kept the hair out of her face. When Ainslie put her leggings back on, the woman attending her said she would be required to wear pants over them. She grunted, put on her sneakers, and laced fur over them, hiding them. Standing there, she blended in with the rest of the boat's occupants. Her guard, Ivor, remained at her side, a constant companion since leaving her assigned hut that morning.

Rannick strode by with his trunk on his shoulder. "Ready for a sea voyage, woman? I am certain ye, being a foreigner, would likely spend the voyage over the side losing yer innards."

She shifted her small, tied bag the woman gave her, filled with a change of clothing, a comb, and other women's necessities. "My brother and I spent years sailing with our da. Being on the water is second nature to me." Let him absorb that. She knew the sea and loved sailing.

Rannick smiled as he moved on.

The men settled into their rows as they prepared to launch. The plank came up, and men on the dock threw the ropes into the boat.

Rannick stood in the rear by the rudder, the rowers pushed the long oars against the dock, and the boat shifted out. The square sail flapped and caught the wind, moving the boat toward the open sea.

The ship picked up speed, and her eyes caught Rannick's. He raised an eyebrow, and she beamed as she gained her sea legs. Ivor sat on his trunk, relaxed now that they were out in the open waters. She huffed a laugh. He figured not much in a way for her to escape since water surrounded them.

****

Later that day, Ainslie sat on a stack of rope, full after a lunch of dried fish and ale, as the longboat sailed smoothly through the ocean.

Rannick approached the mainmast and stopped. "Hail, all. A fighting competition between warriors, one-on-one sparring, and the winner—a solid gold piece." He held up a shiny gold coin, large and round. From her distance, Ainslie saw a pattern stamped on the side.

Loud cheers erupted as the men drew sticks to determine the order in which they would fight.

Intrigued, Ainslie approached and reached out to pull her stick.

Before she got hold of a stick, Rannick grabbed her wrist. "Women do not fight. Women make a meal, a home, and babies."

Ainslie snatched her hand back and huffed. "Where I come from, women do much more than that. Where I come from, women are fighters. We are great scholars, and some are queens leading vast countries. All while still being able to make a meal, a home, and babies." She ticked off the last on her fingers.

Rannick needed a lesson in a woman's ability. Regardless of the time, women were capable of just as much or more than men. Their ability to raise a family with care and brutally fight simultaneously with control set them apart from a man's single-track mind.

Ivor followed Ainslie laughing. "A woman warrior, this I would like to see. I place a wager on the warrior woman that she will best any who fight her."

Rannick waved Ivor off, but the other warriors gathered, making comments. Wagers flew fast, making Ainslie smile. The men's lust for competition forced Rannick's hand, and she hadn't lifted a finger. Men were so predictable.

The fighters cheered as they cleared some chests used as seats for rowing. The men sectioned a small area in the center of the longship off for the fight. Rannick stood beside the keelson box that helped support the mainmast, Ainslie to his right. She removed her overtunic and wrap and stood in only a shirt and pants. Ivor handed her a sword, and she swung it judging its weight.

She glanced up and caught Rannick staring. She

smirked and slashed the blade down, wanting to say, *I'll cut you, Rannick.*

He grinned in return and nodded. "I called the competition. I shall call which warriors battle the woman, the *She Warrior.*"

A warrior protested. "Usually, we go by order of drawn straw. What is this ye play at, Rannick?"

"Fighting with the *She Warrior* is not usual. I shall call upon a warrior for her."

Rannick called the first warrior to fight Ainslie. A young man barely with facial hair approached. Ainslie felt sorry for him because she would knock him on his rear with the first move. He arrogantly strutted. Maybe he was a man intimidated by a strong-willed woman.

She sighed, then took her stance as Rannick stepped back and waved his hand for them to begin. The youth came at her with a forward thrust, and she sidestepped him, blocked him, then used her foot and flipped him on his rear. His sword clattered to the flooring.

She placed her sword at his throat. "Yield?"

The warriors gasped, then cheered for her.

Rannick's eyebrows rose as Ainslie helped the youth to his feet and patted him on the back. Rannick rubbed his neck and looked over his warriors. He called upon another warrior. "Gunnar, come fight the *She Warrior.*"

A large older warrior moved from the crowd, a grin on his face. As Gunnar passed, Rannick patted his back and whispered something, but Ainslie couldn't hear what was said. The warrior nodded as he moved toward her. No matter. She'd fight anyone.

Both took their ready stance, and Rannick signaled

for them to begin.

They circled, weighing their opponent, waiting on who would take the offensive first.

It was Gunnar, with a slice of his blade on her shoulder. Ainslie blocked him well, but he stepped forward and slammed his shoulder into her, knocking her down. Ainslie somersaulted backward to stand, her blade out and ready to defend the next block.

Gunnar glanced at Rannick, who nodded toward Ainslie.

They circled again, waiting to see who would advance.

Ainslie led the next attack with an overhead slash. Gunnar blocked it, pushing her back. He was more substantial, but she was small, agile, and smart.

They circled, and Ainslie went for his middle.

Gunnar blocked and spun, coming around overhead.

She stopped it with her blade and allowed him to slide down hers knowing she could quickly push it aside with his forward momentum. When his sword came to the hand guard, she moved with all her might. He stumbled on a sidestep at the unexpected shift. As he flew past her, Ainslie whacked his rear with the side of her blade. The warriors laughed, and Gunnar came for her in an off-balance rage. She sidestepped and hit his rear end again.

Gunnar leveled his eyes on her and advanced with his blade. Side-to-side attacks came at her fast, backing her into the mainmast, trapping her, obviously trying to end the fight. Knowing sailing and the rigging, Ainslie reached up and grabbed the tack line holding the sail in place and swung herself onto the keelson box beneath the main mast. She landed surefooted and, in her follow-through, swung her sword, connecting with Gunnar's, disarming him. His sword flew out of his hand and clattered against the hull. He stood staring at his empty hand, then tilted his head back and laughed loudly.

He bowed to Ainslie. "Ye are Freyja, the war goddess. Her spirit lives in ye. I have never seen a woman fight. A Valkyrie, and I'm honored to fight with ye."

Gunnar strode to Rannick whose eyebrows remained raised. "She has earned her coin. She has won the contest."

The surrounding warriors cheered as Ainslie stood over them, proud of her accomplishment. She'd battled and won against a trained, skilled Viking warrior. Her da would be so proud. Some warriors grumbled as they settled on the bets made, bringing her out of her musings. Ainslie jumped down and approached Rannick. She grinned at him and held out her hand. "Time to settle up."

Rannick dropped a gold coin in it, then glanced behind her. "Disarm her. She is still our *guest*." Her guard Ivor must be back. The sword pulled in her hand, and she let him take it. He wasn't who she focused on.

She stared at Rannick, her being so tall that they stood almost eye to eye. "I bested yer best. Admit it. A woman can fight."

Rannick's smile grew. "Oh, my sweet, he wasn't my best. He was the one who wouldn't hurt ye."

Ainslie gripped the coin and raised an eyebrow. "I'll take on yer best any day, anytime, and I'd still win."

She flipped the coin and caught it. "I'd even wager the gold coin on it."

She flipped the coin again, and Rannick stepped toward her, catching the coin. They stood close as their breaths mingled. His sweet woodsy scent wafted over her, sandalwood and citrus. He glanced over her face and hair, then trailed to her chest.

His eyes returned to hers, and she raised an eyebrow as he spoke. "Warrior woman from another time or another land, my best would do ye harm. I have vowed never to harm a woman."

Ainslie gazed back into his eyes. "That's all right. Ye'd never get close enough with yer sword to harm me. But I may harm ye."

Rannick stood there a moment, staring into her eyes. She glowered back with the glare of a challenge. She held out her hand for the coin. He took it in his, the rough callouses brushing her skin, sending goose bumps up her arm. He placed her coin in her palm and closed his hands over hers, holding her hand in an embrace.

Without taking his eyes off her, he said, "Ivor, find a second guard. The *She Warrior* might need more than one."

He winked at her, released her hand, and turned, moving away.

****

Later that night, the wind died down. Rannick had the warriors take up the oars to keep the ship going. To pass the time, different warriors told stories while one lightly drummed the beat for the oarsmen.

Ainslie huddled in the boat's front out of the colder night wind.

Rannick sat at the rear in the shadows. He recalled earlier in the day when she wanted to fight.

She flipped the coin, and Rannick stepped closer and caught the coin. They stood so close he saw green specks in her honeyed brown eyes. Her clean scent came to him, lavender, as his eyes roamed her face, petite yet firm, tanned like a man's. His eyes traveled her hair, jet black tresses that fought the ties to be free in the wind. His stare trailed down her chest, where he saw down her shirt. Her abundant cleavage moved with her breath, teasing his senses. His eyes returned to her eyes, and she raised an eyebrow. Defiant, too confident for her own good. She was likely nothing but trouble, and the thought made him smile.

He was ready for her challenge but wouldn't take her on.

Rannick stood there momentarily, staring into her eyes that glared back in challenge. Ainslie's form was a warrior yet also a woman. She carried confidence about her he had never seen in a female before. He had never met a woman like her and doubted he would see another again. She intrigued him.

She held out her hand. Rannick took it in his. Soft yet firm. There was a small callous on her thumb from sword practice. She was truly a warrior. He placed her coin in her palm and closed his hands over hers. His eyes went to her lips. Would they be as soft as her hand, or would her kiss be as firm as her sword arm. A strong fervent kiss from the *She Warrior*? Would she stir him, bringing him to his knees? He blew a huff. She'd likely stab him in the back as she distracted him with her passion.

Without taking his eyes off her, he said. "Ivor, find

a second guard. The *She Warrior* might need more than one."

Being so overpowered by the desire to kiss her, he had to leave. He reluctantly released her hand and turned away.

Gunnar broke into his thoughts, speaking to Ainslie. "Does our *She Warrior*, our Valkyrie, have a story to share with the good men who work to transport her?"

Ainslie grinned. "Aye, Gunnar, I do. The story is about a Valkyrie and a great magic stone. My mother told me this story as a child, and I will share it with ye all now."

Rannick expected Ainslie to decline the offer. But when she accepted, he sat up in his seat.

She settled herself before the attentive oarsmen on the keelson box. The light from the lantern above her lit her dimly but her beauty still shone. She smiled as she began her story.

"A warrior, Sigurd, traveled far away to settle a new land and village and build a sea war army to serve his king.

"During his travels, Sigurd saw a brilliant light in the distance, like a fire burning in the sky. He followed it, curious if it was a god who would make such a bright light. He came upon a worship house, and the glorious light came from inside. He ventured inside, and upon the altar was a warrior in full battle gear, laid out in peace. The magnificent light came from under the stand, lighting the warrior in a fantastic light.

"He approached and noticed the warrior sleeping. He removed the helm and discovered the great warrior was a woman."

Some men gasped.

Rannick grinned as Ainslie told her story. She was an excellent storyteller, using her hands and making eye contact with men rowing by the light of a single lantern above her. He shifted to get more comfortable as she continued her story.

"This warrior woman possessed a beauty unmatched by any other woman he had ever seen. She had jet-black hair, was very tall, and maintained the muscles of a warrior. So, overcome with her beauty, the warrior bent and kissed the woman."

Wee Willie spoke up. "Wait, ye just described yerself. Ye are the warrior woman!"

Ainslie blushed and replied, "Aye, my mother always made me the warrior because I like the Viking way of life, and I like to fight with my sword." Wee Willie grinned, and Ainslie continued her story.

"She woke from her deep sleep and explained that Odin had cast a wicked spell upon her to sleep for 900 years until her true love came. Now awakened by Sigurd, Fiona was a warrior goddess like Freyja, a Valkyrie, reincarnated to bring victory into battle. When her true love came, she would fight beside him in a great fight against a magical evil. Odin foretold only together would they defeat this evil. Apart they would lose."

Rannick grinned into the darkness. Her facial expressions shifted in the lamplight. She was an enchanting creature, almost hypnotizing.

"The battle came, and during the war, they became separated. Both faltered and risked losing the battle. The evil foe captured Fiona and cast her upon a small island that, at high tide, would flood, drowning her.

Fiona prayed for rescue, and a blue light appeared from the ocean on the rocky shore beside her. The light was a magical blue diamond-shaped gem, The Stone of Faith. She picked up the stone and held it to her heart.

"During the battle, a warrior of the evil foe told Sigurd the evil enemy stranded his true love, and she was about to die.

"Sigurd saw his love on the island and sailed to save her. Upon Sigurd's arrival the evil foe hid behind the rock Fiona sat upon and lunged with his sword to kill Sigurd. Fiona, fearing for her love, stepped in front of Sigurd, taking the sword instead. Sigurd, in his anger, cut off the evil foe's head. But his true love lay dying."

Wee Willie spoke up again. "Wait, she dies? What kind of grand story is this? She can't die. Ye're telling the story wrong."

The warrior rowing next to him cuffed him on the shoulder. "Hold, it's her story to tell. I am certain she has more to say." He nodded for her to continue.

****

Ainslie blushed, then glimpsed down. She took a deep breath and glanced up, catching Rannick's stare. She was curious to see his response, for none of them knew she told a story from the *Fae Fable Book*—the story of The Stone of Faith. The book likely didn't even exist yet. It wasn't until she learned that Colin had gone back in time and went to purgatory that she pieced together her ma's bedtime story and the stone as truth. She hadn't seen her ma's bedtime story in the *Fae Fable Book*, but she knew it was there.

The story their mother told Colin as a child was also a Fae fable story. His Fae fable story came true.

75

So, it only stood to reason that the story her mother told her was her Fae fable story, fated to come true. She regarded Rannick as she finished the story.

"Sigurd grabbed Fiona's hands and prayed for her to live. With The Stone of Faith still in her hands, he brought their hands to her heart, praying for his true love. The stone glowed blue, and the light grew. It grew so bright others saw it for miles around. Sigurd called out to his true love, and the light pulsed. Their love healed Fiona, and together they lived happily ever after."

Wee Willie was the first to comment. "See, I told ye she lives."

Ainslie glimpsed at Wee Willie and smiled. "Aye, she lived."

She peeked at Rannick, who focused on her. They sat there locked in a gaze, and time slowed. Her dream flashed in her mind, and Rannick's expression shifted to a grin that slowly spread over his face, touching her heart.

Chapter 8

Balor had his crew sail to the dock at the Isle of Colonsay, Scalasaig, Scotland, a small island close to the mainland but far enough not to garner too much attention—a perfect refuge for him and his thrall.

Standing on the bow, Balor eyed a fat man waiting to greet him, knowing he would be easy prey. He already sensed the weaknesses in the man; mind control would be easy. Time and time again, humans' weak minds were so easily controlled by a simple glance, gesture, or thought.

The man stepped forward and greeted him warmly as his warship slid next to the dock. "Ho, MacDougall warship, welcome!"

Balor wiggled his fingers, commanding his crew as they docked the warship. "Greetings from the MacDougall. I come to rest amid my voyages."

A plank hit the ship's side as the sizeable man stood at the end. Balor, wanting to establish his position as leader, exited first. Standing on the plank over the jarl, they grasped hands. He would not need to use his mind control. This fool already welcomed him with open arms.

The energetic man shook his hand vigorously. "I bid ye welcome to Scalasaig or Skali's Bay, our little slice of heaven. I am Ivor MacLeod, jarl of this little slice of paradise."

Balor moved off the plank, his crew already unloading trunks and goods.

Ivor stood eyeing the goods coming off the ship. "Ye bring news from the MacDougall?"

Balor read his mind trying to discern the best answer to ease any fears. Ivor hoped for good news. He recently had a fallout with the Lord of the Isles. The fool made it too easy.

He used his Scots voice, the one of Balor without the modern American accent of Tony. "The Lord of Lorne sends his greetings and hopes I find yer hall full of hospitality as I rest from trading to return to him with a full report."

Ivor nodded his head. "Aye, ye shall be welcome. I hope ye will take my tidings and vow of service to the Lord of Lorne."

Ivor's gaze moved and froze on the ship. Balor followed his stare.

The crew unloaded Bree, tied, blindfolded, and gagged at his direction. She fought them, not realizing the danger the action posed to her. When her foot missed the plank, and she teetered near the edge, nearly falling, the guard grabbed her, cutting her scream short. She walked the rest of the way tall and proud. Her cream modern pant suit set her apart from the other Vikings, but no matter. Balor could quickly fix it if questioned, changing a memory with the wave of his hand. When they reached the end of the plank, she tripped and fell. Her guard picked her up and followed his crew into the village.

Balor sent a message to her guard using his mind speak. ~Take her to my hut. Bind her. Have a guard posted. No one comes in, and no one leaves. ~

Weak human minds. So easily controlled.

Ivor clapped him on the back. "Come, my friend. Let us eat, drink, and celebrate yer bounty. I am sure ye have goods for trade. We can talk over a good meal in my long hall."

Ivor led them through the village. Balor was nearly blind to the sights and Ivor's senseless prattle.

His powers grew now that he had escaped Fae's purgatory. He grunted. Damn Dagda and the Fae Council for imprisoning him. They thought too highly of themselves. He held power, and they were all envious. He had The Stone of Lust, designed by the Fomoire to track The Stone of Faith. It possessed immense power but also radiated an intense emotion— lust. Balor craved power, but his passion for female human flesh he couldn't deny. He didn't want to.

His wife was human and had died in battle. He had wed and gone against Fae law, that no Fae shall mate with a human, as the offspring could be monsters and not of the human or Fae world. Bah, stupid rule. He had done it anyway and married his love, only to have her felled by their sons. All three fools were born human but became dragon shapeshifters when he cast an ancient spell on them.

Stupid betrayers had turned their back on the Fomoire to fight for the good of mankind for the good Fae, the Tuatha Dé Danann. He cursed them for all eternity, immortal fools.

Arriving in the longhouse, Balor was seated next to Ivor. " 'Tis an honor, my friend, to have someone from The MacDougall in my hall again." He waved to a serving girl, who placed a horn filled with drink in his hand. Before Balor could take a sip, a plate filled with roast lamb, chicken, and various root vegetables was placed in front of him. The scent of grilled meat wafted to his nose, causing his stomach to growl.

"Aye, drink up, my friend. We shall celebrate our wins and praise Valhalla for our bounty." Ivor sat heavily next to him and drank deeply from his horn. "I bid ye welcome again."

Balor only grunted. While he liked the table of a glutton, he couldn't stand their disposition. Digging into his dinner, he eyed the room.

A serving girl passed, and Ivor eyed her, then glanced at Balor. He held no interest in the woman. He only wanted Brielle.

Ivor leaned over. "I saw ye had a thrall tied up like a prisoner. Something tells me there's a story there. Care to share yer thrall's tale?"

Balor sensed the man's lust for Brielle. He smelled it in his sweat, and it disgusted him. The human mind he occupied screamed in his mind. *She's mine, you pig.*

Balor smirked. He liked this human—so much like him. "She's mine, taken as a token of war. She's devious and must always be bound." The mind of Tony kept a rolling commentary on his mind of sex fantasies he wanted to try.

Balor spoke what Tony thought because he liked the perverse nature of Tony and found it entertaining. "I keep her bound for my pleasure, for me and me alone. No one is to go near her, touch her, or aid her. She is serving her sole purpose, my pleasure."

Ivor grated, "A bit fierce in yer treatment of her. A thrall I can easily bring to heel to serve a jarl well. All of mine are happier here as I treat them well. As long as they serve my tribe and me, they shall have good food, nice clothes, and I keep them happy."

Ivor patted the rear of a serving woman as she passed.

She glanced over her shoulder and giggled as Ivor toasted her. "They are even good at playing together, a woman with a woman. Makes for good bed sport." Ivor's boisterous laugh rang in Balor's ears, annoying him.

Balor glanced at the serving woman, young with large breasts. He might like something extra after he used Brielle.

The thought of Brielle brought forth Tony's thoughts, which roared. *She's mine, and I want her now.* Balor leered. He liked this human. Tony proved to be enjoyable to occupy.

Balor stood and bowed. "I thank ye, Ivor, for the fine meal and company, but I must be off to see my thrall. Until tomorrow." Balor toasted his host and headed out the door to his guest hut.

****

Ivor nodded but watched his guest depart. He had a funny feeling whenever he was near this Balor of the MacDougall. He couldn't pinpoint what it was, but it nagged his mind. The thrall was a puzzle, fully bound and gagged. Balor claimed she was the spoils of war, prohibiting him from interfering. But her appearance and beauty captivated all around her. Warriors stopped as they took her through his village. Her regal conduct facing imprisonment was not the behavior of one taken in the height of battle, but one taken against their will. Her clothing was strange and a style he had not seen before. The quality of the fabric, silk for sure, spoke of royalty or relation to one. She must be of noble birth because he'd bet his best longboat there was no way she was common.

His first captain, Tormund, approached, sat next to him, and toasted the evening.

Tormund quietly spoke while he smiled and looked around the longhouse. "His men are typical, nothing to note. They are loyal to him, but there's something off."

Ivor nodded. "Aye, I feel it as well. What did yer men learn?"

Tormund took a chicken leg and bit into it, speaking around his chewing. "It's strange. They speak of loyalty, but they speak in general. No specific locations when asked about raids. And they call him master, not jarl or laird."

Ivor glimpsed across the hall. A few of Balor's men still dined and flirted with the serving women. Very few would be alone tonight—an opportunity to learn information as a woman could gain much more than bed sport from a well-satisfied man. Ivor treated his people well, and in turn, they served him well. He would learn much after tonight.

Ivor lifted his horn and spoke before drinking. "Did ye put a hidden guard on him?"

Tormund nodded.

Ivor toasted him. "To tomorrow."

****

Balor entered his hut and was welcomed to a warm glow as the candles burned low. His guard stood outside with instructions that no one would enter or exit without his permission.

This Brielle, this obsession of Tony's, was a puzzle to him. She must be of powerful mind and heart. There were few whom he could not control their minds. She was immune to his efforts.

He crossed the room to find Brielle lying in bed, still bound by her hands and feet, a mouth gag in place. He'd learned she had a loud scream when she wanted. Balor watched her closely as he approached her. She was asleep, so he softly sat down next to her.

Tony's mind spoke up. *God, she is beautiful, and she is mine again.* Memories flashed through Balor's mind, flipping from one image to the next. Recollections from the past when they were together. Some typical, some arousing. His favorite images were of Tony and Brielle having sex together. The things Tony liked to do for sex play impressed Balor. He'd experienced nothing of the sort. Sex houses were a regular thing in large villages, but the modern world's images were unique and intriguing.

Balor smirked; Tony had just conjured his favorite sexual fantasy with Brielle. Balor allowed the human mind to take control because where Tony wanted to go, Balor liked.

He reached for her face and trailed his finger softly down her cheek.

She moaned and shifted. When her eyes opened, it took her a moment for her to come fully awake. Her eyes widened, and she groaned behind the gag as she tried to shimmy away when she realized who sat beside her.

"Brielle, my sweet. We have finally arrived at our island heaven. Now, ye will take me to paradise." Balor took the ropes holding Brielle's hands and untied the top part, leaving her hands bound.

She struggled against the bonds. Balor jerked the ties tighter, making Brielle whimper in pain.

Tony leered inside. Hurting Brielle aroused him like nothing before. All of Tony's anger at her surfaced as Balor's arousal sought the same sexual desire and power. Following Tony's lead, he tied her hands to the bedpost.

She stared into his eyes, pleading.

Tony roared in Balor's mind. *God, she's so vulnerable.*

He pulled his dagger and moved it before her eyes, which widened again.

Tony chuckled lowly. *I love the knife. She's so afraid of it.*

His gaze roamed her body. Too many clothes for what he had in mind. He moved his dagger to her cheek, then her breast, and trailed it down her side.

She shifted away but couldn't get far.

At her ankle, the tip caught in her pants leg, and he slipped the knife inside and ripped it from ankle to hip.

Brielle tried to scream, but her yelling had reduced her voice to a rasp.

Balor grinned and shifted to the other leg, repeating the tear. He stripped her pants off, exposing her underwear bare on the rear.

Tony smirked. *Thongs. I love thongs.*

Yes, Tony's mind was a place Balor could like, possibly love. He trailed the knife under Brielle's blouse and flipped the tip, traveling up her chest, popping off the buttons one by one. He brushed the shirt open and cut her bra off in one quick twist. He inhaled her scent, roses mixed with a tinge of sweat. The kind that held a metallic edge of fear underlying body odor.

Brielle cried softly and closed her eyes.

Tony roared in Balor's mind, *God, she's beautiful.*

Balor allowed Tony free rein and sat back to enjoy the evening.

Tony leaned over Brielle as he grabbed her breast, squeezing hard, hissing, "Open your eyes, Brielle."

She shook her head.

"Open and look at me, now!" he screamed.

She opened her eyes and stared into his.

"Good. I will have you as I have always wanted you. You would never allow me to tie you up for my pleasure." He trailed the knife along her breast's side, bringing out a shiver. "Now, I will take you like the slave you are."

****

Brielle whimpered. She had to close her mind off, as she had done when Tony played his perverse sex games. She conquered that fear when Colin showed her what sharing true love was like, not this fiendish sex play. But now she needed the mind-numbing escape, the one she had learned from a friend. Brielle had to go away. Her body was not where she was. She needed to go. She shut her mind off, going away. *I am not here. I am not here.*

Chapter 9

Rannick escorted Ainslie through the village at Oban Bay. "Stay close, woman. Something has crowded the village today."

They'd docked that morning and traveled through the thriving Viking village to Dunollie castle to see the MacDougall. Ainslie examined the town and surrounding area as much as she could, but everything seemed different. She figured it would be since there was a one-thousand-year difference, but even the curve of the land appeared changed. No, not changed. In the future, man would change it.

Following Rannick through the crowded village, she tried to compare the past to the future to know what to expect. The outer building she called home at Dunollie an ancestor built much later, closer to the sixteenth century. They'd used part of the original Dunollie castle stones that stood as a ruin for the foundation of the new modern house. When they sailed into the bay, she saw the familiar square stone tower from a distance. Much different in the past, Dunollie castle was a full tower with wall walks lining the cliff the building stood on. She surmised there was a large bailey inside and a village where the manor house she knew as home would be in the future.

She bumped into Rannick's back, and he turned.

He grunted as he nodded to a group on horseback

leading other horses. "The castle sent an escort to the village after seeing my warship dock. We'll make our way quickly to the castle. My men typically stay on the longship in Oban, but I stay at the castle." He eyed her up and down. "Ye can ride, can't ye?"

Ainslie rolled her eyes as she folded her arms across her chest and nodded.

Rannick huffed a short laugh, turned, and hailed the group of warriors riding toward them. Before she turned back, Rannick lifted her onto a horse. As they made their way up the cliff to Dunollie castle, he and five of his men surrounded her.

Rannick rode closer to her. "I've sent word ahead. They are expecting us. Dougal doesn't like—surprises."

Ainslie smirked. She would surprise her ancestor, whether he liked it or not. Appreciating the short ride instead of the long walk, Ainslie gathered her thoughts. She needed to devise a way to mention the Fae and the Stones of Iona without being overheard by a room full of guards and retainers she imagined were in attendance. With the village this crowded, the MacDougall was probably holding meetings. Ainslie had read they were called a "Thing," but she needed to find out if this was the case today. She glanced at Rannick. Maybe he could help.

She leaned over, murmuring, "I need to speak with the MacDougall in private."

Rannick barked a laugh. "That will not happen."

Ainslie huffed, "I have to prove I am truly part of the family. To do that, I must reveal a family secret."

Rannick shook his head. "Dougal is never alone. There are no family secrets."

Ainslie turned and smirked. "Says the man who is

not a MacDougall."

Rannick glanced at her and then ahead. "Ye must convince him of a private audience if ye want one. I doubt he will believe ye." Chuckling, he added, "I hope he doesn't decide to throw ye out of his hall."

Ainslie shrugged. "He won't. But I think he may not like me, for what I say will surprise him."

As they approached the cliff, a large market came into view. Farther down the road to the right, warriors held fighting games, with men watching, making wagers. Next to them was another game where there was a tug of war between groups of men, all yelling and cheering. The outside of the castle resembled one of the reenactment events Dunstaffnage held in the future, resembling a giant party. Ainslie took it all in with a smile. She loved those events and was smack dab in the middle of a real Viking party. She almost giggled.

As she turned to Rannick, he huffed. "He must be holding a Thing. Damn, it will be hard to gain his attention as he will be busy making judgments. Today is not a good day to come, Ainslie. I hope he treats ye well."

She was right about the history; her knowledge of Viking lore came in handy. Ainslie's hopes dwindled at Rannick's comment, but she kept a positive outlook. The man was her ancestor, after all. Family—he wouldn't throw out family.

When they approached the gates, guards greeted Rannick and his men with cheers. As they dismounted, they handed horns of ale to each man as lads led the horses away. A horn was shoved into her hand, and she drained it, thankful for the reprieve. As Ainslie handed her horn to a lad, she stepped beside Rannick as he and his men entered the castle and marched toward large, open double doors.

When Rannick and his men entered the main hall, a boisterous voice boomed off the walls, sounding too much like Ainslie's da. "Rannick, to what do I owe the pleasure of a visit from ye? I hope nothing's gone wrong. I sent ye to Loch Etive a month ago to make the settlement. What brings ye to my doors so soon?"

Rannick turned and bowed as did his men, so Ainslie followed suit. When they rose, a large man in extensive robes hugged and clapped Rannick on his back. He was taller than Colin but had the trademark MacDougall jet-black hair. His hair was in a long ponytail, and his beard carried braids.

When he turned to examine Ainslie, she gasped. If not for the full beard, he was the spitting image of her father. She almost said, "Da," but stopped herself.

Her expression must have shone because the MacDougall stopped and beamed. "What have ye brought with ye, Rannick? A beauty to grace my hall? Someone special, eh?"

Rannick frowned and leaned over, muttering in Dougal's ear.

Dougal's eyebrows shot up almost to his hairline.

Ainslie stood waiting, her palms sweating as heat rose on her neck. Would they declare her a liar and toss her out? Or would she gain the same welcome?

Dougal stood there momentarily, his eyes moving up and down as if gauging the truth of the story she had yet to tell.

Dougal shook his head. "I do not know this woman, Rannick. I do not have a relative named Ainslie. She is a liar. A beautiful face and a nice pair of tits have taken ye in."

The surrounding men roared with laughter.

Dougal turned and strode away.

Ainslie turned red, fisting her hands at her sides. "I am yer relation, and I can prove it."

He didn't even glance back at her declaration. Tears gathered in her eyes. His turning away and calling her a liar was like her da doing the same. It hurt just as bad.

Desperate to get her audience, she called out. "I know why Rannick settles the area. I know why ye must build a castle there."

One of Rannick's warriors she recognized from their longship laughed out loud. "Warrior woman, ye will have to do better than that. Everyone knows Rannick's task."

Dougal arrived at the dais, turned, and sat in an oversized ornate chair. A serving woman brought a horn of ale, and he drank deeply from it, staring at Ainslie over the rim.

Ainslie stepped toward Dougal. Guards grabbed her arms, stopping her advance. She glanced at Rannick, who shook his head. Her gaze moved back to the MacDougall, who sat staring her down. It was now or never.

She took a deep breath and spoke firmly. "I know a family secret. One each laird will only pass to the first son. One that begins here and lasts for hundreds of years. Shall I speak this aloud, or can we speak in private?"

Dougal smirked. "The MacDougalls have no secrets. Yer games are not welcome here, wench." He bowed his head, waving a hand. "Take her away."

The guards pulled on Ainslie's arms. When they turned her away, her gaze shot to Rannick, who stared at his feet. He *had* warned her.

As they dragged her away, she called out. "What if I told ye a story of the Fae and magic stones? Stones to be kept safe for all mankind."

"Halt!" Dougal's voice echoed in the hall.

The guards turned her to face him fully yet held her arms tight. Dougal rose, jumping off the dais and striding briskly toward her.

He bent, speaking softly, "Are ye a witch or a Fae?"

He studied her eyes, then her face, as if trying to see more than what was plainly in front of him—a human woman. "A trick to get me to talk of that which I cannot. What game do ye play?"

Ainslie whispered, "I am not a witch and not of the Fae. I suspect ye know Brigid. I am yer relative from the future, and we need to continue this in private."

Dougal eyed her, his glare unnerving.

He glanced at Rannick and then back at her, barking, "Rannick, attend to me in my chamber and bring the wench with nice tits."

****

Ainslie sat with both men in a smaller room off the hall. Between her and Dougal was a desk filled with scrolls and burning candles. A fire blazed in the fireplace, chasing the chill away.

Rannick told the tale of her arrival and their trip to see him. Ainslie sat and gaped at Dougal, having an almost out-of-body experience. There were moments Dougal looked so much like her da. After a while, she saw unique characteristics between the two strong, merry men, one modern, refined in his manner, the other blunt and rougher in his way and form. Dougal's was clearly a body used to the roughness of the twelfth century.

At the moment, Dougal laughed so hard he couldn't breathe.

Rannick laughed with him. "She unarmed Gunnar in a sword fight. Goodness, I never would have thought it of a woman."

Dougal caught his breath and leveled his gaze on Ainslie. "Out with it, girl. What's yer story? How do ye know of the stones and the Fae?"

She nodded, knowing now was the time, and told him everything. The future, the portal, the Fae. The MacDougall family's duty to the stones and how Dagda, the King of the good Fae, scattered them in space and time before an evil Fae found one. She glanced between the men, who weren't giving her trouble. Both must know of the Stones of Iona. When she got to the part about Brielle's kidnapping and how she followed her through the portal, that's when the questions started.

Rannick sat forward. "There's a portal in the woods?"

Ainslie nodded. "Aye, it's the chapel door in the future."

At Rannick's raised eyebrow, Ainslie added, "A worship house. Brielle's assignment was to renovate the chapel since it fell into ruin. That's when she met my brother, Colin, and they fell in love. He will, for sure, follow. He has traveled through the portal before. He would definitely come for his wife, Bree."

She turned to Rannick. "Yer man will bring him,

won't he?"

Rannick nodded. "Aye, if yer brother comes, my first will bring him here."

Dougal rubbed his chin. "So ye say the future. How far?"

Ainslie knew this question would come up and feared both men wouldn't believe her. Colin and John mentioned they couldn't share too much about the future. These people shouldn't change the past as it would likely affect the future. And knowing too much about one's future could lead to disaster. She had to be careful about what she shared. Her da always said to stick to the truth, even if it sounded false. His voice came to her mind. *Truth shall always prevail.*

She spoke steadily. "Around one thousand years."

Rannick whistled.

Dougal tilted his head. "Are all women warriors in the future?"

Ainslie laughed and tried to keep it as simple and truthful as possible, but she couldn't easily answer this question. "Well, not the way ye're thinking. We exercise and fight, but wars are fought differently in the future. I like Viking history, and my da taught me to fight the old way. He taught my brother and me together."

Rannick grinned. "That's how ye bested Gunnar. Ye'd already fought men."

Ainslie blushed. She had fought men and used his lack of knowledge about her training to best his warrior and win the competition.

Rannick glanced at Dougal, then back at Ainslie. "I see a resemblance."

Ainslie nodded at Dougal. "Aye, when I first saw

ye, I almost called ye Da. Ye are the spitting image of my father."

Dougal sat up taller. "I'd like a son like me. I hoped the gods would grace me with many sturdy boys."

Ainslie grinned and thought one future tidbit couldn't hurt. "Aye, ye will."

He stared at Ainslie, his expression softening, a smile spreading.

He glanced at Rannick and sighed. "So, this must be the delay in the stones' arrival. I thought it was because ye hadn't finished the hall yet, Rannick. It seems the Fae don't have the stones."

Ainslie shook her head. "Not exactly. Well, we've recovered two, The Stone of Love and The Stone of Fear."

Dougal's head snapped up. "Fear? The Fae only mentioned three stones: Hope, Faith, and Love."

Ainslie glanced between both men. "Brigid told Colin when the Fae scattered the stones in the future, the evil Fae created three evil stones to hunt the three good stones. Fear hunted Love; they've now recovered both stones from different times. There is still Lust which hunts Faith and Doubt which hunts Hope."

Rannick stood and moved to the fireplace. He stared into the flames as he spoke. "The story, the Fae story ye told on the ship, it mentioned the Faith stone. Is that part of the Fae and the stones?"

Ainslie nodded, glad he caught on so quickly. "There is a *Fae Fable Book* the Fae gifted the family centuries ago that keeps the stories of the stones. Each story tells how to find the stones—in a roundabout way."

Dougal frowned. "I don't have a book from the Fae."

Ainslie swung her gaze to Dougal. "Well, ye don't have the stones yet, so I assume the book will come with the stones."

Rannick spoke lowly from the fireplace. "The story of the woman warrior. Is it foretelling? This story will come true?"

Ainslie glanced down. "Yes, and no. The Fae wrote the stories as fables, like folklore stories. Based upon our experiences, the way it occurs in real life will differ, but the outcome is the same."

Rannick frowned into his horn and uttered, "The warrior woman is ye, is it not?"

Dougal interrupted. "What is this story? Ye must tell me."

Ainslie told the story to Dougal in a much less animated form, shorter, making sure all the facts were there. He met each part with either a raised eyebrow or an exclamation.

At the end of her tale, Dougal frowned. "The Stone of Faith is on an island here?"

Ainslie shrugged. "I don't know for certain. But what I know is I need to get to Bree. She is in danger."

Dougal huffed a sigh. "There is no telling where this madman took her. I've not had any reports of a kidnapping or even a raid. It has been peaceful for months."

A knock rapped on the door.

Dougal answered. "Enter."

The door creaked open, and the guard glanced at Dougal. "The Thing, my king, they await yer judgment." He cleared his throat. "Uh, yer brother started a drinking match."

Dougal groaned. "He will get the entire hall drunk in mere minutes if I don't intervene. Last time he had the warriors stripping their damned clothes off, comparing the size of their…"

Rannick coughed loud enough to echo in the room, making Ainslie blush, knowing what they referred to.

Dougal glanced between them, laughing out loud. "What Rannick doesn't want ye to know, girl—he won. The size contest, that is."

Ainslie gasped as Rannick spoke loudly again. "Dougal, it's time ye rejoined yer Thing."

Dougal stood and winked at Ainslie. "I'll send out messengers to all my villages asking about a stray longship with an unfamiliar captain holding an unwilling thrall. If he is out there, we'll hear within a week, two at most. In the meantime, ye both are guests here. Stay in the castle and join the feasting and games. I suspect it will last a fortnight." He turned and left the room.

****

Earlier, Rannick quietly observed Ainslie as she retold her story. She was an intelligent woman, a warrior as well. She didn't realize her beauty or didn't seem to care as most women did.

He thought over the story as she repeated the fable, and his worry for her increased. She was not afraid of danger, but she should be. She mentioned there was no telling how or if the story would come true. Rannick didn't want to see her hurt, stabbed by a blade as she saved her true love. He wondered who her true love was and became very jealous of a man he didn't know.

He glanced at her, and Ainslie sat staring into the

flames, tears gathering in her eyes.

Rannick considered the warrior woman. One who was so strong showed weakness. "What's wrong, Ainslie? Dougal is doing all he can."

She sniffed. "I know, but a week is a long time for Bree to be in the hands of her ex-boyfriend. Two is even longer. He used to abuse her."

She glanced at Rannick as a tear trailed down her cheek. Beat a woman. It was his vow never to harm a woman. Women were worshiped and revered as lovers, wives, and mothers. He wouldn't stand for it or allow Ainslie to think he was less of a man for not standing up for what was right.

He set his horn on the mantel and went to her, kneeling in front of her.

He took her hands in his and held them to his heart. "Ainslie, as soon as we hear where yer sister is, I vow my men and I will sail there and take her back. I will return her safe."

He kissed her hands and gazed into her eyes, for this oath was one he did not take lightly, the safe care of a woman. "This I pledge to ye."

Chapter 10

Ivor sat at his table, enjoying his morning meal. The thrall he assigned to care for his newest guest approached. He hated the man, Balor, but he was a MacDougall ally. Ivor had doubts and hoped the messenger he'd sent to the McDougall soon returned with welcome news. He would love nothing more than to toss Balor out on his arse.

She bowed before him, and he nodded, allowing her to approach.

She crossed to his side and bent, whispering in his ear, "He insists we serve him. He won't come to the longhouse unless it's a feast."

Ivor grunted but nodded, encouraging her to continue.

"The guard will not allow me inside at his *master's* command. I offered to clean his hut, but they shouted at me."

Ivor didn't like the sound of these developments. "The woman, his thrall?"

She sucked in a breath. "He hasn't permitted her to leave."

Ivor turned his head and pulled it back to stare at her. "What? Not even to bathe or relieve herself? It's been days."

The serving woman shook her head. "I peeked once when the door opened wide for food. He's tied her to the bed."

Ivor snorted, not liking what he heard. Thrall or not, treating any woman with such abuse was wrong. While he understood and held with basic discipline, he had a certain level of respect for the necessities of life: good food, excellent drink, and a clean body. The thrall was likely in poor shape, and he didn't want her death on his conscience.

Balor declared he'd gained her in a raid. Considered spoils of war, any human captured could become a thrall at the command of a jarl. Viking law prohibited Ivor from taking the thrall for poor treatment alone.

He nodded. "Continue to serve him."

The woman nodded, went to leave, but turned back. "My lord, we, yer thralls. We are happy with yer treatment. Many of us have better lives here. Some women talk. They want to help her, Balor's thrall. What he is doing isn't right."

Ivor nodded at her. "Aye, ye are all good and serve me well." He scratched his chin. "If ye can get close to the thrall and speak to her, find out her story if ye can. If we can get her away, we will. Get other women to help ye. I have a suspicion she isn't a thrall at all."

She nodded and moved away.

His first, Tormund, approached and sat next to him. He and Ivor smiled and drank as if they discussed the weather.

Ivor spoke first. "Well, what is yer report?"

Tormund grunted and drank again. He shifted in his seat, fidgeting a bit. Ivor sensed something was wrong, for Tormund was never at a loss for words.

Ivor spoke sharply. "Out with it, man. I must

know."

Tormund spoke softly but firmly. "We cannot get close enough to get to her."

Ivor grumbled. "The guard ye positioned outside the hut. He is still there?"

Tormund growled. "Aye, he has offered to risk his life to free her."

Ivor nodded. "The woman assigned to care for his hut reported the thrall has not been out at all."

Tormund nodded. "Aye, his treatment of her has angered yer warriors. They argue over who is next to watch in case a chance to rescue her arises, each eager to free her. I am surprised his guard hasn't noticed our man."

Ivor rubbed his neck and spoke lowly. "I suspect there is more to this Balor than he shows. Something isn't right with his warriors."

Tormund glanced around the hall and then gazed at Ivor as he spoke. "I cannot explain it. It is a sensation I get when I speak to his warriors. The way they speak, 'tis not natural. I don't understand."

Ivor suspected that all wasn't right with Balor, and he didn't like his gut reaction when he was around the man. When Balor was close, he sensed darkness that crept into his soul. He hated the man for bringing evil to his little isle of paradise. He needed to distract Balor to get to the thrall. If his suspicion was correct, she was of noble birth and wanted by her family.

He sat momentarily, recalling all Balor had revealed in their short time together. He was a master of his men, controlling. He, like Ivor, enjoyed the finer things life had to offer. He liked a woman like Ivor did, but that's where the similarities stopped. Ivor would not permit any human abuse outside of earned punishment. And even then, he was lenient. He needed to distract Balor to get to the thrall. Something to entertain Balor so she could be away from his treatment, giving her time to heal.

An idea formed in his mind. Why hadn't he thought of it before? Men like Balor were driven by the same thing—lust. All he needed to do was use Balor's weakness as his asset. He sat and allowed his idea to grow. The more he thought, the more the idea seemed to be the best answer for all.

He chuckled as he spoke. "Spread the word. Let everyone know there will be a feast tonight. Add much to the meal. I want a full feast." He chuckled low in his throat. This was perfect. "Send me Edna and Ingrid. I wish to speak to them."

Tormund's eyes widened. He laughed as their eyes connected. Aye, Tormund understood his plan. This would be a fun game to play, and Balor was the main participant.

Tormund nodded. "I shall send an invitation to our special guest to ensure he attends our feast and show."

Ivor nodded. "Aye, do that."

Tormund rubbed his hands as he rose and left the longhouse.

Ivor sat and fretted over Balor's thrall. A woman, likely of noble birth, trapped on his island and abused. He didn't like it all.

****

Balor belched, knowing it was much later than he planned to stay.

Ivor leaned over to him. "Enjoying the feast, Balor?"

Balor, long into the drink, blinked, trying to stay focused. He hadn't known his human could consume so much. He had a hard time keeping a grasp on Tony's mind. Balor sat up and shook himself. Ivor had addressed him. He turned to his host and replied, his words slurred. "Aye, it has been delicious, but I think I should seek my rest."

Ivor clapped him on the back and shouted, "More drink for my friend."

Ivor turned to Balor speaking low, "Ye cannot leave. We have a special surprise for ye. Something I know ye'll thank me for. May even reward me with a boon."

Ivor waved, and two young women entered, covered in furs. One was blonde and the other brunette, both beauties. They moved to the center of the room, glanced at each other, and giggled.

Ivor leaned over and spoke lowly to Balor. "Pretty, aren't they? Good friends they are." Ivor signaled them, and both women dropped the furs, exposing naked bodies to all in the hall. The men cheered loud, filling the hall with drunken calls.

Inside Balor, Tony roared to life. Two women naked together was a fantasy of his for a long time. The women turned to each other, kissing. Tony's desire surged through Balor. The two women fondled each other and occasionally peeked at him. Tony's mind took over, and in his drunken haze, Balor allowed it. Tony had watched many women together and often dreamed of joining. He'd never had two women at once, and his lust surged. His hand went straight to his crotch, and he stroked himself through his pants, imagining the two women fondling him while touching each other.

Ivor laughed. "I thought ye'd like Edna and Ingrid. They came to me together from a raid. They like this play, so I let them entertain me occasionally." He groaned. "They will amaze ye with what they can do to each other and together to a man."

Balor allowed Tony free rein, for his desire had risen, and his cock was hard. He stroked himself harder and rasped, "I must have them both together."

Ivor leaned over, speaking low in Balor's ear, "A bargain I shall make with ye, then."

Balor never took his gaze from the women. The brunette dropped to her knees and moved her head between the blonde woman's legs. The blonde enjoying the other's tongue, ogled Balor, moaning with each lick from her friend. The blonde tossed her head back, running her hands through the other woman's hair.

God, Tony was beside himself with desire. He'd do anything for a night with them together. Panting with lust, the words barely came out of his mouth. "What is yer bargain, Ivor?"

Ivor chuckled. "I give ye both women for the entire night. Have them as often as ye desire, for they enjoy it." Balor groaned as Ivor spoke. "But yer thrall, ye allow her to rest. Let my women take care of her."

Balor stopped his movement, but his eyes never left the two women who lay on the furs rubbing against each other, kissing. The blonde rolled the brunette onto her back and made eye contact with Balor. Keeping her eyes on Balor, she sat up and crawled toward the brunette's face, placing her sex over the other's mouth. The woman on the bottom slid her tongue in the other's folds. The brunette eyed Balor and crooked her finger at him, inviting him to join their play.

"My thrall is mine; she is my prisoner."

Ivor nodded. "Aye, and she will remain yers, but allow us to heal her. Ye can enjoy these while yer prize rests."

Balor closed his eyes as Tony roared in his mind. *Take both women. Take them now!* Balor opened his eyes, and both women were at his side. They helped him up and led him to the door.

He stopped halfway across the room and turned to Ivor. "My thrall will remain secure. She disappears, and I will take yer life."

Ivor nodded as he signaled his captain.

****

When Tormund returned, he sat next to Ivor. His sigh and somber expression spoke much about his longtime friend's concern. "She is frail, but the women help her. Balor said her name was Brielle."

Ivor stared into the flame of the fire. "Women are strong, stronger than men. She will heal."

Tormund shook his head. "I fear for this one, friend. She won't speak or make eye contact. She lives on the outside but is dead on the inside."

Ivor drank his ale. "Maybe Edna and Ingrid should have an extended stay with our guest. And send a guard as a lookout for the messenger from Oban. I need to know what the MacDougall has to report."

****

Tony was jolted from a nightmare with a yell. A soft female hand reached out and smoothed his left shoulder. He tried to catch his breath, and the woman to his right sat up and grabbed his cock. He lay back down and allowed both women to soothe him, trying to banish the vision from his thoughts.

He searched his mind, and Balor wasn't there. He exhaled. Balor was a cruel man and hard to have inside his head. As both women stroked his body, he relaxed more but still couldn't get the images out of his head.

He dreamed of the Scot, the bastard that took his Brielle from him. The dream came to him in slow motion, each detail a vivid image he'd not easily forget. MacDougall came to him with a sword. Tony watched from outside of his body as a bystander, but his heart and soul felt every moment as if it happened to him. He knelt on the rocky ground, half in frigid ocean water. The sting of the salt hit his cuts and bruises, and the cold sent a shiver over his body. His head raised, and the Scot moved for him, sword raised. He only had time to turn his head, but the blade came at him in slow motion. The shift in MacDougall's muscles accentuated the arc. The expression of sheer rage was clear on his face. Spittle flew from his mouth as the blade arched downward. Tony lost focus, and the world went numb. The cut to his neck sliced slowly as the blade progressed. His face froze in shock, stuck forever. The head dropped and bounced once, then rolled into the depths of a black sea, never to be seen again.

He shivered, then closed his eyes as the sensations the women aroused took over his mind. One moved down his chest while the other sucked his cock. With a giggle, one offered his cock to the other. Both women were greedy and now took turns sucking him. He envisioned Brielle doing this to him, her mouth on his shaft, her lips wrapped around him. He imagined Brielle liking it, and he grew harder. She was his and his alone.

Chapter 11

Dunstaffnage Castle, present day

John stood outside the study door and smiled at the scene before him.

Squeals of laughter reverberated off the walls as Marie pinched the bridge of her nose, obviously fighting another headache. Doug and Ewan played "Save the Pretty Princess from the Pirates" as they chased each other around the couch in the Great Hall. Said pretty princess, Evie, sat poised in her chair with a paper crown and a tartan wrapped as a cape. In one hand was a cookie, and in the other a cup of juice. Sitting prim and proper, she resembled royalty.

John crossed to Marie, leaned down, and kissed her. "Ye sure, not one more? Maybe another princess to add to the brood?"

Marie groaned. "I never thought looking after three kids would be so hard. I like it when Doug plays quietly alone."

John laughed. "Yea, until ye find he has been making mud pies in the garden, and ye have to clean him and his clothes." They both laughed.

Evie primly took a nibble of her cookie and sipped her juice. "Ye will have one more child. A girl, and she will be my bestest friend."

Marie patted her on the arm. "I'm sure ye'd like a friend to play with, as Ewan has, but maybe John and I

106

are done, eh?"

Evie shook her head. "No, next year. A girl. Brigid told me so when I asked for a sister. She said I'd get something better than a sister, a best friend, Doug's sister."

Marie gasped, and her gaze shot to John, who shrugged.

John stood using his parenting voice. "I have a surprise for everyone."

Ewan stopped running, and Doug ran into his back, causing both boys to grunt.

John hid a smile, trying to look serious. "Actually, if we all wait here, I suspect it will walk through the doors any moment as I spied Ronnie's car from the window." The boys jumped up and down and clapped.

Ewan asked, "My da's come back with Ma?"

John and Marie exchanged a look.

John shook his head. "Not yet, Ewan."

The doorbell rang, and John moved to the castle's main doors, knowing who was on the other side.

He opened them, greeting Dominic DeVolt. "I saw ye come up the drive. Come on in. Ye haven't met the rug rats. Allow me to do the honors."

Dominic put his luggage beside the door. Ronnie McTavish, one of the regular workmen hired to the castle from the wharf, hefted another inside that John recognized as Brielle's luggage.

John waved Dominic ahead into the great hall to a sight John had never seen. Three young children stood still and silent, staring at the newcomer.

Hiding his shock behind a cleared throat, John addressed them all. "Kids, I'd like ye to meet Dominic DeVolt, Brielle's brother from the States."

The boys' mouths fell open in near unison.

Doug was the first to recover. "The fighter pilot?"

Dominic chuckled. "The very same. Are you Ewan?" Doug, wide-eyed, shook his head slowly.

Ewan stepped forward, pointing to himself. "I'm Ewan. He's Doug. For a fighter, ye aren't that big. I figured ye'd be bigger than me da."

Dominic laughed. "Well, Ewan, nice to meet you." He ruffled the boy's hair. "Size doesn't always make the best fighter."

Evie moved between the men, her gaze constant on Dominic.

Marie glanced at John as he shifted to her side, patting her shoulder as he muttered, "He insisted on coming. He's demanding answers, and I don't know how I will lie my way around a United States Air Force Special Ops officer."

Marie rose and took his hands in hers. "Ye'll do the right thing, I'm sure of it. I suppose a distraction for the tykes is in order so ye both can speak in private?"

John nodded at Marie, who announced, "Ye know, I thought I saw Mrs. A with some new treats. Let's all go to the kitchen and see what she has today."

The kids cheered, and Ewan and Doug followed Marie toward the kitchen.

Evie stood quietly next to Domonic as she took his hand.

Dominic turned and bent to her level. "Yes, Evie?"

John spotted Evie's serious look as she put both hands on either side of her uncle's face, whispering, "I know ye can help find Mommie. Ye're a special pilot, and I'm glad ye came."

Dominic took her hands from his face and held

them together. "I hope so too, princess. Now go get some treats before the boys eat them all."

As Dominic rose, Evie skipped off toward the kitchen.

He turned to John as his eyes leveled on him. "I've brought Bree's luggage from Houston and am here to get some answers."

John sighed. "Aye, I suspected ye'd show up, eventually. Let's go to the study and have a dram."

****

From behind the desk in Colin's seat, John put his glass down. "Dominic, what is it ye think I can answer that the police, FBI, and the security service Colin hired have not yet?"

Dominic reminded John of Colin. John had to be careful. Dominic DeVolt could be just as, if not more, cunning than Colin. He needed to proceed carefully.

Dominic smacked his lips together, holding the whisky glass up to the light. "Scot's whisky never disappoints." He put the glass on the desk and stared at John. They sat staring at each other for a moment.

Dominic smiled, but it wasn't a full grin. It looked practiced, like Colin's law expression. *He will not let me off easily. What exactly does this bloke do for the United States military? Bree said he was a fighter pilot, yet being special ops hinted at much more.*

Dominic shifted in his chair. "Why don't you call me Dom, as Bree does?"

John nodded. "All right, Dom, what can I do for ye?"

"I need more answers, John, and you are the one to give them to me. First, where exactly is Colin?"

John knew this question would come and had

prepared for it when Dominic called, saying he was already in Scotland.

He put on his best blank face. "I already told ye and the authorities that he is out of town, and he has kept his whereabouts…private."

Dominic gave him that expression again, setting his nerves on edge. "Are you in touch with him?"

John shook his head. "No, I cannot communicate with him at this time." And that was no lie. Colin's ancestors built the castle later in the twelfth century. Where Dagda sent Colin chasing after Bree and Ainslie was in the beginning of the twelfth century. This trip would have no scrolls from the past. The mantel didn't exist back then, leaving John out of the loop.

Dominic watched him momentarily and nodded as if concluding John didn't lie. His face changed this time, more relaxed. "John, you know I'm special ops, right?"

John nodded. "Aye, that I do."

Dominic leaned forward, resting his elbows on his knees. "People these days, John, are easier to track with the technology we have: cell phones, video cameras everywhere, and facial recognition. It's tough for a person to disappear and not show up in an airport, a security camera in Mexico, or even the background of a social media post by accident. Too many cameras around to just…disappear."

Dominic exhaled. "I have access to just as much or more resources as the FBI, John. My sister disappeared in that alley. She's off the grid. Her cell, any trace of her traveling from that spot, doesn't exist. It's as if she vanished."

John glanced down, trying to hide his reaction and

likely not doing a very good job of it.

Dominic continued in his soft, monotone cadence. John had heard Colin do the same, likely purposely to get John to let his guard down. He couldn't do that. The Iona Stones' secret was paramount to Colin successfully returning with Bree and Ainslie safely.

The soft voice spoke, soothing. "Colin, he's gone off-grid. I've traced his cell. The last ping was here days ago. Bree's in the US, Colin's here…both vanished."

John glanced at the *Fae Fable Book*, hoping it looked like he looked out the window.

Dominic's voice floated to him. "I think there is more to this than what I see. You are too calm about this, and I think you know where they are." Dominic stood, put his hands on the desk, and leaned into John's face. "Where did the madman take my sister? Please tell me Colin has gone after her."

John groaned and ran his hand through his hair. He stood, picked up his whisky, and moved to the mantel, gulping the rest in one swallow. Hell, this was all getting out of hand. Dominic was an intelligent man with resources different from typical authorities. If John told him of the Fae, the stones, could Dominic do more to help from this side?

This time too many people outside the informed ones saw too much Fae activity: the private security detail who filed a police report; eyewitnesses near the museum where Bree vanished. When Colin, Bree, and Ainslie came back, which he prayed for daily, someone would need to deal with the authorities. Someone with knowledge and experience to create a plausible tale and navigate the agencies to leave no suspicions on the family.

He briefly prayed to his Fae, Morrigan, and turned to face Brielle's military brother. "Sit, Dom. This will take a while. Aye, I'll tell ye about the Fae and the Stones of Iona. But for all that is holy, this must remain between us. Even with yer work for the special ops. No investigation, no government. It's a centuries-old family secret, and it must remain that way."

Dominic nodded and sat in the chair in front of the desk.

John crossed, sat at the desk, and folded his hands. The beginning—that's the best place to start.

John told Dominic about the Fae and the Stones, the brief version. He told him what he knew of the events when Bree and Ainslie went through the portal, and how Colin went after them to the twelfth century. For an American, he took it very well. He wasn't familiar with the oddities of Scotland's history, heritage, and the land's mysteries—how they interacted with the modern world. When John got to the part about Ainslie grabbing Bree's hand, Dom gave his first real reaction.

Dominic sat up. "Wait, Colin's sister Ainslie went through the portal as well?"

John nodded. "Aye, saw it with my own eyes. Ainslie runs fast when she sets her mind to it."

Dominic barked a laugh. "The amazon woman is back in the twelfth century. God, I wish I was there to see it."

John laughed. "Amazon woman? Is that what ye call her?"

Dominic nodded. "Well, she's six feet and fights like a man. At least that's what Bree says."

John sighed. "Ye know Ainslie followed Colin and me around when we were lads. She carried a wooden sword until her da finally relented and allowed us to train together."

Dominic's eyebrows rose. "She's trained with a broadsword?"

John nodded. "Aye, damn good at it. She knocked Colin and me on our asses repeatedly. It's not her I'm worried about. Dagda already said she was in good hands." John exhaled, his voice dropping as he spoke. "It's Bree I'm worried about. She tends to get into trouble, especially when she goes back in time."

Dominic's gaze swung to John. "This isn't her first time-hop?"

John shook his head. "No, she accidentally followed Colin back to the eighteenth century to find The Stone of Love. She brought him back from purgatory. Well, their love did."

Dominic shook his head. "Astounding. How did she do it?"

John rose from the desk and moved to the *Fae Fable Book*. "She read from the *Fae Fable Book*, and the Fae showed her the way. It was in The Stone of Love fable."

Dominic followed him to the book. "The book you said that tells fables which tell the outcome of the stones?" He looked at the glass case. "How the hell do you read it? It's in a case." His hands traveled around the edges as most did when they first saw it, trying to find the seam where there was none.

John breathed. "There's no seam in the glass and no lock. It's a Fae spell."

Dominic rested his hands on the sides and studied

the book. The book pages flipped fast while still locked in the case.

Dominic tried to pull his hands away, then jerked his whole body. "John, it's got my hands. They're stuck."

The book slammed in the case once and stopped open to a page. John and Dominic leaned over the enclosure, and only two sentences were on the page.

Dominic read it aloud.

But those who have hope will renew their strength. They will run and not grow weary; walk and not faint; they will soar like wings on eagles.

Once Dominic read it aloud, the case freed his hands. He jerked them back, bumping into John, who caught him by the shoulders to steady him.

John dropped his arms, and Dominic turned to him. "What the hell does that mean?" Dominic lifted his hands. "And my hands. They were stuck to the glass."

John strode to the desk, picked up his glass, turned to the whisky decanter, and poured a healthy portion. He offered some to Dom, who followed, picking up his glass and offering it for a fill. John spoke as he filled Dominic's glass. "The book reveals what it will when it wants." John set the decanter back and took a sip of his whisky. "I've never seen that quote before and don't know what story it goes to, but for some reason, the Fae wanted ye to see it."

Dominic took a generous sip of his whisky. "I've seen some things in my special ops, but nothing like this. A chapel door that's a time portal and a book that reveals only certain things." Dominic sat and sighed. "What's worse is we do not know how things are going back in time. I want to jump up and run to their rescue."

John sat back in the chair at the desk. "Aye, I know what ye mean, but ye get used to it. The Fae do things in their way. Ye have to have faith."

Dominic took another sip of his whisky. "Yes, faith."

Chapter 12

Dunollie Castle, Twelfth Century

Ainslie made her way to the main hall at Dunollie. She had been there for a day, and had immersed herself in the festive celebration. Her history had been correct. A Thing was a judgment day for the lord and his jarls over the lands he ruled. The event resembled a gigantic party that lasted for days or even weeks. The castle was on day four, and Ainslie only had one night. She knew she could drink most modern men under the table, but Viking warriors—they were a whole new breed.

Upon entering, Dougal was in his usual seat, and his wife Fiona sat beside him. Her long golden-brown hair was artfully styled in intricate braids which sat atop her head like a crown. Beads were woven through, accentuating the image. Ainslie figured this was the origin of her middle name, making her happy. Fiona was a strong woman and a delightful companion to Dougal. They greeted Ainslie like family as she sat at the end of the family table. A serving girl brought her hot porridge with nuts, dried fruit, and a cup of mead. Rannick was at a lower table with his men. When he glanced her way, Ainslie blushed.

Dougal loudly cleared his voice. "Ainslie, cousin, I have heard the tale of yer fighting skills. Today is more fighting games and a contest between Rannick's rag-tail bunch of warriors and mine."

Shouts and cheers rose in the hall. Rannick's men shouted foul at the insult and Dougal's men cheered.

Dougal turned and addressed her. "I'd like to see the fighting skills of a woman today. Tell me, which group shall ye fight for?"

She glanced at Rannick, who watched her intently. Rannick had boasted he was the best. She wanted to see his skills for herself.

She smirked. Feeling a little reckless, she replied, "My king and cousin, why I can only fight for my family. I challenge Rannick to a contest of skill."

She glanced at Rannick, who glared at her over the top of his horn of ale. Around them, the hall erupted in cheers. She raised an eyebrow at Rannick, who kept his eyes locked on hers as he slowly lowered his horn.

She waited for the cheers to die down before she spoke softly, "That is if a mere woman could best him." The hall erupted again in cheers and jeers.

Rannick slowly rose and moved toward Ainslie, watching her with hooded eyes as he approached.

When he arrived, he bowed and rose, addressing her. "Alas, my sweet, I cannot fight a woman. I have taken a vow—a vow I take seriously. I cannot fight ye for fear I will hurt ye. But for sure, I am the best warrior in the kingdom."

Dougal scoffed. "Rannick, ye cannot still carry a grudge against yer father after all these years. Ye settled that debt when ye killed him."

Ainslie gasped as Rannick frowned at the floor. "I made a vow. A vow I will keep."

Dougal stood. "I will make an exception, a fight till the first one disarms the other. No blood, no injury. I wish to see the warrior woman fight, and I wish to test her against my best."

Rannick glared at Dougal and shook his head, causing Dougal to frown. "I command it as yer king."

Rannick stood still. His hands fisted as his face turned red.

Ainslie glanced between Dougal and Rannick. Would Rannick go against his king?

Ainslie lowered her voice so only he heard. "Rannick, it will only be a fight to disarm. This is no real fight. I won't be injured."

Rannick glowered at her as a muscle ticked on his cheek. Had she gone too far? Was it not right for her to assure him not only of her skill but his? She knew he would not harm her.

He turned and bowed to Dougal. "My king, yer wish is my command."

Rannick turned and strode from the hall.

Fiona patted Dougal's hand. "Ye push him too hard, my husband."

Dougal took his wife's hand in his and kissed it. "He has to let the past go." He winked at Ainslie. "This will be entertaining."

****

Ainslie spent the morning wandering the market stalls with Fiona and her retainers.

Fiona took her arm in hers. "Ye have quickly made friends and adapted well to Viking life."

Ainslie strolled with the queen, liking her the more they chatted. "Aye, I enjoy the banter of the women. Learning to barter for goods seems it's not only a way of life but a challenge." They stopped as one of the queen's retainers argued with a rug maker. In the next stall, another's voice rose as she bantered for a bracelet.

The two beside them spoke to each other. "Ulna, did ye see the jeweler try to fool me with tin saying it was silver? I would know the difference in the weight of silver rather than tin."

Ulna made a sound from the back of her throat. "The leather smith wouldn't take a coin and insist on raw gold only. These merchants don't know the coin is gold!"

Ainslie huffed a laugh as Fiona turned to her. "Something amuses ye?"

Ainslie shrugged. "Well, this is just like home—the women, that is. They make business deals like men. Some barter for goods for the home and others for jewelry."

Fiona eyed her. "Ye do not own much jewelry. Allow me to buy ye some for the feast." Ainslie owned little jewelry in modern times, here nothing at all. But Viking women wore lots of it. Ainslie shook her head, and they continued strolling the market lane.

She stopped at another jeweler as she looked over the pieces. Maybe she should have something, to fit in. A necklace caught her fancy, silver beads on strands draped in loops connected at the center by a large silver locket. She wondered if the locket opened where one could place a photo inside. In this age, it would be a small painting, one delicate and dear to someone.

As Ainslie fingered the necklace, a warrior from Fiona's guard approached her. "A pretty piece for a pretty woman. Shall I buy the warrior woman a lovely necklace? Or maybe an armband set?"

Ainslie smiled at the warrior as a familiar voice spoke from behind. "A woman of such beauty doesn't need adornment, Ulf."

Ainslie turned, and Rannick stood staring at her. She blushed as Rannick nodded to Ulf, dismissing him.

Rannick waved ahead. "Walk with me, please."

She nodded, and they strolled side by side, glancing at the wares on display. They passed a jewelry cart filled with necklaces, arm bands, and earrings. Then a leather crafter who had an assortment of bags, belts, and other clothing. The next booth held brushes and combs. Ainslie stopped and admired some.

The vendor approached her. "A comb and brush set for yer lovely tresses, my dear." His focus slid to Rannick. "My man, a gift for yer wife."

Rannick moved close to her and spoke near her ear. "She is not my wife, but if she wants a set, I'd love to purchase her one."

When the vendor offered one for her to try, Ainslie shook her head. She moved aside and strode ahead. Rannick quickly caught up. They strolled on quietly through the stalls.

Rannick was the first to break the silence. "Ye seem to have adjusted well to our way of life."

Ainslie grinned. "Aye, I have always liked the Viking time. I studied it extensively. It almost became my major in college, but I took to teaching instead."

Rannick glanced at her. "College?"

Ainslie huffed a laugh. "Education. I teach children."

A young boy flew out of a booth and fell before them.

The merchant yelled, "Ye're worthless. Can't even walk without breaking something."

Ainslie ran to the boy and helped him up. The small boy stood, wiping his tears, and limped away.

Ainslie noticed his issue right away. He had one leg shorter than the other. Ainslie walked after the boy, grabbing his shoulder. "Stop! I can help."

The boy stopped. "Ye'd help me?"

She glanced at Rannick. "Where is a cobbler's stall?"

At Rannick's blank look, she picked another word hoping it would make sense. "A shoemaker. I need a person who makes something for yer feet."

He nodded and led her down the aisle, then crossed, moving toward a tent where all sorts of shoes hung from hooks and more were laid out on a table. Ainslie held the boy's shoulders steady, making sure they were even. She bent and placed a rock under the boy's shorter leg, measuring the difference. She adjusted his hips, chose another rock, and measured again to ensure his hips were even.

Sitting at eye level with the youth, Ainslie stared at his dirt-smudged face. He was barely even eight, not old enough to work for anyone, and too thin for her liking. Her heart went out to him as she asked, "What's yer name?"

The boy blushed and muttered, "Attar. I am or was with the merchant. He tossed me out." He took a breath seeming to fight tears. "C-Can ye fix my leg?"

Ainslie patted his leg and gazed at him. "Aye, ye will walk without a limp as long as we make one shoe with a higher sole to raise the foot."

Keeping her hand on the youth's shoulder, she spoke to the shoemaker. "I need ye to make the left shoe with a taller sole, the heel as tall as this and the toe a bit lower." She showed him two rocks held together at the right height she measured for the boy. "The other shoe needs a regular sole."

The shoemaker frowned but listened and agreed to deliver the shoes in the morning. Ainslie took the gold coin she'd won on the longship to pay.

As she reached out to give it to the man, Rannick grabbed her wrist. "I'll pay." He grinned at her. "Ye should keep yer winnings." He winked at her and paid the merchant.

The boy beamed at Ainslie and Rannick. "Thank ye so much. I owe ye both, but I have no way to pay." He toed the dirt as he looked down. "I am homeless now that the merchant tossed me out."

Ainslie stared at Rannick, hoping he would step in and help the youth.

Rannick nodded at her expression. "Attar, seek my men at the dock, the longship named *RanGun*. Seek Gunnar and tell him Rannick said to put ye to work. Ye are part of the crew now. Work hard, and ye will have a home within our new village we build for the MacDougall."

Attar hugged Rannick, then nearly tackled Ainslie with a hug. "The new village? Thank ye! I will serve ye well." He took off, hobbling quickly.

Ainslie called after him, "I'll bring yer shoes to the ship tomorrow."

She turned and found Rannick staring with a smile. He waved her before him, and they continued strolling through the market.

The scent of spiced grilled meat reached her, and her stomach loudly growled.

Rannick chuckled. "I suppose the Warrior Woman has a warrior's appetite."

Ainslie blushed. "I am hungry."

Rannick stopped and bought them both ale and meat on a stick from a merchant. He handed her a horn, and she sipped sweet mead that quickly became a favorite of hers. She bit into the meat, the juices dripping down her chin. Lamb grilled over an open flame reminded her of camping trips with Colin and her da. Rannick drank deeply from his horn, then tore into the meat as they strolled.

Between bites, Ainslie asked, "*RanGun*? I don't recognize those words. What does it mean?"

Rannick grinned. "Goddess of the sea at war. She is my warship when I raid." He moved his hand holding the stick of meat like a boat sailing through the waters. "She is light and fast."

Ainslie nodded as they moved on. Rannick waved her to a tree overlooking the bay of Oban. Ainslie sat, and Rannick sat close, both leaning against the tree's trunk. They finished their food, and she gazed out over the bay, marveling at the simplicity of it during this time. The village and dock seemed busy. The area was a large thriving community. The MacDougall Thing was obviously popular with his kingdom, bringing merchants and visitors together. Yet, to her, the land remained untouched. There were no signs of modern man, steel, concrete buildings, and mass production. The ocean, the earth, and everything in her sight was made from nature. The people built conforming to the land, not molding or changing the land to fit man's or society's needs. In this time, she found the village so peaceful and comforting.

Rannick grumbled next to her, causing her to glance at him.

He glimpsed at her and turned away. "I wish to ask

about the boy, his leg. How did…how did ye know what to fix?"

Ainslie smiled. "I work with special-needs children."

Rannick tilted his head. He wouldn't understand the words "special needs." She sighed and looked over the cliff at the bay, trying to find the easiest explanation to a man from a time that didn't understand the need for accommodating those who were challenged.

She turned to him hoping her explanation was enough that he understood the kids' needs. "Not all children are alike. Some are born with a shorter leg, like Attar. Some have a hard time speaking and understanding. Some are just born different. I help those children. I teach them how to adjust to life."

Rannick looked at her as she explained how she helped children. At first, his expression was hard, but his face softened as she spoke of each condition. He was quiet and seemed to contemplate what she said. He looked at her. "Ye are a healer, then?"

Ainslie shrugged. "I guess ye could say that. I am not a healer of illness, but I heal their problems and challenges. I make living day to day easier for each one."

Rannick stared at her, and the wind blew her hair loose. He leaned close, brushing her hair away from her face, and gazed into her eyes. "A warrior woman and a healer. The goddess Frejya of war and the goddess Idunn of youth wrapped into one woman." He cupped her chin and brushed his lips across her softly. He spoke, and their breaths mingled, his beard tickling her chin. "A warrior for the children."

She brushed her lips across his, craving his touch.

He groaned and deepened the kiss, bracing his hand on her neck, his soft beard touching her skin. Ainslie gasped, and he took advantage of her open mouth, delving his tongue inside. He tasted of meat, ale, and a sweetness that was only Rannick.

She wrapped her arms around his neck, and he pulled her into his lap, kissing her deeper. His lips were soft, yet his kisses were firm, causing her to moan.

He stopped placing his forehead against hers. "Ainslie, ye tempt me beyond reason. Why is it I find I cannot resist ye?"

She smirked. "I don't know. But ye need to reserve yer energy for today. I will best ye in our fight and keep my coin."

Rannick froze and glared into her eyes. "I will not fight ye."

Ainslie replied, trying to keep it light, "Rannick 'tis only a game, and Dougal commands it."

Rannick set her from his lap and rose. He moved away but quickly turned back. "Fighting is no game, Ainslie. If I fight, I worry I will hurt ye."

She stood as Rannick growled and marched away. Ainslie watched his retreating back. She understood there was more to this and hoped he'd get over it soon. Their fight was that afternoon.

****

From his raised dais Dougal called the roaring crowd to order. "Ho! I call our warriors to the field. MacDougall and MacRaghnaill standoff."

Ainslie's gaze traveled over the crowd gathered around the fighting field. The crowd was immense. Ainslie wondered if anyone was left in the castle or the village even. Warriors made wagers as the group was excited to see the test of skill between the best man and the warrior woman. Dougal's first set Ainslie up with pants and a short tunic, a shield, and a sword close to her size and weight at home. Hers had been custom-made in Edinburgh for her size, and she wielded it well.

Dougal's warriors lined up behind her, cheering her on. Across the field, Rannick stood silently with his warriors cheering behind him.

Dougal called over the crowd. "Silence!" Eventually, everyone quieted.

From the platform, Dougal spoke with dramatic command. "A fight, a contest of strength and skill between my best warrior." His left hand waved to Rannick. As he spoke the next, he waved his right hand to her, "And the warrior woman. Both of ye, approach." He brought his hands together indicating they should approach the dais.

Ainslie strode toward Dougal, and Rannick stepped beside her as they approached the dais together.

He stared ahead but spoke so only she heard, "I will not fight ye."

Ainslie didn't respond.

They stopped in front of Dougal, who spoke for all to hear. "The first one to disarm the other wins. Ye have agreed to fight to disarm. No injuries and no bloodshed. Do ye both agree?"

She nodded and peeked at Rannick. He stood still, and she feared he would defy his king. Her focus went between the two men. They were close, more friends than a king and subject. But as Dougal's expression changed from expectancy to anger, Rannick pushed his luck.

As she took a deep breath to speak, Rannick

nodded to his king.

Dougal growled and signaled them to take their places in the fighting field. They each were allowed a sword and a shield as they faced each other.

Ainslie took a fighting stance to prepare to fight.

Rannick stood still, his sword pointing to the ground, but his shield was held at the ready.

Dougal roared, "Fight."

Ainslie circled Rannick, who turned, keeping her to his front, but did not take a stance or raise his sword. She took the first offensive, a swipe from overhead. Rannick blocked with his shield but did not answer with his sword. She circled the opposite way, him following, keeping her in sight. She took another offensive, trying to swipe sideways at his head. He blocked but refused to engage her, allowing her sword to slide off his shield.

The crowd groaned, and someone yelled at Rannick, "Fight, man! She's only a woman! Sweep her and be done with it!"

Ainslie came at him again, a sword smack from the side going for his shoulder, but she did not back away this time. She held her sword on his shield, and she pressed her blade hard. "Fight me, damn ye!"

Rannick said nothing and grunted at her push. Her sword slipped off his shield, and she spun, swiping at his feet with her follow-through. He easily blocked with his sword. She turned in the opposite direction and swiped at his head, hitting his raised shield. She smacked his guard with her sword with each word she spoke.

"Fight!" *whack!* "Me" *whack!* "Damn" *whack!* "Ye."

Rannick refused to engage, shaking his head, but the tic in his cheek contradicted his control. His face turned red, and his brows crunched.

She came at him again, an overhead hit, which he blocked again. She came at him under his shield, at his head, at his middle, all he blocked without lifting his sword in offense. Ainslie grew tired. She should yield. She figured he waited, knowing she'd tire if he allowed her to have a few good hits. Then he could safely disarm her—smart tactic, but she wouldn't let him get off that easily. She came at him again, another swipe at his head blocked by his shield. She moved in, pushing against him, and when she was close, she hissed, "*Huglausi.*"

Rannick's eyes widened. She called him cowardly as she ensured no one heard her but him. He growled, shoving her away. He stood staring at her as a muscle ticed at his eye, and he heavily panted. His expression shifted, the relaxed openness replaced by a hard set of his eyes, a grim tilt to his mouth. Ainslie understood the moment he changed his mind and readied herself. He would fight, and she needed to be ready. She'd poked the bull, and now he would charge.

Rannick shifted his grip on his sword and advanced on Ainslie. He struck toward her head, and she blocked, nearly faltering. Damn, the man was strong.

She taunted him, hoping to bring out the brutal warrior inside, aching for a good fight. "Aye, now we're talking." She came at him again, an overhead attack he blocked with his sword. He struck her, forcing her to drop the point to the ground. But she held her grip hard. Dropping the weapon meant she would lose, and Ainslie wasn't a loser.

He turned and swung at her middle, which she blocked but lost her shield from the strength of his hit. He didn't pause but spun the other way and hit her side with the flat of his sword. She grunted but turned and came at his head, which he blocked with his shield.

Using the flat of his blade, he spun again and whacked her arm, causing her to fall to the ground. She cried out, but she still held her sword. He tried to hit her with his sword, and she rolled, but his flat side connected to her side, striking true. Her groan was drowned out by his roar as he came for her side again with the flat of his sword. When he hit her, she screamed out and curled into a ball but still held her sword.

At her cry, Rannick stopped and pulled back. "By the gods, Ainslie, did I hurt ye?"

He dropped his shield, kneeling at her side. *He fell for it, just as I planned.*

Ainslie's sword shot out from under her and swiped at Rannick's, sending it sliding along the dirt in a puff of dust. He watched in dismay as his sword skidded away. When he glanced back, she held her sword point to his throat. Rannick froze. If he moved, the blade would nick him.

Ainslie kept her eye and sword on him as she slowly rose. She had to keep her other arm wrapped around her middle. It hurt like hell. Rannick wasn't kidding when he said he was the best fighter in MacDougall's force. She couldn't stand up straight, but damn it, she had won.

The crowd went wild, and Dougal called for silence. "Rannick, ye have lost. My mighty warrior bested by the warrior woman."

A burst of laughter loud enough to carry across the land caused the crowd to turn, exposing a man. As he stepped from the crowd, he slowly clapped as he approached. He moved close to Ainslie. She spied muscular legs and a MacDougall plaid draped near his knees. Wait, she knew those knees. Was he here already? She couldn't stand up; she dared not take her gaze from Rannick's as she still held the sword at his throat for the win.

The man beside her spoke in an all too familiar taunt. "I come all this way. Spend two days on a longship chasing ye across the western isles. Figures, I would find my sister with a sword pointed at a warrior."

Ainslie gasped and turned to the familiar voice. "Colin!" He took her in his arms, and she cried out as he embraced her.

Rannick growled from the ground.

Colin stepped back and held her carefully against his side.

He spoke with an edge to his light tone. "Did he bruise ye, sister? Shall I run him through?"

Ainslie gripped her middle. "No, brother, it was a fair fight. The bruises I earned."

Dougal stepped down from the dais and strode purposefully toward them. "Ainslie, this is yer brother?" When he got close, he spoke softly, "Yer brother from the future?"

She nodded and spoke so only the people standing nearby heard. "Laird Dougal MacDougall, Lord of the Isles, this is my brother Laird Colin Roderick MacDougall, thirty-first laird to the clan MacDougall." She leaned over and whispered, "Yer grandson from the future."

Colin nodded and bowed slightly, making Ainslie gasp as he addressed Dougal. "I've come for my sister and wife."

Rannick stared at Colin from the ground. "Well, ye found yer sister. But we don't know where yer wife is."

Colin growled. "I will move heaven and earth to find her. She's in the hands of a madman, an evil Fae."

Ainslie turned to look at her brother, noticing the pin on his shoulder. She gasped. "Colin, is this the Brooch of Lorne?" Colin nodded as the gems in the pin winked in the sunlight, one purple oval over a deep red heart.

Ainslie gaped at her brother's face. "Colin, are those what I think those are?"

"Aye, I am to send the bastard to purgatory and recover my wife on a mission for the Fae."

Dougal huffed, "I've had messengers sent out. We should hear soon." Dougal clapped Colin on the shoulder, speaking low. "But for now, a show for the people attending the fight." He called out, speaking loud for the crowd, " 'Tis a celebration we shall have!"

Colin gripped his ancestor's shoulder.

Dougal grinned at Colin. "Good to meet ye finally. We'll speak later, but I have some unfinished business." He dropped his hand as Colin dropped his.

Dougal turned to Ainslie and Rannick, calling out loud for the crowd, "Ainslie, ye have won the contest. What token shall ye ask of Rannick for yer win? Gold, jewels, rich cloth?"

As Ainslie moved her sword away from Rannick's throat, he groaned as he stood.

Colin hid a smile behind his hand as he laughed, knowing material objects would not win her over.

Ainslie shook her head but turned to Rannick. "What I ask for is not for me but for the people of the new village ye build, the one where a MacDougall castle will stand."

Rannick turned to Ainslie, his expression open, ardent. "What is it ye ask of me, warrior woman?"

She handed her sword to Colin, who nodded at her as he took it. She took Rannick's hands in her own. "The children. I ask for the children. No matter how they are born, able or not, I ask that they have a place, a duty in the village. An undertaking they can do, and people that help care for them all. I ask ye to care for the special ones like Attar."

He bowed and kissed her hands. "Aye, warrior woman, I can do that."

Colin growled beside Ainslie. "Ye bruise my sister in a fight, then kiss her hands. Yer intentions better be honorable."

Dougal laughed. "Come, let's toast our family and plan how to find yer wife." Dougal broke out a wide grin. "I think we'll get to go a-raiding."

Chapter 13

Balor stormed into the longhouse and marched to Ivor. Before he reached him, two warriors rushed forward, restraining him. Ivor barely blinked.

Balor struggled and yelled at the obese sod stuffing his fat face. "What is the meaning of this? Why won't yer guards release my thrall?"

Ivor sipped his mead as he glared at him over the rim. Slowly lowering his mug, he tilted his head. "Ye have already tired of Edna and Ingrid? That cannot be possible. They are a delight to enjoy." Ivor waved his hand. "Go back to yer hut. If ye are nice, I can send another thrall and make it three women to enjoy."

Balor yanked his arms out of the guard's grasp. Ivor couldn't do this. The human woman was his, his to take and enjoy. This man was no jarl. He was a fat lazy bastard.

Balor ran his hand through his hair. "She's mine, *my thrall*. Mine to enjoy, and I want her now!" He screamed as spittle flew from his mouth. Fury boiled inside him, leaving him red in the face and panting in anger.

Ivor picked up some meat and ate it, his other hand signaling Tormund. Balor's gaze traveled the room as the rest of Ivor's warriors silently rose. When he glanced behind him, one stepped outside, and a few more filed in, making a wide circle around him.

133

After Ivor swallowed, he spoke low. "Ye mistreated yer thrall. She still heals. I am saving her from the damage yer lust has done. Ye should thank me, not bellow in rage. I shall send another thrall for ye to enjoy." Ivor waved to the vacant seat next to him. "Relax, eat, enjoy some mead. Yer thrall will be well soon."

Balor took a deep breath and then another, The Stone of Lust called to him as the red receded from his face. This man was nothing. The stone would make this right. Then he, Balor, will have it all—the village, his army, and her, *Brielle*.

Balor reached into his bag and held the magic stone. Grasping it, he sensed the energy in the stone pulse. His mind focused solely on Ivor and the will to command him to do his bidding. Powerful energy filled him, making him strong.

He eyed Ivor, focused his will upon him. He fixated on the command, waving his hand as he spoke. "Ye will bring my thrall to me now." He glared at Ivor, waiting for him to do his bidding.

Ivor stared blankly back.

Balor concentrated harder and waved his hand again, sending the mental command more forcefully. *Ye will do as I command.*

Ivor growled and frowned. "I hear ye in my head, Balor. Whatever power ye possess to do that won't work. I have a stronger will than ye think. I will not bring yer thrall now." Ivor waved him away. "Go and enjoy the women I have offered, for I am certain they have a greater skill of seduction than the ill thrall."

Balor's fury grew, and his rage boiled. He held The Stone of Lust, closed his eyes, and commanded the men under his control. ~ *Prepare for attack. Retrieve my thrall at once.* ~

His men in the longhouse stood as one and marched out. Ivor glanced around. His warriors had their hands on their swords, ready to defend themselves should an attack come.

Balor slowly opened his eyes and leveled them on Ivor. "I thank ye for yer hospitality. My men and I shall depart." He closed his eyes, waiting for a signal from his warrior.

~I have her.~

Balor opened his eyes to stare at Ivor, then smirked. "With my thrall."

Ivor signaled his men, who closed in on Balor. Balor waved his hand, and a flash of light erupted, taking him to his longboat.

****

Brielle lay on a warm and clean bed for the first time in a week. The people whose home she was in were friendly but spoke in a strange form of Gaelic she couldn't quite understand. Occasionally, a word or two sounded familiar, but Brielle couldn't grasp enough to understand or communicate. The pain had faded from the beatings, and being quiet allowed her to focus on thoughts that made her happy.

She made her little mental cocoon where Colin spoke to her. He told her how much he loved and cherished her. The twins played in the yard, their squeals of laughter as Colin, growling like a bear, chased them around filled her mind. She smiled, and grimaced as it hurt her split lip.

Brielle sighed and pictured Colin caressing her face and kissing her softly. Would she ever see the family she grew to love so much again? She shifted in the bedding. She was clean yet felt dirty and raw, ugly. Would Colin ever find her attractive again? Brielle was relieved there wasn't a mirror, fearing she would fall apart if she saw what she looked like now.

There was a commotion at the door. A man yelled, and the woman tending her ran to the door. A warrior burst through, stabbing the woman, cutting off her scream. The fighter glanced around the room and spotted her on the bed. He strode toward her as she scooted away. But not soon enough. He scooped her up, furs and all, flung her over his shoulder, and marched out of the hut. Brielle screamed, beating his back and kicking her legs, but it made no difference.

He hauled her through the village. From her upside-down position, there were warriors in battle all around them. He carried her through the carnage without care. Screams erupted in the air, and grunts of men fighting reached Brielle. The smell of blood mixed with mud made her queasy as she bumped in his steady gait. He dropped her, and she hit the back of her head on something solid as stars danced before her eyes. Coming to, she glanced around and saw she was in the front of a longboat again. When she moved, bindings cut into her hands and feet. Damn, he'd tied her.

She gazed up, and Tony's face replaced the warrior's. "Miss me, darling? I missed ye."

Tony stood shouting for his warriors, who jumped into the longship. The boat shifted in the water, and oarsmen rowed as men continued to climb into the ship. Tony held the black glowing stone to his chest and yelled an order.

Brielle closed her eyes, trying to find her cocoon

136

again, but the surrounding sounds drowned her thoughts as tears stung her eyes. She was in hell, and she desperately wanted out.

Brielle woke as someone picked her up, and she dangled over a warrior's back again. It was dark, making it difficult to see where they were. She almost laughed. They handled her this way so much that she should have gotten used to it, but it still hurt and made her nauseous.

Tony shouted orders in Gaelic. Turning her head, she caught an upside-down glance at men running around, unloading supplies, and making camp. The guard took her to a tent and set her on some fur, still tied hand and foot. The warrior strode out, leaving her alone. A brazier warmed the tent, and a lantern on the center pole provided light. Her hands were in front of her, the ties too tight to undo, but she managed to untie her feet. She wiggled to her knees and stood holding onto the pole. She plodded to the tent opening.

Tony entered, his shocked expression near hers.

He grabbed her ties and jerked her to the furs. "Going somewhere, my sweet? I think not." He took her ties and secured her to the bottom of the pole. She huffed in frustration as she lay there on her side.

Tony sat beside her, leaning against the pole. A warrior entered with a steaming plate of food. The scent of freshly roasted meat sent her stomach into spasms of hunger. Her mouth watered, but her throat went dry, her thirst palpable. It seemed they'd set up camp while Brielle slept in the boat. Her stomach growled, filling the tent with its rumble. Tony laughed.

He picked a piece of meat, waved it before her, then popped it in his mouth. As he chewed slowly, he took out the black stone. It did not glow, but he held it up to the lantern light.

"I've watched ye for a long time now, Brielle. Did ye know that?"

She looked away. The change in Tony's voice told her the Fae spoke now. She'd gotten used to the difference and knew who spoke when.

He continued as he ate another bit of meat, speaking between bites. "Aye, I saw ye the first time in the Great Hall at Dunstaffnage, in the eighteenth century. The sunlight on the window glinted off yer face. The gods made ye only for me." He finished the last bit of meat, leaving nothing for her. Brielle closed her eyes, willing him to stop speaking, trying to block him from her mind. She needed her cocoon, needed to survive.

His voice drifted to her. "Aye, I fell in love with ye then. Much like my wife, *lust* at first sight."

She opened her eyes. Her stomach growled again, this time caving in on itself, forcing the acid to rise in her throat. She lay there wishing for a drink or something to eat, but she'd never beg, not from Tony or the Fae inside him.

Tony picked up a mug and gulped the rest. He smacked his lips, then audibly moaned as he set the tankard down.

He held the black stone farther into the light. "Lust, Brielle, lust is a powerful emotion, almost as powerful as love."

The stone glowed, and he closed his fist around it. "Do ye feel that, Brielle? Do ye feel the lust I have for ye?" He glanced at her.

She closed her eyes. She sensed him lying down

beside her. She smelled his sweaty body odor as it fouled her appetite. He grabbed her hands, and she cried out, not expecting his touch.

He forced her hands open and placed the stone in them, then closed his fists over hers, holding them tight. "Do ye feel it now, Brielle? My lust for ye? Tell me ye feel lust for me as I do ye?" He closed his eyes, and his breathing slowed.

Brielle feared moving might set him off, so she lay still and stayed that way for some time. The stone warmed in her hands. A vision came to her, fading in her mind's view. She sat on a small rocky outcropping with waves crashing against it, an island in the distance. It played out like a movie. Dougal MacDougall, a clan elder from the seventeenth century she had spoken with when asked to write the Family Book for Roderick, was visible. Well, Colin pretended to be Roderick in the past. Dougal's voice came clearly as if he sat next to her now.

You must believe and have faith,
the one who doubts is like a wave of the sea,
blown and tossed by the wind.
The one who has faith is like the rock.
Standing solid against the waves.

She still saw the island in her mind's eye. The scene flipped like a movie. In a blink, she sat on the isle gazing toward the shore. The sun shone brightly, and the day was clear and warm, pleasant. She looked around at the beauty surrounding her—the island, the ocean, the lush shoreline in the distance.

She glanced down at the rocks beside her feet. In the water lapping against the island's rocky shore was a blue gem glittering in the water, winking in the sunlight. She reached into the water and picked up the blue diamond-shaped stone. The rock glowed brightly, and her heart filled with faith. She called to her true love, begging him to sail to her rescue.

She blinked, and the scene changed again. She sat on the same island at night, the waves crashing harder now, closer and closer to her. Ainslie spoke, but Brielle didn't see her. Ainslie read from the *Fae Fable Book*.

"Upon arriving at the battle, the prince fought hard and searched for his true love. As he fought on, going deeper into the enemy camp, The Stone of Love burned brightly in the brooch on his chest, and The Stone of Fear glowed purple behind it.

"During the battle, a warrior of the evil foe told the prince his commander had stranded his true love on an island, and she was about to drown when the tide came in. The prince panicked and sailed to save her.

"When the prince approached the maiden, the evil foe lunged from behind the rock she sat upon with his sword, intent on killing the prince. The maiden, fearing for her love, moved before the prince. The blade pierced the maiden; the blade jutted through her back, the tip coming from her chest stabbing the prince in his, missing his heart. The maiden cried out, and the prince roared, gripping her to him. He held his true love as the evil foe withdrew the sword screaming. He had stabbed the maiden by mistake.

"The maiden sobbed as the prince held her up. 'True love or a lifetime in purgatory; you once cheated The Stone of Love. Now the story shall come true.' The maiden opened her palm, and The Stone of Lust glowed black. She pressed the side of the brooch, and a secret compartment opened.

"She inserted The Stone of Lust and closed the latch. 'But it's not me going to purgatory.'

"The prince lowered his love carefully to the ground, and the gems on his shoulder glowed brightly. The light grew brighter, then his arm glowed. He pointed his hand to the evil foe, and light shot from his hand, capturing the foul enemy and freezing him in a circle of light. The prince concentrated all his energy on the evil foe and, with a roar, swiped his other arm holding his sword, cutting off the evil foe's head.

"The prince dropped his sword, fell to his knees, and gathered his true love in his arms. He begged the Fae to spare his true love's life as she lay dying. Dagda, the king of The Tuatha Dé Dannan, appeared. 'I am sorry, Prince, I cannot help you. A deed by the evil Fae I cannot undo.'

"The prince roared and held his true love as she died in his arms.

"Dagda spoke. 'When lust is conceived, it brings forth sin. Sin, when it is finished, brings death.' "

Brielle gasped. She was the maiden, and Colin was her true love! Brielle saw her death. She gripped the black stone, for she now realized she held The Stone of Lust, which showed her the blue stone on an island by the shore—the location of The Stone of Faith.

A warrior called for Tony from the entrance. "Master, the boat is too close to the reef. We must move it before it crashes against the rocks."

Tony jolted awake, quickly sitting up, his head shaking from side to side.

Tony rose and shouted to the warrior, "The boat! We must save the boat! It's my only way back to the portal!"

As he left the tent, Brielle hid the stone in her clothing, hoping Tony or the Fae inside him would forget he'd given it to her.

Alone again, she closed her eyes and prayed for Colin to arrive. She knew he would not stop until he found her, knew he would come. She prayed he would know what to do. He'd changed the ending of The Stone of Love fable when the time came. Had he read the *Fae Fable Book* now? Did he know the outcome? She prayed he could change the end of The Stone of Lust fable. If not, she would die in his arms.

Brielle hugged herself and moaned, "Please, Colin, hear me. Come soon. Come chase my storms away."

Chapter 14

The healer still heated the pot as she mixed the herbal poultice at the fireplace. Ainslie lay on her stomach with only a sheet covering part of her, leaving her bare to the waist, her back and side in full view.

A low growl filled the room. Its cadence didn't belong to Colin. She rose slightly, turning her head, only to cry out in pain. Rannick stood staring at her. Ainslie rested her head, gazing back.

He glanced down and heaved a sigh as he clenched his fists repeatedly.

She spoke softly. "Ye are not to blame, Rannick. Mine is a warrior's body. I get bruised sometimes."

Rannick's eyes moved over her back and side. She knew what he saw. She'd peeked in the mirror earlier.

He huffed. "Ye get bruised like this always? Purple and black marks mar yer perfect ivory skin. I can clearly see welts in the pattern of the side of my sword." He sniffed. "One has broken open along yer lower rib, oozing blood." His gaze came back to hers. "By the gods, I fear I've left ye scarred."

His eyes traveled slowly down her body. This time, his expression told her he admired her curves, making her face flush with heat.

His eyes returned to hers, the hunger evident in the expression he settled on her. "It is a woman's body, Ainslie, and I put those bruises there."

She glanced down, embarrassed that Rannick admired her form, naked, under the sheet. Heat flushed her body and awareness of his attraction came over her.

The healer turned from the fireplace, her items in hand, ready for her patient. "Rannick, ye should know better than to be in here. Yer mother would skin ye if she knew."

Rannick never took his eyes from Ainslie.

His expression softened at the woman's scolding. "Agnes, I hurt her. I wish to heal her, please."

Agnes shook her head. "I doubt the woman hurt wants ye in here. She's not decent, Rannick."

He stared at the healer and scowled. " 'Tis part of my vow. I hurt her. I heal her."

Agnes huffed as Ainslie spoke up. "Agnes, it's okay. Where I come from, men and women are healers. I do not fear him, and he can't see anything too alarming."

Agnes puffed a sigh. "I'll stay to make sure all he does is heal ye."

Ainslie laughed at her comment as Agnes handed Rannick the bucket with the fabric soaked in the herbal mixture. "Ye were always such a willful child, Rannick."

Agnes settled in a chair by the fireplace, ready for a nap.

Ainslie smiled, easily picturing Rannick as an unruly child. She imagined him ignoring his chores and working his sword day and night, dreaming of becoming a great warrior. He obviously had a soft spot for his ma. When Agnes mentioned her, his eyes softened.

He approached and set the bucket on the floor, took

some of the paste, and lightly rubbed her back and side, careful when he came upon the cuts. Ainslie winced at the first touch, but as the mixture warmed her skin, it soothed her bruises. She closed her eyes and inhaled. Mint, camphor, and whisky scents filled the room, folding over one another. Each aroma fighting to be the strongest, the camphor winning.

Rannick said nothing. He gently rubbed her back and side with the herbs. At times he massaged a tight muscle, but when he came to the cut, he lightly fingered it. The sting from the herbs faded fast into a dull ache, then numbness. When he began humming, she eased. He had a lovely baritone voice, and his touch was gentle but firm, confident in his ministrations. He'd done this before. Her mind drifted, and she relaxed fully.

She wondered what it would be like to live here in the Viking time. Would they permit her to continue to be the warrior woman they had taken to calling her? Would Dougal allow her to train and fight with the men as she dreamed of, like how she trained with her da? What would living as a woman in this time provide for her? A home she would certainly have as a relative of the Lord of the Isles. Would she take part in the settling of Dunstaffnage, its beginning? Rannick oversaw the settlement. Would he like her to stay and live there? Did he have a woman, a wife, chosen for his life? Would he want someone like her, a modern woman, a warrior woman?

When he placed a hot wet cloth on her back, she started. As he spread it over her side, she relaxed again. He tucked it around her, ensuring the fabric covered every bruise yet noticeably avoiding the sides of her

Margaret Izard

breasts. Rannick gently rubbed the rest of the herbal mixture on the warm material, leaving it to soak.

Ainslie was almost asleep when he whispered in her ear, "Rest, warrior woman, a warrior for the children. I shall fight by yer side but never raise a hand to ye again."

****

The chill of the wrap woke Ainslie, and she found herself alone. Dreading moving, let alone rising, she lay there enjoying the rest.

It didn't last long.

Colin stormed into the room. *Well, no rest for the weary.*

Colin slammed his fist on the mantel. "Damn it, Ainslie, I want to go find her now!" The mantel was solid stone and didn't budge. She wondered if he'd broken his fingers.

"I've just come from a private conference with Dougal and Rannick about Bree. They wait for messengers and refuse to begin a search without further information."

Ainslie knew this. If she hadn't been injured, she would have been part of the meeting. Now she needed to soothe her brother—a nearly impossible feat when it came to Bree.

Ainslie exhaled. "Colin, it would be a waste of time to chase up and down the western isles if ye don't have a clue where he took her."

Colin growled, but Ainslie continued, familiar with her brother's anger. Glad he took it out on objects only. Mrs. A kept an ample supply of whisky glasses, as that was his usual target.

"Colin, ye found us in time. Tell me, was there a

new fable from the *Fae Fable Book*?"

Her brother grunted. "Aye, it was similar to the one Ma told ye as a child, but parts were different."

Ainslie moved to see her brother better. "How so?"

Colin growled, "I'd prefer not to say. It describes the ill-treatment of a woman and a man's greed, hinting at Bree and her damned ex. The Fae didn't give us the end. It left the woman on the island begging for her love to rescue her."

Ainslie mulled that over for a moment. "Colin, no end must mean it's still left to play out. Maybe there are different endings, depending on how successful we are?"

Colin huffed. "The only way we'll be successful is if I get out there and search for my love."

Ainslie shifted, getting more comfortable. "Dougal seems confident his messengers will return with information soon. Once that comes, Rannick promised we would sail for her immediately. He vowed he would bring her safely to me."

Colin glanced over his shoulder, raising his eyebrow. "He vowed, did he?" Colin turned and leaned against the side of the mantel. He crossed his arms over his chest, his feet at the ankles, and stared at her. He stood there waiting for a response.

Her shoulders nearly moved to her ears under his glare. There were times he saw straight through her, and it unnerved her. This time, he wouldn't get a glimpse of her thoughts, her feelings for Rannick.

Ainslie refused to look at him as she spoke. "What?"

Colin glanced at his feet, then her face. "What have ye been up to here in the Viking times, little sis?"

Ainslie blushed and turned her head to face the other way. That did not distract Colin. He moved to that side of the room within her line of sight and leaned against the wall.

Ainslie groaned as Colin laughed. "Out with it, sis. What is going on between ye and this Rannick?"

Ainslie tried to sit up and gasped in pain, only making Colin chuckle.

She rolled her eyes. "Nothing, Colin. He's helping us find Bree and the madman. Who happened to take his newest longship and hijacked his men. He wants them back."

Colin heaved a long sigh.

Ainslie felt for him. His heart was torn apart. Bree was the best thing to happen to Colin. As his true love and the mother of his kids, he'd move heaven and earth to get her back. She tucked her hands under her chin and gazed at her brother, his raw emotions clear on his face. "Colin…"

His pained expression shifted to Ainslie.

She sniffled, her eyes watering. "We'll get her back. We'll get yer wee Bree back."

Colin stared at his sister, and a tear trailed down his cheek. "I know we'll get her back. I only worry there won't be much left when we do." He took a shuddering breath. "It is killing me knowing she's in that madman's hands. I must force myself to stop thinking of all the things he could do to her. And I am…" He waved one hand in the air. "…stuck here waiting, allowing it all to happen."

Ainslie reached her hand out to her brother, and he kneeled, taking it between his. "Colin, whatever has happened to her, we'll deal with it. She's a strong, smart woman. For all ye know, she's outwitted him and sits in the corner eating chocolate cake."

Colin huffed a sob, and she knew he thought of his and Bree's first dinner together, where they shared chocolate lava cake and chocolate kisses. Ainslie joked with them about it constantly, as they ate chocolate cake often. When Bree ate chocolate, she instead on chocolate kisses from her husband.

He gripped her hand as he slid sitting on the floor. "I vowed I would kill the madman. The King of the good Fae, Dagda, demanded I send the evil Fae inside Tony to purgatory first, but I don't know. The anger inside me commands I kill Tony, and I hope I can hold out. Dagda said if I didn't send the evil Fae away first, he'd haunt the family till we do."

As a sob broke from Colin, she squeezed his hand. "Ye'll do it. I'll be here to help. Rannick and Dougal have pledged to help. All we need is to know where he took her. We'll get her back, Colin."

Colin rested his head on their hands as he quietly sobbed.

She'd never seen her brother like this. Ainslie was a warrior. She could fight like any man and followed Bree through the portal to save her. Ainslie swore she would do anything in her power to save Bree. If she saved Bree, she'd save her brother.

****

After a night and full day of rest from her fight with Rannick, Ainslie went into the crowded great hall for a special feast. Thankfully the soreness and bruising had faded, and she walked with ease. For the special evening, Dougal's wife, Fiona, gave Ainslie a silken overtunic for the special feast the Lord of the Isles hosted in honor of her and Colin.

Stopping inside the great doors, she smoothed her hand down the front of the garment. She wanted to look her best this evening, and with the Viking dress, she felt more like a princess than a warrior. A maid styled her hair with a series of braids intertwined with glass beads. A crown of intricately twisted tin, shaped with Celtic knots, held more glass beads, and pearls sat across her upper forehead. She patted the back of her hair to ensure it was in place. Multiple bracelets borrowed and worn at Fiona's insistence clinked and flickered in the candlelight.

Her brother's deep voice rumbled behind her. "Ye are like a Valkyrie princess, warrior, and queen, all wrapped in one."

Colin wrapped his arm around her, hugging her, and she winced. Seemed not all the soreness had faded.

"And I'll gut that damned Rannick for hurtin' ye. He should have pulled back before his strike would hurt. It was a fight to disarm only."

Ainslie turned, patting his shoulder. The Iona Stones in the Brooch of Lorne winked in the candlelight. "Ye will not. It was a fair fight, and I goaded him, anyway."

Colin laughed. "I am certain ye did. The same way ye goaded John and me time and time again. 'Tis still no excuse."

Ainslie stared at the candles that blurred as she recalled Rannick's visit to her room. His quiet declaration, another vow to her. Guilt ate at her. She'd used his weakness to win the fight. Underhanded but strategically better than his tactic, to not fight at all. Sometimes winning wasn't everything. She blinked, and the candles came into view. "I likely owe him an apology."

Colin made a huffing sound.

She glanced at him and almost grinned at his raised eyebrows—she'd shocked him.

"He had an oath not to hurt women. Something about his da—I forced him to break it by egging him on. I likely deserved a good whack or two."

Colin frowned. "Still, a good whack doesn't bruise like that."

The very person they discussed approached with an older woman on his arm. She was tall like Rannick but had blonde hair with silver streaks that reminded Ainslie of flowing white caps of ocean waves. She moved gracefully, and her expression glowed brightly when she glanced at Rannick.

When he reached Colin and her, she still gazed at Rannick when he spoke. "Ainslie and Colin MacDougall, I'd like ye to meet my mother, Astrid."

Ainslie grinned as she spoke. "Astrid, it means beautiful and loved."

Astrid nodded as she peered at Colin, then Ainslie. "I am happy to meet the warrior woman who has helped heal an old part of my son's heart. I am pleased his grudge against his father is over." She glanced at Rannick, then back at Ainslie. "It was a long time coming. But worth the wait since it was ye who healed him." Rannick glanced down, and Ainslie spotted a blush on his neck.

Astrid took Ainslie's hands into her own and stared into her eyes. Astrid's eyes traveled over her face and hair; her hands warmed in Ainslie's. Astrid's eyes were the same ice blue as Rannick's, and Ainslie found she couldn't look away if she tried. Astrid patted her hands and placed them in Rannick's. She closed her eyes and murmured something Ainslie could not hear.

She stared fondly at her son. "She's a strong spirit with a kind heart. A warrior for the children is the right name for her, my son. I am happy for ye." She turned and walked to the dais to speak with Fiona and Dougal MacDougall.

Rannick pulled something from his pouch, holding it in his hand. "Ainslie, I have a gift. A token of my regret for hurting ye. I shouldn't have lost myself."

Ainslie smiled, remembering the market the previous day. "I thought a woman of beauty needed no decoration."

Rannick's cheeks flushed. "Ah, her wit is as sharp as her blade…true, a woman's true worth is not in her appearance but in the hidden person of the heart. Where her imperishable beauty lies." He paused, gazing at her. Could he see her hidden person, the individual she was, a hardened warrior and a vulnerable woman?

Glancing at his hands, he broke the connection. "But for ye, I wish to give ye this. Please turn, and I will place it on ye."

She turned as Rannick placed a necklace around her neck, his fingers brushing her when he closed the clasp, sending shivers down her neck. She glanced down. It was the necklace from the previous day, the one she admired in the market—silver beads on strands draped in loops connected at the center by a large sliver locket twinkled in the candlelight.

His hands rested on her shoulders as he whispered in her ear, "Please forgive me."

Ainslie turned, gazing at him over her shoulder.

Their faces were close, breaths mingling. "I forgive ye."

Colin grumbled next to Ainslie, who shot her brother a dry expression.

Rannick took Ainslie's hands and placed one on his arm. "Allow me to lead ye to the dais. Dougal insisted ye both dine as honored guests tonight."

Dougal was all too happy to see his guests again. Standing, he hugged Ainslie. "Ah, the warrior woman. Hopefully, ye have healed well."

Ainslie nodded, and Dougal moved on to Colin with a bear hug and patted him on the back. "Colin, please sit beside me; we have much to discuss."

Everyone settled into their seats, Colin to Dougal's right and Ainslie to Fiona's left as she sat beside her husband. Rannick sat to her left, and his mother next to him.

Dougal banged his metal chalice on the table, and everyone in the Great Hall quieted. " 'Tis with great pleasure I honor our guests and distant relatives, Colin and Ainslie MacDougall." He raised his cup for a toast. "To the warrior woman and her brother." Everyone raised their cups, and a cheer went through the hall. Dougal sat as Fiona signaled the servers to bring out the platters of food.

Astrid leaned over Rannick, speaking to Ainslie. "I want to hear about Attar, the boy with the leg that is short no longer."

Ainslie set her cup down as Rannick filled their shared trencher with food. She turned to his mother. "It really was nothing, only extra leather to build up the shoe of his shorter leg. I saw him this morning, and he walked easily."

Astrid smiled widely at her.

Rannick leaned over to speak to his mother. "She's being modest. Ye should have seen the boy run. He said he had never sprinted so fast or smoothly in all his life. Claimed it was like a longship gliding in the ocean." Rannick glanced at Ainslie, a grin on his face. He took her hand in his and kissed the back. "He cried tears of joy."

Astrid beamed and nodded. "He will be loyal, Rannick, now that ye have given him the gift of walking easier. He will serve ye well for his life now."

Rannick squeezed her hand and set it down as Ainslie studied their trencher. Rannick had piled it high with various foods. There was roast lamb, salted fish, and fresh root vegetables on the plate, and plenty of fresh bread sat in a bowl in front of her. He was already slicing the meat and placing the tenderest pieces on her side. She speared the lamb, put it on her tongue, and it melted in her mouth.

Colin spoke to Dougal from the other side of Fiona. They spoke low, but if Ainslie focused, she could easily pick out her brother's deep voice. Dougal asked about the stones and Fae and Colin quietly responded.

Ainslie puzzled over the Fae fables, both so similar yet so different. One with an ending and one without. What did it mean? Was there no ending for Bree, or did the Fae not want Colin to know Bree may die? Then there was hers, one not from the book but from her parents. The female died in that one, but Ainslie knew from Colin and John's experiences with the fables that they didn't come out exactly as told. The actions and conclusions were personifications of the truth. Having both had to mean something, but what?

Rannick glanced at her, tilting his head as he did. "Is yer side still paining ye, Ainslie?"

She smirked and took a bite of her food. "Would it bother ye if I said yes?"

He huffed and turned away. He was still angry with himself for losing control during their fight. Likely upset with the fact Dougal's greatest warrior had lost. He fisted his hands and heaved another sigh. He beat himself up over his concern for hurting her. She felt guilty for teasing him and should put him out of his misery.

She set her knife down and took his hand in hers. "I am truly fine. A little bruised, but nothing I haven't had before." She looked down. "I think it made Colin happy to know someone finally landed me on my ass."

Rannick patted her hands. "Ye must tell me if ye hurt, then I can take ye to yer room, make sure ye rest."

Ainslie waved over the room. "I would much rather be here where the party is."

Rannick gave her a side glance. "Party?"

Ainslie took her hands away and waved in front of them. "The feast. This is a party."

Rannick's gaze traveled the room, then he grunted. The serving women brought in a fresh fruit dessert and a little honey on buttered bread, setting a platter before them.

Ainslie ate a fruit as she studied Rannick's profile. "Tell me about the vow, the one about yer father."

Rannick sat up and turned to look at his mother by his side. She spoke with Gunnar, their heads bent close. He studied them for a moment.

Ainslie stared at Rannick and followed his focus,

moving to his mother, wondering what Rannick thought.

Gunnar bent his head to Astrid's ear, only to have her blush and look away. She peeked at him from under her lashes. A person might miss the flirting if they weren't specifically watching, but both flirted. Her eyes returned to Rannick.

He exhaled, and she hoped he would approve of the courtship. Gunnar seemed to be a good man and a better warrior. Rannick took a handful of nuts, popped one in his mouth, and chewed.

Ainslie tapped his arm. "The vow?"

Rannick glanced back at her. "It is nothing ye need to concern yerself with."

Ainslie took his left hand in hers and faced him. "I wish to know. I want to understand."

He removed his hand and took a long pull on his ale. He stared into the mug, then set it down with a thump.

He dumped the nuts on the trencher and spoke in a low voice. "My father was one of Dougal's greatest warriors and a good friend. My father trained Dougal in his youth before his da's death, and he took over as Lord of the Isles. Fiona and my mother are best friends. Astrid is a mother figure to Fiona, who lost hers at a young age." He sighed. "My father loved my mother deeply. He courted her for a full year before her father relented and allowed the match. For a time, they were happy."

He peered at his mother, and Ainslie's eyes followed.

Astrid turned her head to the side as Gunnar whispered in her ear. She put her hand on his chest, and he raised his head and gazed at her with longing. Astrid returned the look and grinned.

Ainslie turned to Rannick, and he smiled. The elder couple seemed happy, and she bet it was long overdue.

He fisted his hand as he spoke again. "It was the drink that got him angry. He raided for Dougal and was away often when I was young. Another's husband, who was injured and couldn't raid, took to helping her with chores and supplying food from his hunts." He took another long drink of his ale. "My father's drunkenness and jealousy led to his anger, which kept coming out of his fists."

He glanced at his mother. "My mother is a healer and weathered the bruises well, but one night, he was hard on her and knocked her out. I'd just started training with the sword, and we argued. I thought he'd killed her. In my stupid youth, I killed him to avenge her death."

Her heart went out to him, and Ainslie placed her hand on his arm. "Ye were young and defending yer ma. It took a lot of courage to stand up to yer da like that. What a difficult thing to deal with as a young man. To face off with yer father to protect yer mother. A fight for both the people ye loved most in the world yet forced to pick one over the other."

He laughed bitterly. "That's what Dougal said. Declared me innocent of wrongdoing and demanded I move in with the warriors training at the castle. He said I would make a great warrior one day." He stared ahead. "That was when I vowed never to hurt a woman. I pledged to defend them."

Ainslie rubbed his hand as she still held it. "And ye have, Rannick."

He tightly fisted the hand she held. "My anger at my father cost him his life. I should have better control over my fighting. Not permit the bloodlust to control me."

Ainslie smoothed her hand over his firm fist, and he relaxed it a little. She understood his warrior's heart. The desire to control the fierce energy within him that wanted to wage war but still needed to be gentle with his friends and family. The people he loved deeply. Maybe if she explained how she saw the bloodlust, he might understand the balance between the two.

She continued to caress his fist as she whispered, "Bloodlust is something every fighter has, Rannick. Even women."

He stared at her hand, gently stroking his, and he relaxed a little more.

Her fingers trailed along his knuckles. "Fighting comes in many forms, not just the sword a warrior wields, but a mother's fight to bring an infant into the world, a husband's fight to hunt for food for his family, a warrior's fight to defend his land."

She opened his fingers and lightly brushed hers along his palm, from his fingertips to his wrist and back. "A child's fight to survive in a hard world." She slowly traced the lines in his hand. "Using the bloodlust for the right reasons and causes is the art of being a great warrior."

Rannick glanced at his hand, then her face. His free hand came to her cheek and caressed it.

He used his thumb to tilt her head till their eyes connected. "Warrior for the children, woman of war. Is yer bloodlust only for the children?"

Ainslie gazed into Rannick's bright blue eyes and

became lost. She spoke before she thought. "Everyone, I fight for everyone. Who does yer bloodlust fight for, Rannick?"

He leaned toward her, and their breaths mingled. "I fight for many things." He licked his lips and spoke softly. "But tonight, I use it to pursue the woman I love." He brushed his lips on hers, and they paused for a moment, a breath, as they stared into each other's eyes.

The room erupted in a roar of cheers, and they broke apart.

Ainslie dropped her head, her face heating. They'd forgotten where they were.

Dougal slammed his cup on the table. "Rannick, my man. Seducing a woman at my feast table? And in front of her brother? Ye grow bolder by the day!"

Colin growled next to Dougal.

Ainslie peeked at her brother, who glared at her.

Colin smiled, nodded, and spoke loudly for all to hear. "Ainslie is a rare woman, a bright spirit. She has a will of her own, and I permit her to pursue her heart. I desire her to find true love as I have."

Dougal turned to Colin. "Aye, and as I vowed before, we shall find yer true love. I suspect my messengers will return soon, and when they do, we shall go raiding and bring her back."

Ainslie shifted in her seat, wincing from her injury.

Colin turned to her. "Ainslie, ye should rest from yer injury."

She glared daggers at him. "I am fine, brother." Her sharp response brought a smirk to Colin's face.

Rannick spoke to Colin. "I shall see her in her chamber." He turned to her and rose, helping her up.

"Goodnight, all." He glanced at her, smiling. "Good party and good rest."

****

Colin watched them leave, Rannick carefully escorting his sister from the hall. Her gaze was only for Rannick. Love grew between them for all to see if one only looked. He turned and sat staring into his mug. He hoped what he saw in Ainslie was love, and then again, he hoped not. Ainslie in love would make traveling back to their time that much harder.

Chapter 15

Rannick escorted her from the hall toward her room, ensuring he held her as they climbed the stairs. The ascent became more difficult the farther she went. At the top, she paused momentarily, and Rannick turned to her. She waved him off before continuing down the passage. Her room was pretty close.

The torches flickered in the hallway, lighting their way, creating a warm, soft light. They strolled arm in arm, and when they reached the door, Ainslie opened it and entered the room. She poured mead into two cups, turned, and moved to Rannick, who stood in the doorway.

Ainslie handed him a cup and turned as she sat in the chair before the fireplace. From the corner of her eye, she saw that Rannick leaned on the frame and sipped as he settled his gaze on her.

She turned to him, waving a hand at the chair beside her. "Rannick, I wish to speak to ye. Please come sit by the fire."

Rannick frowned into his mug and responded without looking up. "I should not be here, Ainslie. 'Tis not proper."

She patted the chair next to her. "I'm the warrior woman. I've already broken propriety rules. Where I am from, sitting and talking is no crime."

He glanced up and raised an eyebrow as he stared

at her a moment. His eyes moved over the room, landing on her sword and shield propped next to the bed.

She patted the chair. "I won't raise my sword. All I want to do is talk."

Rannick shoved off the doorway and closed the door softly. He smirked as he moved to the offered chair. "Ye may not raise yer sword, but ye might punch me."

Ainslie laughed at his comment and sipped her mead.

Rannick sat, leaned back, and crossed his feet at the ankles, stretching them before the fire. With a sigh, he took a sip of mead, rested his head on the back of the chair, and closed his eyes.

Ainslie studied him for a moment. In his silent stillness, he looked younger. Laugh lines crinkled at the edges of his eyes, attesting to his good nature. He seemed less warrior and more a mere man in his relaxed state.

Ainslie recalled her dream, where she'd seen him before coming to the twelfth century, before she'd even met him. She remembered her feeling when his light blue eyes electrified her with his gaze, and she sensed true love. Outside her dream, she wasn't sure it could be true love. They were centuries apart in their lifestyles, yet they held the same values and drive for life. Ainslie sensed, in her heart, that she loved him.

His head came up, turned, and he settled those electric blue eyes on her now, holding the same expression she'd seen in her dream. Her heart skipped a beat, and she recalled what she wanted to say, and earlier she thought it would not come easy for her.

But staring into his eyes, the words came easily. "Rannick, I wish to speak about our combat. About what happened."

Rannick sat forward, breaking eye contact, resting his elbows on his knees. "There is nothing to discuss. It won't happen again."

Ainslie touched his arm. "I wish to apologize, Rannick."

His head shot up. "For what? I am the one who beat ye black and blue. 'Tis my fault."

Ainslie waved her hand. "Rannick, it was I who egged ye on. It is my fault for pushing ye beyond what ye wanted. If I hadn't goaded ye, ye would not have let loose yer bloodlust."

He sat still, staring at her. Maybe she'd shocked him.

Ainslie set her cup on the side table and kneeled before Rannick. "I am asking for yer forgiveness. Please forgive me."

Rannick set his mug down and brushed her face with his hand. "Oh, Ainslie, it is I who has asked for forgiveness from ye."

She sighed. "Then we are both forgiven."

Rannick took her hands in his and kissed them.

Ainslie rose to fill her mug with mead and winced.

Rannick stood, reaching for her. "Ainslie, ye are in pain. I will call Agnes."

She put her hand on his arm. "Nonsense. It is late. She has already returned to the village."

Rannick took her hands in his. "I'll get my mother. She can heal ye."

As he turned to leave, Ainslie caught her hand on his elbow. "She is enjoying herself at the feast. Leave her be, Rannick."

Rannick turned to her, those corners of his eyes wrinkling at the corners.

Ainslie brushed her hand on his cheek. "Rannick, I want ye to heal me. I need ye, Rannick."

Rannick took a deep breath, and his nostrils flared. "Ainslie, do ye know what ye ask?"

Ainslie nodded. "Aye, Rannick, please. I want ye."

Rannick bent to kiss her, timid at first, uncertain about it. When she returned the kiss, his hands cupped her face, a low moan vibrating her lips. At her gasp, his tongue swooped in to taste her—devour her. He wrapped his arms around her, tilting his head as his mouth moved, sending shivers over her body. As his woodsy citrus scent came to her, she rose on her toes, trying to kiss him more.

As he bent her over his arm, a pain shot up her side, forcing her to wince again. Rannick growled, sweeping her in his arms.

He carried her to the bed and laid her on the covers without breaking the kiss flaring between them. Rannick shifted her carefully off her side as he slipped off her overtunic, tossing it away and letting it land in a heap on the floor.

He stood as he removed his tunic, exposing his expansive chest, the tangle of black hairs dusting the chiseled planes of his body.

She smiled as his hands went to the top of his pants. He undid the ties slowly one by one, and she shifted, trying to get a better view as his chuckle filled the room. When he bent to pull them off, she lost sight of his nakedness.

But when he stood, her mouth went dry as her eyes

traveled slowly up his body to his face, and a wide grin met her stare. "Does the warrior woman approve of her combatant?"

Her eyes met his smoldering look. "Aye. Join me, Rannick. Please come conquer yer warrior woman."

Rannick slid onto the bed next to her and took her in his arms. He kissed her and stopped, staring into her eyes. "Ainslie, for a man and woman to do this...for me to take yer maidenhead, it means marriage."

Ainslie caressed his face. She knew he would ask this. He honored her thinking of her virtue. Ainslie had an answer ready since she wasn't sure how much time they had together before she had to return, but she wanted to enjoy what moments they could share.

"Rannick, I know ye cannot offer me marriage, and things are very different in my time. Can't we enjoy the time we have? I won't require a commitment from ye."

Rannick bent to kiss her, then stopped. "But ye will give me yer maidenhead. It will ruin yer chances of a good marriage."

Ainslie laughed. "Rannick, it's okay. I've already lost it, and in my time, things are different. Trust me, please." She caressed his face and whispered, "I want our time together to be enjoyable. Please don't worry. Make love to me."

She ran her hands down his naked chest, marveling at the ripple of muscles.

Smiling, Rannick untied the top of her shift and lowered it to free one breast. He massaged it and bent, laving the nipple as Ainslie moaned. He moved to the other side, lightly sucking the other. Ainslie arched into him as tingles shot through her. She ran her fingers through his hair. She stripped her shift off between kisses, and Rannick sat back on his knees to gaze at her body. His hungry eyes took in each detail like a starved beast. Rannick's expression softened when his eyes landed on her side, the bruising still visible. His fingers gingerly traced the remaining bruises.

He bent and placed feather-light kisses on the darker ones, murmuring, "I am sorry, so sorry." He trailed his fingers farther down, kissing one another. "I want to heal ye."

Rannick's concern touched her. The vow to his father reminded her he respected women and wanted to cherish them. His apology moved her like no other.

She leaned up and kissed him full on the mouth. Between kissing her lips, he worshipped her breasts, laving them with his tongue time and time again. She caressed his back and arched into the attention he gave her.

He trailed kisses lower, slowing at her bruises and softly kissing them again. He shifted, nibbling her inner thigh, making Ainslie sit up and wince slightly.

He set his hand on her chest. "No. Lie back and enjoy my attentions. I will see my warrior woman scream in delight."

Ainslie raised an eyebrow but lay back with her hands on his head. A boyfriend had done this once. It wasn't the mind-numbing experience her college roommate claimed it was, but the promise in Rannick's expression as he hovered sent chills over her.

He licked her folds once, and she squirmed. Rannick parted the folds and licked her fully, enticing a gasp. He licked her quickly, drawing his tongue over and over her folds as she threaded her fingers through his hair. Placing his mouth on her nub, he sucked,

166

making her cry out. He focused on her nub, and Ainslie arched and panted, her bruises forgotten.

This was what she wanted and needed. A man worshiping her, taking her to heights she'd never experienced before. The desire built inside of her as his mouth continued its dance. He inserted a finger and sucked harder. Ainslie lifted her hips, wanting more of what he offered.

Rannick stopped and blew on her folds.

Ainslie wiggled. "Ye devil of a man, why did ye stop?"

He slowly slid his finger along her folds, spreading the juice around, and smiled as he stared into her eyes. "I want to watch ye come apart for me. I want to see ye release from my mouth." He returned to sucking as he watched her.

Ainslie lifted her hips and moaned. He increased his pace, and she grabbed at the bedding beside her, needing something, anything to hold on to. He kept his pace and watched her from his place with his mouth on her. She arched into his attention, the pressure building tighter this time as her breaths became shorter. His driving force demanded a response. It was all too much. She threw her head back as stars danced behind her eyelids. Her walls clenched around his finger as she screamed his name. He drove into her again and again, only to make her come apart and scream. When she returned and tried to catch her breath, he stroked her softly with his finger.

He licked her folds again as she wiggled in the aftereffects of her climax. "Good God, that was amazing."

Rannick kissed his way up her body to her mouth.

Her hands framed his face, and she kissed him thoroughly, tasting their love on his lips. She trailed her fingers down his chest and encircled her hand around him.

Rannick lifted his head and sucked in a breath. She stroked him softly, and he dropped his forehead to her chest. She squeezed him, then ran her thumb along the tip, catching the bead of moisture that had escaped. Rannick raised his head and kissed her hard.

She swirled the moisture around the end and stroked it again as Rannick's hips bucked. "Woman, ye're driving me mad."

Ainslie shifted closer to him. "Make love to me, Rannick. Make me yers."

She rubbed him over her juices near her entrance, reveling in the hardness against her sensitive skin.

Rannick kissed her as he slowly slid into her folds. He got partway and stopped. "By the gods, ye feel so good. I wanted to go slow, but I don't think I can."

Ainslie raised her hips, taking him fully into her. "I am yer warrior woman. I don't want soft. I want all of ye, Rannick. I want all ye can give."

Rannick growled and withdrew slowly, then drove into her. She cried out in ecstasy, gripping his shoulders. He pulled her legs around his back, and her hands slid to his rear, gripping it tightly. He pumped into her again and again, taking full strokes each time. As he drove in her, she grabbed his rear, pulling him closer, trying to bury him deeper, closer to her heart.

Having him so deep, so close to her soul—this was what making love was—the melding of two souls into one pulsing motion. Her eyes connected with his as he continued his onslaught—the intensity in them, the fierce emotions crossing his face. It was a connection like no other, and her heart nearly burst.

Her walls clenched, and her pants came faster. She was close, and Rannick swelled inside her. He kissed her hard, and her world exploded as she arched her back and shouted his name.

Rannick arched and, as he roared, released his seed into her. They froze for a moment in sheer ecstasy, arched together as the wave of their orgasm flowed from their cores. Rannick pumped once, then again, panting as he came down from his high.

Ainslie wrapped her legs and arms around his body, not wanting to release him. Her breath subsided. Rannick rested his elbows beside her head, their bodies still joined.

He caressed her face and looked into her eyes. "Warrior woman, my warrior of love." He kissed her lightly and gazed into her eyes.

She trailed her finger down his cheek. "I am conquered."

Rannick slid from her and gathered her in his arms. She rested her head on his chest, and they slowed their breathing, held in each other's arms.

Ainslie shivered, and Rannick pulled a fur over them. She had never slept overnight with a man. He ran his fingers up and down her arm as shadows from the fire cast patterns upon the ceiling. The soft brush of his caress, his even breathing, his steady heartbeat, and his warm chest soothed her, and her eyes drifted closed.

****

Rannick glanced at her. From her relaxed face and even breathing, she had fallen asleep. That was good. She needed rest to heal.

He ran her Fae fable story through his mind again, retracing each part. He'd concluded he was the man in the story and she the maiden easily enough, which made him very happy. If it was another man, he knew he would kill him. He didn't want her hurt and thought of ways to keep her safe, knowing his warrior woman would plant herself in the battle to save her brother's wife.

Earlier, when he, Colin, and Dougal met, Dougal confided that he thought a messenger would return within a day and had told them they needed to be ready. After hearing Ainslie's Fae fable story, Dougal narrowed the island location down to Colonsay, as there was a point precisely like the one Ainslie described in her story. Some called it Selkie Point. Others called it Mermaid Point. Either way, a jetty of rocks ended on an island that, during high tide, became nearly submerged. From the ocean, rocks surrounded it, making sailing treacherous and challenging to reach. Waves battered the jetty, so walking from the mainland to the edge was dangerous. Anyone there would get tossed into the sea and thrown against the rocks.

Rannick thought Colin had held something back during the meeting, but he couldn't pinpoint what exactly it was. Colin was beside himself with worry over his wife. He would feel the same. Colin was angry and upset, and rightly so.

How would he feel had Ainslie been in her brother's wife's situation? She moaned and shifted in her sleep. Putting the answer from his mind, he pulled her closer to him. He didn't like that thought at all.

His thoughts turned to Ainslie. The only way to keep her safe was to keep her by his side. In the story, if fate separated them, it meant failure for them both. He wouldn't allow that to happen.

Ainslie moaned again in her sleep, and Rannick gathered her in his arms and kissed her forehead as her honeyed lavender scent washed over him.

He caressed her cheek and tilted her chin to kiss her lips. "Warrior woman, my warrior of love from the Fae and the future. I vow to keep ye safe."

Chapter 16

Rannick was in the most erotic dream. He had never been so hard in all his life and stroked in a warm, wet fashion. There was a sucking sensation in the tip that sent shockwaves through him. His lower back tightened, and a jolt went through him, forcing his hips to buck. The warmth covered him again, pumping him. Each time he entered the wetness, something squeezed his tip, sending that shock through him again. God, he could explode at any moment. Ainslie's face, aroused in passion, flashed before his eyes, and he remembered the night before and where he was.

He came awake in astonishment and raised his head to find Ainslie's mouth covering him. She sucked as he laid his head back and moaned. His hands threaded through her hair, and she began pumping as he pushed against her. By the gods, he had never had a woman do something like this to him. He was close, so close. Ainslie cupped his balls, and he exploded into her mouth with a roar. He froze, his entire body tense then lay back with a huff and a panted.

She shifted away, wiping her face. Shortly she returned, resting her head, smiling at him from his stomach.

He closed his eyes and willed his heart to calm down as he came fully aware and awake. That was the most erotic thing a woman had done to him. Bless the gods, he wanted her to do it all over again.

Ainslie climbed up his body to snuggle against him. "Good morning, my warrior."

Rannick heaved an enormous sigh, finally catching his breath. "Woman, ye will be the death of me."

She kissed his cheek and pouted. "Ye did not enjoy the way I woke ye this morning?"

He glanced at her face, flushed from her exertions, and smirked. "Ye wake me like that every morning, and I shall give ye all the jewels in the world."

Her expression faltered. "I don't want jewelry."

Ainslie turned, trying to get out of bed, but Rannick grabbed her and kept her by his side. "I want to spend as much time as I can with ye. Please don't leave my side."

She kissed him again.

Bam! Bam! Bam! The door flew open. Colin rushed in and stopped. He folded his arms over his massive chest as Ainslie squeaked and ducked under the covers.

Rannick lay back, settling his arms behind his head, and stared Colin down.

Colin growled. "Both ye, make yerselves decent and be in the great hall. There are messengers, and we know where Bree is. An island called Colonsay."

Rannick raised an eyebrow. "My longship and my men?"

Colin nodded once and glanced at the mound hiding under the covers then back at Rannick. They glared at each other for a moment, not moving.

Colin raised an eyebrow, glanced at the mound again, and then nodded once. Rannick smiled as Colin turned and slammed the door.

Rannick sat for a moment, waiting for Ainslie to emerge. He thought he might have just received Colin's approval for his relationship with Ainslie. Still, he would speak to Colin today and explain his intentions.

****

For Rannick, the day went by in a typical blur as they prepared for the raid. Plans in place, supplies loaded, and the crews assembled. They were to set sail for Ivor MacLeod's village on Colonsay that evening. He'd only met the man once but found him a fair and jovial jarl. He suspected he'd find help and support in retrieving Colin's wife plus his men and longship.

He had difficulty getting Colin alone but finally stopped him on the dock. "Colin, I need to speak with ye." He and Colin stepped aside to a tree by the landing.

Colin frowned at Rannick. "If ye had not come to me today, I would be very disappointed in ye."

Rannick crossed his arms. "I am an honorable man. Yer sister has different ideas than we do. I see that. I love that in her."

Colin leaned against the tree, silently watching him. Seemed he would make this hard on him as most brothers did.

Rannick uncrossed his arms, staring at the Bay of Oban, trying to find the right words for the brother from the future. "Yer sister is a rare woman."

Colin snorted a laugh.

Rannick rubbed his neck. "I not only ask this because I have bedded her…"

Colin growled, and Rannick rushed on. "…but because I love her. I wish to have her for my wife."

Colin stood there as Rannick waited for his answer.

He ran his hand through his hair, sighing. "I know why ye offer for her hand. And I know why ye come to me to ask. It is the way ye do things in the twelfth century."

Colin turned and gazed at the bay. "In our time, things are vastly different. Everything is so…modern."

Rannick tried to visualize what modern would be or even meant and couldn't.

Colin turned to him. "In the future, the women are all outspoken, like Ainslie. They have careers and duties independent of men. In our time, they are equal to men." Colin shook his head. "She will want to be *yer equal* as a warrior but also be yer wife and the mother of yer children. Do ye understand?"

Rannick nodded. "Aye, I think I do."

Colin slapped his shoulder. "Good! Well then, it will make sense when I tell ye the decision is hers, not mine."

Rannick stepped back. "Hers?"

Colin smiled widely, so widely Rannick's stomach fluttered. "Aye, it's the way it is in the future. Ye must not only ask her to marry ye, but ye must convince her she *wants* to do it. That she wants to stay here with ye instead of coming home." Colin patted him on the shoulder. "And just so ye know, if she says no, it means no. I will support whatever decision she makes."

Rannick stood stunned as Colin chuckled and strode away.

Rannick called out, "Colin, I have another question I need to ask ye." Colin stopped and turned as Rannick caught up. "The Fae fable, the one Ainslie told that talked about the island and the stone. Is that how it will be?"

Colin glanced at the bay again. He stood still as

Rannick stepped closer to speak low. "There's more, isn't there? More to the story."

Colin glanced at him and nodded.

Rannick inhaled. "I thought ye held something back from the MacDougall in the meeting. Ye need to tell me. I need to know what we face."

Colin stood there staring at him, maybe measuring him as a warrior, as a man.

Rannick wasn't certain what test he faced. But what Colin saw in his face that he needed to proceed, he seemed to gain.

Colin nodded and spoke. "Aye, that is true. The *Fae Fable Book* told more than one story for The Stone of Faith. Our parents told Ainslie's story, but the Fae never showed it in the book. The Fae's story revealed before I traveled back in time seems to target Bree, not Ainslie."

Rannick took a deep breath and let it out in relief. "So, the enemy won't stab Ainslie? I don't have to worry about protecting her?"

Colin rubbed his neck. "That's hard to tell. The stories are a guide, not fact. The outcome is what we make of it. I've changed the outcome once but at a high cost."

Rannick crossed his arms. "So, what do we do?"

Colin grunted. "I need ye to keep Ainslie close. Don't get separated." He glanced at the bay. "I'll need to focus on Bree, saving her and dealing with the evil Fae. As long as I know ye've got Ainslie, it's one less thing I'll have to worry about."

As Rannick nodded and turned to leave, Colin grabbed his arm. "For what it's worth, I think Ainslie loves ye, and I would be happy to have ye as me brother." They clapped a hug and went back to loading the supplies. Fable be damned, Rannick would do everything in his power to protect Ainslie. She would become his wife.

****

Closer to sunset, Ainslie stood beside her brother on the dock, waiting for the last supplies to load into both longships. As the time to sail drew closer, Rannick became gruffer, more demanding.

Rannick came to them, and Ainslie turned. "I will travel on Erik's boat with Colin."

His face went red as he yelled, "For all the gods, woman, ye will travel with me."

She huffed. "Ye haven't even asked. What if I *want* to travel with my brother? Be at his side helping him rescue his wife?" God, one night in his bed, he already thought he owned her. Men! All the same, no matter the century.

Rannick advanced on her, his face close to hers. "I have spoken, woman. Ye will do as yer *jarl* commands."

She folded her arms and glared at his face as their breaths mingled. She might kiss him if she wasn't so angry, but argh!

"My jarl? Ha! Ye're doing nothing more than chauvinistic bullying." She pointed, hitting his chest when she spoke. "*I* am not *yers* to command, Rannick!"

He roared into her face as she smiled.

His expression changed, and he stood up. "What is this chauva…chauva—"

Colin leaned over. "Chauvinistic. It's French, and it means ye are being an arse to a woman."

Colin glared at her with an all-too-familiar

177

expression. "Ye will need to ride with Rannick. We will be together when we arrive. All will be *fine*, sister." Damn him, *the laird* had spoken, and she must do as he commanded.

Rannick grinned and strode away. He might have won that round, but Ainslie vowed that when the time came, she would be beside her brother.

Colin turned, took her arm, and pulled her aside. "Ainslie, I haven't spoken with ye since this morning." Ainslie blushed to the roots of her hair and glanced down, avoiding Colin's glare.

Colin gripped her shoulder, his voice softening as she glanced up. "I have never pried into yer relationships with men, and I don't want to now, but circumstances are different. Ye toy with a man from the twelfth century. Courting, relationships, the meanings of things are different here than in our time."

Ainslie glared at him and rolled her eyes. "I can handle my own, Colin."

He rubbed the back of his neck and leveled his eyes on her. *The laird* expression was back. "Ainslie, ye need to think on this carefully."

She blinked at him and then glanced away. Rannick was on his ship overseeing the last loading before they were to sail with the evening tide. Attar and Wee Willie helped load items together, already forming a friendship. As they passed Rannick, he nodded to both and clapped Attar on the back, giving him support and approval. Attar looked back at Rannick with growing respect.

Ainslie loved being in the twelfth century with the Vikings. She fit in and knew there was a place for her here. The wind ruffled her hair, and it seemed her ancestors brushed past her, saying, *aye, ye belong here.* She found her true love, but her heart fell. Once they found Bree, they would have to return to their time.

She took a deep breath and turned to Colin, who observed her quietly. "I see ye now realize what I refer to." He took her in his arms and hugged her, holding her like her da did when she was sad—tightly, and a little longer. Her eyes watered, and she wished her da was here. His stalwart advice would, for once, be welcome.

She hiccupped as Colin patted her back. "We have a lot to get through before we make it to the portal. Before ye must decide. Whatever ye want, I will support ye. I am yer brother, and I love ye deeply."

He breathed as he held her, and a tear escaped. "It will kill me if ye choose to stay with him. But if ye love him and this is what ye want, then that's what ye should do."

Another tear escaped, and they stood like that for a moment more.

Colin stepped back and held her shoulders. "Ye are my wee warrior, and I will always love ye, no matter what time ye live in."

She smiled through her tears and nodded.

Colin turned and moved to Erik's ship.

Ainslie took a moment to gather herself. She watched the last loading, then gazed out at Oban Bay in the setting sun. She adored her brother, her family, and all the people in the future. But she was in love with Rannick and the Viking world as well. They both fit but were so different.

Rannick approached her. "It's time, Ainslie. We need to sail." She nodded, and he took her hand, guiding her to his longship. She climbed aboard, and both boats set out to sail to Colonsay and Ivor MacLeod's village.

As they cleared the bay and hit the open ocean, the ships sailed side by side. Ainslie stood at the boat's bow, watching the sun fade on the horizon. She glanced at Erik's ship, and Colin stood on the bow, poised as if he was the vessel's commander. His kilt flapped in the breeze; the Stones of Iona in the Brooch of Lorne winked in the setting sun. She stared at him knowing he could command, anywhere in any time, the strong laird that he was. They would recover Bree, and everything would be all right.

Rannick approached and wrapped her in an embrace. She glanced at him and saw his love for her in his expression. She gazed into his eyes and knew she had found her true love. Rannick kissed her, held her in his arms, and they watched the sunset as they sailed away.

****

Colin sensed Ainslie watched him. He'd kept his face carefully tilted so he saw her without her knowing. Colin knew last night she'd fallen in love with Rannick, and it was no surprise to find them in bed together this morning. He wasn't a stupid man.

He smirked. He'd bedded Bree before they wed as well. He hoped Ainslie was happy and would find happiness in the Viking time. In a way, it made sense. She'd spent most of her time daydreaming of the era. It seemed fitting she should find true love here and choose to stay.

Rannick embraced her, and her focus left Colin. He knew what her choice would be. He took a deep breath and released it slowly as the pain hit his heart.

This was the only time he was thankful his parents were dead. If he had to return to the future and tell his ma and da that he'd left his sister in the twelfth century for true love, it would destroy them. Colin sighed. Rannick was a good man. He would care well for her. He stared at them a moment more and realized how much he would miss his little sister, his wee warrior.

Chapter 17

"Aye, right bugger he was. He introduced himself as Balor. I recognized the MacDougall warriors but hadn't seen that longship before." Ivor MacLeod and his first, Tormund, met them at the dock, not surprised two longships arrived loaded for raiding.

Ivor escorted Rannick and Ainslie through his village, updating Rannick on all that had happened since Balor had graced his shoreline. Colin followed behind, listening to the conversation but not commenting. He needed all the info he could get to determine what to do next with the evil Fae that had taken over Tony. But more so, he needed information on Bree. Where was she? Was she okay? Did the madman still have her? It was all he could do not to tackle the man and demand answers. But he and Rannick had agreed to allow Rannick to lead the conversation, being MacDougall's captain.

Ivor nodded as he spoke to Rannick. "Ye say the longship he has is yers, stolen?"

Rannick fisted his hand. "A new design for my fleet. Aye, he stole it and the crew as well."

Ivor led them through the village. Colin's eyes roamed, taking in the situation, searching for any sign of Bree. Men repaired damaged huts. Charred trees came into his view. A man poured sand, covering a wide pool of blood. He turned and counted over a dozen such sand piles.

Ivor turned from the sight and huffed. "Aye, his men were not right. I didn't like any of them."

Rannick glanced back at Colin, who only nodded. The two had agreed they needed to keep Ivor from learning about the Fae and the Stones, but that depended on what Ivor had witnessed and figured out on his own. It seemed not much. Colin explained to Rannick that as soon as he rid Tony of the evil Fae, Rannick's men would be out of the Fae's mental grip. He'd signal Rannick to call them to him with the war cry. Colin kept strolling, waiting for news of the thrall, his wee Bree. It killed him, but he waited.

Rannick continued moving with Ivor. "My longship wasn't at yer dock. I assume he has left. Do ye know where he is now?"

Ivor nodded. "Aye, just the other side of the isle near Selkie Island. It's treacherous to sail that side. He's camped there. I have a guard rotation to see what he's doing. I knew my messenger from MacDougall would return soon. After Balor instigated a battle, I knew he wasn't with the MacDougall, but I needed word on how to proceed."

Nothing of the thrall. No word of a prisoner, a woman, or any hint that Bree was still with the madman. It tore Colin up inside, all this talk of Rannick's damn longboat. What about his wife, his true love? He had to know. Colin couldn't hold it in.

He burst between the two men. "The woman he's held captive. What has he done with her?"

Ivor stopped and squinted at him. "She's yers, isn't she?"

Colin growled. "My wife, kidnapped."

Ivor glanced down and sighed.

Colin grabbed his arm. "Tell me. I must know. How is she?"

Ivor glanced at Rannick, then at Colin. "He claimed she was a thrall, a prize from a raid preventing me from intervening. I sensed she was from a royal family."

Colin loosened his grip and ran his hand through his hair. "Sh-She's a MacDougall. I am cousin to Lord of the Isles, Dougal MacDougall."

Ivor stepped back, his hand at this chest. "Had I known, I would have done more. I distracted him with two female thralls to entertain him while my women healed her. When we refused to return to her, he attacked our village. Stole her back and sailed to Selkie Island."

Beside Rannick, Ainslie gasped.

Colin clenched his fists and spoke through his teeth, trying to keep himself in check, "Why would my wife need a healer?" This man better have some answers. Why had he permitted a woman to come to harm?

Tormund came beside him. "He left her tied without tending to her basic needs. She wasted away, and we didn't want her to die. When I learned of it, we distracted him and got her away."

Ivor nodded and turned to Colin. "He demanded her back. Going against Viking law, we denied him. He attacked in response. All my warriors fought, wanting to honor her, but he still got her. We lost three men in the battle."

Colin stood momentarily, staring at both men, absorbing what they said. It struck him speechless. Bree hurt, and he couldn't care for her.

Ainslie stepped close to Ivor. "Ye healed her. She's alive then?"

Ivor peered at Ainslie, and a tear escaped her eye. "Please tell me…" Ainslie glanced at Colin. "He's my brother. She's his wife. We are family."

Ivor nodded. "She lives."

Ainslie whimpered and put a hand over her mouth.

Colin fisted his hands with his head bowed. She's alive, healed. Ivor said healed. He would find her, take her home. He would stop at nothing to get her back.

Rannick took Ainslie in his arms and held her. "I promised I'd get her back, and I will."

Ivor waved them toward the path. "Let's meet in my longhouse and plan a raid. I know the area well, and we will prepare our attack."

He turned to Tormund. "Send a replacement guard to Selkie Island and have the recent guard report to me as soon as he returns."

As they filed along the trail, Colin followed. "Rannick…"

Rannick glanced over his shoulder as Colin spoke. "Balor, he's mine. Ye make sure in the battle, I kill Balor."

"I would have it no other way, Colin."

****

In the longhouse, Rannick and Ainslie sat next to Ivor, with Colin next to Ainslie. A guard stood tall before Ivor, appearing honored to give his report. Colin had a hard time sitting there waiting for news about Bree.

Ivor still questioned his guard. "So, it's as we suspected. He's camped there, but why?"

Ainslie leaned over Rannick. "Ivor, ye mentioned Selkie Island. Is that the island in the fable of the Selkie woman who married a human man?"

Ivor hummed. "Ye mean the story bards tell of the man who stole the sea woman to make her his wife, only to have her return to the ocean as a selkie? Aye, some say she haunts the point, though we have never seen her. We don't sail that side of the island. The rocks are dangerous, and the island floods at high tide."

Ainslie gasped, and Rannick bent to her. "What is it?"

Ainslie shook her head.

Colin took her hand from her other side and whispered in English, "They cannot speak English. Ye figured out that is the island in the fable?"

Ainslie slowly nodded.

Colin's eyebrows creased in what she recognized as anger. "That's where Bree will be."

Ainslie stared at her brother. "Or me, depending on which story the fates follow. Yers or the one Ma told me as a child."

Colin sliced his hand down. "Either way, we will be ready. Ye must stay close to Rannick and do as he commands."

Rannick glared at them, tapping Ainslie's arm, but Ainslie waved him off.

The guard spoke again, answering a question from Ivor. "No, he still waits. For what we do not know."

Ivor had not asked about the thrall.

Impatient and tired of waiting, Colin demanded, "What of the captive, the woman?"

The guard's gaze shot to Colin, then back to Ivor.

Ivor nodded his permission to answer.

The guard huffed and fisted his hands. "She is in his tent. He has not let her out."

Colin spoke firmly, wanting answers now. "She is my wife. How does she fare? What has he done to her since he arrived?"

The guard faced Colin and spoke in a softer voice, "He has spent little time in the tent. The rocks made it hard for him to beach the ship. He anchored the boat, but it came loose. The problem has taken all his attention, so they don't lose the longship on the rocks."

Rannick growled. "If he crashes my longship into the rocks, I'll take great joy in torturing him."

Colin's desire to charge the camp rose, but he tamped it down. Better to be wise than quick. Colin's voice came out bitterly when he spoke. "He's mine."

Ivor spoke to his guard. "Ye have served me well. Ye honor yer family well. Take yer leave and rest."

The guard bowed to Ivor and turned, leaving the longhouse.

Ivor and Rannick spent the rest of the time mapping out a plan of attack to retrieve Bree and overtake Balor. Information from the guard on the camp layout and the location of Bree's tent made a plan easy to formulate.

Their chatter faded as Colin frowned into the fire, his mind occupied with what went on with Bree. Was she healed and well? How far had Balor or Tony taken his abuse, and in what state would he find his wife? Tears threatened as he tried not to picture what all that madman might have done to his wee Bree. They flipped from one scenario to the next, each mental image ended in him torturing and killing Tony. He needed to focus and rid Tony of Balor first. Then Tony would die.

****

A servant approached Ainslie. "MiLady, please come with us to bathe and freshen up with the women."

Rannick paused mid-sentence. "Go on, Ainslie. I'll update ye on the final plans over dinner."

The woman took Ainslie to the bathhouse, and a tub awaited her. The Vikings were as fond of a full bath, a luxury, as Ainslie. She sighed as two other women attended her in her bath in silence. As they removed her clothing, she took her ease in the quiet, running the events of the last few days through her mind. They helped her into the tub, and she sat back, allowing the warm water to relieve her aches, her mind.

As Ainslie relaxed in the warmth, one woman spoke up. "Ye are the family to the captive woman? The one we tried to save?"

Ainslie sat up in the tub, forcing water to slosh over the side. "Aye, I am. What can ye tell me of her?"

The woman sat beside her and held Ainslie's hand. "They placed her in my hut to heal. I am Thyra. The bad men killed my servant. I was most honored to serve her, for I knew she had to be royalty. They say her husband is the large man in the funny tunic."

Ainslie smiled at the description of her brother's kilt. Kilts would not come into fashion for a while, but Colin was comfortable in them.

"Kilt, it's a kilt. And yes, Colin is her husband and my brother. She is his true love. We are cousins to the MacDougall, so by yer standard, she is royalty."

Ainslie needed to know. "How was she?"

Thyra glanced down, and Ainslie's heart dropped. "At first, she was frail and had many bruises. That man had beat her." Thyra glanced at the other women, who nodded. "Jarl Ivor had a thrall try to enter the hut to clean, but Balor refused."

A tear escaped Ainslie's eye, and she wiped it. "Please tell me all of it."

Thyra nodded. "We worry about her. She would not speak. We tried, but she acted like she was away."

Ainslie took Thyra's hand. "Bree cannot speak yer language well. She may not have understood."

Thyra stared at her as her brow wrinkled. "I fear she lost her will to live. She would not make eye contact. She will need a long time to heal."

Ainslie swallowed and nodded. "We will care for her well. Thank ye for all ye have done. We will get her back."

****

Ainslie arrived at the longhouse late for dinner but refreshed and wearing a tunic dress provided by the women. Rannick and Ivor still discussed plans, going over the finer points.

Ivor spoke as Ainslie sat. "We will raid before sunrise and surprise Balor and his camp."

Ainslie nibbled her food but didn't have an appetite. She searched for Colin, but he wasn't around.

She rose, and Rannick grabbed her hand. She leaned down, whispering, "I search for Colin."

Rannick nodded and returned to his conversation with Ivor.

She went outside, and he wasn't far, sitting under a tree with a full cup of ale in his hand.

Ainslie stood back as he stared at the bay of Colonsay. It was a beautiful sight in the moonlight. She knew Colin didn't see it. It would take Colin and Bree a long time to heal from this.

"I can hear ye behind me, Ainslie. Ye do not need to hide."

Ainslie grinned. She'd never been able to sneak up on Colin.

She moved and sat next to him, leaning against the tree. "Ye cannot sit here tearing yerself up, Colin. We will get her back, and she will be fine."

He hiccupped and sounded as if he had been crying. Her heart went out to him, her big brother.

His voice pitched a little when he spoke. "I cannot get the vision out of my mind. I see him taking her over and over, and I die inside. Then I think of Bree and how she must feel, and I want to kill him repeatedly. I see me doing it, killing him again and again, and it's not enough." His breath hitched. "Then I think of what's next. I get her back. Then what? Will she be whole again?" He took a deep breath, then let it out. He beat his own emotions raw with each word he spoke, and by the end, Ainslie wanted to shake him.

Ainslie grabbed his arm. "Stop, Colin. Stop it. The women, the ladies who took me to the bathing house. They healed Bree."

Colin dropped the mug and grabbed Ainslie's shoulders. "What did they say? God, please tell me, even if it's bad. I must know."

Ainslie jolted at his grip. "I will, but ye must let me go, Colin. Yer grip is tight."

Colin dropped his hands. "Sorry, sister. I'm worried. Please tell me all, no matter how bad."

Ainslie took a deep breath and spoke. "The woman who healed her spoke to me. She was ill, weak from hunger." Colin drew in a deep breath. "They bathed her and cared for her. They said she wouldn't speak, but we know she doesn't know this language well."

Colin mumbled, "She should learn Gaelic fully." He stared out at the bay.

Ainslie put her hand on his arm. "Last they knew, she was well, healing each day."

Colin drew in a sharp breath and groaned, "Thank God." He dropped his head in his hands and cried soft sobs.

Ainslie sat beside her brother and held his arm. She didn't know what to do. Before coming to the twelfth century, she had only seen Colin shed a tear at their parents' funeral. Another time was when he broke his arm, but that was pure pain. This was a different pain, one that cut deeper—hurt more. He was never one to show such emotion, but he'd never been in love before. She wished there was more she could do. She desperately wanted to help him, to help her sister-in-law, Bree.

A footfall came from behind them, and Colin raised his head. "It is Rannick. Go, get some sleep. Before dawn, we will take the camp."

Ainslie paused, but Colin spoke loud enough for Rannick to hear. "I can smell ye from here, Rannick. Ye need a bath. Take my sister and take yer rest."

Ainslie kissed her brother's cheek. "Ye need rest too."

He patted her arm as she rose to join Rannick.

****

Colin waited till the sound of their footsteps faded. He sat there staring at the bay in the moonlight, knowing Bree was nearby. The Stone of Love didn't glow, but it would soon. He came for his true love, and nothing would stop him from saving her.

Chapter 18

Ainslie shivered, and Rannick wrapped his arm around her as they walked through the village. "Ye worry for yer brother. I would as well."

She leaned her head on his shoulder as they continued to walk.

She sniffed and giggled. "Colin was right. Ye need a bath."

Rannick stopped and gathered her in his arms. "Aye, but the bathhouse is full of stinking warriors. So, I had a small bath placed in the hut. Care to bathe yer warrior?"

Ainslie frowned as he pecked a kiss on her lips. "So, I am to serve ye now? Is that it? I am no thrall, Rannick."

She turned to step away, but he caught her in his arms. "Ahh, woman. Not my slave. I want ye to bathe me." He kissed her deeply. "I want ye to rub soap all over my body till it hums with excitement. Then I may do the same with ye." He kissed her again, and she wrapped her arms around him, responding to his kiss. Heat gathered in her as his tongue danced with hers.

She lifted her head and teased, "Then will I get to dry ye off?"

Rannick chuckled. "Aye, I would like that very much."

He picked her up and walked to their hut. Inside

was small, but she liked the cozy setting. A small wooden tub, like a hip bath half full of water, sat by the fire. Over the fire, a large pot heated with steam rising from it. Rannick set her down and quickly undressed. Ainslie raised an eyebrow at his nakedness.

Rannick hissed, "Hurry, woman, it's cold. Pour the warm water in and I'll climb in." Ainslie stood there and folded her arms. Rannick came to her and gathered her in his arms. "I see ye need some persuading." He kissed her deeply and ran his hands under her dress, his icy hands gripping her bare back.

Ainslie yelped. "Yer hands are freezing."

Rannick laughed as he shifted closer to the tub. "Aye. Pour the water so I can bathe, and then we can warm each other in bed."

Ainslie grabbed a rag and hefted the pot from the fire. She poured it into the tub, sloshing a little over the edge. "Sorry. Where I am from, we have showers."

Rannick climbed into the tub and sank into the heat, sighing a long sigh. Ainslie rolled her sleeves up and kneeled by the tub. Rannick grabbed the soap from the stool, soaped his hair, set the soap bar back, and dunked quickly. She noted a rag sat by the soap. She took the soap, wet the rag, and began washing Rannick. A familiar woodsy citrus scent came from the soap. Must be a popular recipe. She'd never bathed a man before, and she found the chance to explore his body exciting.

Rannick leaned back and mumbled, "Shower, what is a shower?"

Ainslie picked up Rannick's arm. It was heavy, but she rubbed the soapy cloth down to his wrist, taking care to get every groove and crevice clean. Ainslie picked up a small cup and scooped up water. She held his arm up and poured it near his wrist. She watched the water flow along his muscles, then he stretched his arm behind his head and offered her the other one as he lay back with his eyes closed.

She took his arm, rubbing the soapy cloth along his muscles, allowing herself the time to examine him. "Well, ye know when it rains from the skies. It's like that, water sprinkling over yer body."

His well-developed muscles were impressive from afar, but up close, they mesmerized. His chest was wide as a barrel, and she had to bend over him to scrub the entire width. She sat back, lightly rubbing the cloth on his chest, and stared at his face. He was a handsome man. The strong chiseled lines of his jaw were visible under the beard, now less angular in his relaxed state, making him look younger, vulnerable even.

As he shivered, she washed his arm and lowered it into the water.

He bent forward. "Scrub my back, woman."

Ainslie sat back, staring at Rannick. "Another command for his thrall. She will give him no reward tonight. He may be left wanting."

Rannick glanced over his shoulder. "It would bring me great pleasure if ye scrubbed my back." He turned his head away. "Then I will bring ye great pleasure for doing it."

Ainslie smirked as she began scrubbing. "Promises, promises."

He sighed. "That feels so good." Rannick moaned as she continued to scrub his back, dipping to his lower back under the water.

She knew saying water sprinkled down wouldn't

be enough for Rannick. He'd want to know how it worked. So, when he asked, she wasn't surprised.

He glanced at her from his bent position. "If the water comes from above, how does it get there? Over yer head?"

She slowed her scrubbing to a slow massage. "Well, we send the water through pipes and push it over our heads, making it rain upon us to clean our bodies."

Rannick sat up and squinted at her. "Is it similar to dunking a bucket of water on yer head?"

Ainslie huffed a laugh. "Yes, and no. It's like a trickle of constant water on yer body. It's very relaxing."

Rannick leaned back in the tub and closed his eyes. Ainslie set the rag on the edge and reached between his legs with a soapy hand. He drew his knees up, and she found her favorite part of his body, making him groan as she stroked him.

"A shower sounds nice. More room than a bath like this one." He sat forward, grabbing her hand and kissed her deeply. "I wish to be in bed where I can enjoy ye while not bent like a twig."

Ainslie giggled and rinsed her hands off.

As she reached for the drying sheet left by the fire, Rannick stood. Her gaze traveled his form. His muscular chest flexed as he reached for the cloth. She stepped back and her eyes traveled down his body to the staff standing tall at attention. He stepped toward her, reaching for the cloth, and she stepped back again, but seeing his shiver, she relinquished the warm cloth.

He took the sheet and began drying. "Ye keep looking at me like that, and I won't bother drying off."

Ainslie turned and walked to the bed. It wasn't far

as the hut was small, but it was warm. She reclined on the bed and watched Rannick finish drying his body. His arms flexed as he rubbed his body. The muscles rippled as he bent to his task, causing her to swallow a gasp. When he bent over, she got a very nice profile of his ass, round and firm. She recalled grabbing it the night before and shivered.

"If ye are cold, get under the covers, Ainslie." Heat rose on her cheeks and Rannick stopped drying.

He turned fully, gazing at her, and grinned. "Ye aren't cold, are ye?"

She smiled back, twisting her body so he saw her rear.

He set the sheet aside and crawled into the bed, covering her. "Ye have entirely too many clothes on." His clean scent wafted over her, sweet wood and citrus, like soap.

He kissed her as he undressed her, kissing each spot as he removed each piece.

Rannick sat back as he took off her tunic, and he bent and kissed her neck. She had to wiggle to divest herself of the full tunic. As he dropped the shift down her torso, he kissed her bare shoulder. When he slid it past her breasts, he stopped to kiss one. He peeked at her and moved to the other breast, and this time he suckled, making her bend her back and moan. He laved her nipple as he caressed her back, encouraging her arches at each lick and suck of each breast.

She ran her fingers through his hair as he played with her like a musician playing his instrument, making sweet music. When she lifted her rear so he could pull the garment away, he kissed her hip. As he dropped the garment to the floor, she lay back on the bed, opening her arms in a relaxed stretch, allowing Rannick full sight of her naked form.

He sat up. His gaze roamed Ainslie from the tips of her toes to her hips, then the juncture in her legs. He quirked an eyebrow and his gaze trailed up her side to her breasts. His eyes widened, and she took a deep breath, causing her breasts to rise, then fall. His eyes roamed her face then her hair as if he tried to sear her image in his memory.

"Beautiful," he whispered.

Rannick's fingers touched her ankle, traveled up her calf. She twitched at the tickle, causing him to chuckle. He bent and kissed her ankle, then her calf as his hand continued to her hip and his tongue leaped out to lick her. His hand moved up her side to her breast, and he cupped it, allowing his thumb to rub the tip, enticing a hitch in her breath. His hand traveled to her cheek, where he cupped her face as he kissed her deeply.

He covered her with his body, kissing her lips and delving his tongue into her mouth.

He lifted his head and trailed kisses from her cheek to her neck. "By the gods, Ainslie, ye feel so good."

Rannick kissed his way down her neck, making her sigh. He swirled his tongue around her nipple, and she arched in his mouth. His hand slid between her legs and cupped her mound, making her moan.

Her hand reached for him, stroking his length. He groaned as he sucked her nipple hard. She increased her pace as he suckled a breast. Rannick's breath picked up, so she kept pumping her hand as her eyes met his. He slid a finger inside her, and her legs drew up, welcoming him.

His gaze held hers as they pleased each other. "Ainslie, ye are like no other woman." She stopped her hand. He continued his assault on her folds, making her hips buck.

He smiled at her. "Warrior woman, ye have raged a war on my heart." She moved her hand along the length of him, and he tilted his head back moaning, and he drove his finger quicker, making her pant. She felt her excitement build, and she arched as her wall spasmed around his finger.

She cried out, "Rannick!"

He shifted between her legs. "I cannot wait. I want ye now." Ainslie stretched her legs open as her hands spread down his chest. She gripped his staff and guided him inside her, moaning when he easily slid into her.

He slowly filled her and then he exhaled. "I have found paradise."

Ainslie pleaded, "Take me, Rannick. Take me to paradise." He kissed her deeply, caressed her face as he filled her time and time again. She kissed his neck as he slid deeper. He sucked her nipple as he rose slightly. Between the mingling of their bodies, it was hard to tell where one began and one ended—as if they were one.

Ainslie felt her tension rising. She arched and moaned. Rannick answered with an increase in pace, and soon he rode her hard, filling her with each deep stroke. She cried out first in a sudden burst, and he answered with a final swift thrust and a roar. He froze above her, in a tense orgasm. Rannick released his breath and almost fell on her, but he rolled to the side, taking her with him held tightly in his arms.

He tried to catch his breath as Ainslie ran her fingers through the hairs on his chest. Rannick seemed spent. He hadn't even opened his eyes. She lay there quietly, waiting for him to relax. When he did, she figured he must have dozed for a moment; he was so still.

Rannick took a deep breath and when he spoke, his voice was drowsy. "I wish to ask ye something, but I am so tired." He took another deep breath, as if he tried to stay awake. "I…Ainslie…stay. I want…ye…to…" and he released a long sigh, falling into a deep sleep.

****

Ainslie wasn't tired. She had a lot on her mind as she lay in Rannick's arms. Had she been able to catch Bree before being dragged through the portal, then Tony wouldn't have taken her back in time. She glanced at Rannick and sighed. If she had not followed, she never would have met Rannick. There was Colin to think of as well. When they finally got Bree back, if Tony had badly hurt her, she knew Colin would come apart.

All the thoughts swirled in her mind as sleep eluded her. She had to do something. A plan quickly formed in her mind. She was a warrior in her own right. She listened in the planning between Ivor and Rannick, knew the layout of the encampment and where the tent that held Bree was located. It would be a better plan to have one person sneak in and grab Bree before anyone was wiser than to risk hundreds of lives in a full attack. If she went alone, snuck in and rescued Bree, there would be less bloodshed and she could have Bree back by sunrise before the raid even started.

She rolled out of Rannick's arms and quietly dressed. Rannick snored lightly, making her smile. She took her sword, shield, and the wineskin. She packed what food she could grab, for she knew Bree would need sustenance. As she crept from the hut, the Fae fable ran through her mind.

When her true love came, she would fight beside him in a great fight against a magical evil. Odin foretold only together would they defeat this evil. Apart they would perish.

She tamped the warning down. That story hadn't appeared in the *Fae Fable Book*. Colin said a different one had that he thought pointed at Bree. Still, this was all her fault. She had to save Bree.

****

A few hours later and closer to sunrise than she wanted, Ainslie crept near Balor's encampment. She tied her horse farther away so he wouldn't make noise and give her position away. Ainslie knew Balor had to have guards out, but she didn't know where they were. She'd have to keep an eye out; she didn't want this to be over before she could spirit Bree away. She stared at the tent she knew had to be Balor's, for it was the largest one, when someone pressed a knife against her throat. Her breath hitched and damn if a guard didn't catch her.

The voice near her ear was cold. "What do we have here? A gift from the gods?" A hand slid around her front and gripped her breast. "Aye, with nice tits as well."

"Shit." She'd run out of luck. She was a prisoner now, and God only knew what Balor would do when he found out who he had.

The guard dragged her into the camp, and yelling followed. Two guards held her by the arms, and she knelt before Balor's tent before she knew it.

Balor stormed from his tent. "Who the hell has woken me before sunrise?" Ainslie groaned but didn't look up. She recognized that voice. Damn, she'd really screwed up now. Maybe she could come up with a good lie, so he wouldn't learn of the coming attack. Someone grabbed her hair and jerked her head back.

She frowned at Tony as he stopped and glared at her. "Ye! How did ye…" In his expression, she saw Balor in Tony's mind putting the pieces together. His face registered shock, then his eyes shifted side-to-side as he turned, apparently placing all the events in order. If she was here, then others were as well and come for him. God, she'd gone and ruined everything.

His face locked on hers as he roared, "Guards, everyone! Wake up now! We are going to be attacked. Wake everyone and prepare."

He stepped toward her and sneered. "I need to welcome Colin. He has come for his wife."

The guard dropped her head.

Tony spoke flatly. "Bring her into my tent with the other woman. Keep them tied. We need to set a trap for the Highlander and welcome him with a present. And I know exactly what to do." His laughter rang through the encampment, evil and insane.

Ainslie feared she had unleashed a demon.

Chapter 19

"Colin, is Ainslie with ye?"

Colin turned from the longship he helped load to find Rannick approaching. It was hours before dawn and minutes before the group set out for the attack on Balor's encampment. Colin glanced around and replied. "Last I knew, she was with ye, Rannick."

Rannick waved for Erik, his first to join them. "She was last night, but her sword and shield were gone when I woke." He turned to Erik. "Search the area. Ainslie has gone missing. Report to me if anyone has seen her."

Colin ran his hands through his hair. "She did not. She would not." He searched the area and knew it in his bones. Ainslie had gone ahead of the raiding party to rescue Bree. He leveled his eyes on Rannick. "I told ye to keep her by yer side. If separated, ye both will fail."

Rannick fisted his hands at his side. "I know. I slept, and she snuck off."

Colin grunted. "Nothing short of tying her down will keep her from doing something when she sets her mind to it. Damn, now we'll have two women to rescue."

Rannick's head snapped toward Colin. "The Fae fable, the island. That's where she'll be."

Colin nodded. "Aye, both of them, and it will be hell getting to them."

Rannick examined both longboats. "We'll have to use my smaller longboat and have Erik take the other. The raiding boat sits higher in the water and is faster. It will be our only chance of getting to the island without breaking up on the rocks." He studied the sky. "We'll have to go soon. The highest tide is as dawn rises. We'll need to reach them before the island floods, but when the water is high enough, so we won't break up in the rocks."

Erik ran to Rannick. "A horse is missing. The guard saw someone leave shortly after midnight."

Rannick turned to Colin. "It is as ye thought. I'll tie her down when I get my hands on her."

Colin scanned the area. "I'll find Ivor. Alert him of the change in the sea approach. We'll have to drop off warriors first, then make a break for the island. Hopefully, the attack from the sea and land will be a distraction so we can get to the women without anyone noticing. Can ye handle the longship alone while I go on the island to get the women?"

Rannick settled his eyes on Colin. "Of course, I can. We'll retain four oarsmen to keep the ship light in the water." Rannick rubbed his chin. "Won't Balor be on the island? That's what the Fable said."

Colin grinned. "Aye, he will be. And I'll be ready for him."

****

The boat bobbed deeply in the waves and bumped against rocks. It would have been hard enough to sail on the rocky shoreline in daylight and nearly impossible in the dark with lanterns as they were.

Tony yelled at the man steering the boat. "Get us closer, man, I need to get on the island." The man steering cursed and tried to get closer to the island again.

Ainslie sat next to Bree, both tied by hand and foot. There had been little opportunity to chat, as Tony was with them the entire time. Now, with Tony distracted trying to sail near a small island with a precarious rocky shoreline, Ainslie took her chance to speak to Bree.

Ainslie leaned over and whispered in English, "Bree, how are ye faring?" Ainslie worried about Bree. She gazed into the distance and allowed everyone to drag her around like a rag doll. Bree needed to snap out of it. She needed Bree awake and aware if they were to get out of this alive.

Ainslie hissed louder, "Bree!" The oarsman closest to her turned his head and glared at them, but she lowered her face, trying not to draw attention.

A moan came to her. "Ainslie, is that you?"

Ainslie drew in a breath. "Aye, ye must be quiet and still. Can ye do that?"

Bree sobbed softly. "I never thought I'd see anyone again. I…I had to go away, someplace else."

Ainslie sniffled and whispered, "We are here. Colin is here. He's coming."

Bree tilted her head and peered at Ainslie for the first time since Ainslie had joined her. "Colin? Oh, God. He can't see me like this. I can't."

Ainslie shook her head. "No, Colin loves ye. He's coming for ye." Before Ainslie could take another breath, someone slapped her hard. Her head bounced off the side of the longship.

"I said no talking." Tony bent over them, his face so near she could smell that his breath stank.

Bree curled into a ball.

Ainslie leveled a hateful glare at Tony and spat in his face.

Tony wiped the spittle and licked his hand.

He turned to the warrior behind him. "Bring them both. When we get on the island, untie them and get this longship away. I'll wait for our guest here. Command the men. Kill anyone who attacks the encampment."

Tony jerked Bree's ropes, bringing her into his arms. "When everyone is dead, return to get me and my prize." He kissed her hard. "I'll enjoy both women when we win."

****

A fog rolled through the area as Colin and Rannick approached the rocky shoreline. The Stone of Love warmed and glowed red for the first time since arriving in the past.

Colin whispered, "Bree, she's close." He closed his hand over the stone, and it pulsed. Covering the gems with his plaid, he hid its light so Balor couldn't see their approach.

As the men unloaded as close to the shore as Rannick dared to get, he leaned in, gasping at Colin. "Yer stone glows. I've seen nothing like it."

Colin nodded. "Ye will when the Fae deliver the Stones of Iona. This is The Stone of Love, which glows when my true love is near. Over it is The Stone of Fear. I will use them together to send Balor to purgatory. 'Tis why I need ye to focus on the women while I deal with him."

Colin glanced around him. "The fog grows thicker. It will be hard to see the island."

Rannick replied, "The gods are with us. Balor will

not see our approach. I'll know the way from the waves. Don't worry."

The last man jumped into the surf, and Rannick turned to the four oarsmen. "Silence. Hand signals only."

The men nodded. Each knew his duty and the price of failure. From this point on, they sailed in darkness and silence.

Rannick steered the longship as the rowers rowed, dipping the oars in the water on the edge to make only the slightest noise. The only sound in the night was the water lapping against the boat and the oars dipping into the water, almost in time with the waves. In the silence, the oarsmen kept perfect time with each other. The farther into the fog they traveled, the rougher the water got, but Rannick kept on course with the moon to the south.

Colin placed his hand under the plaid touching The Stone of Love. It pulsed with his heartbeat, and he knew Bree's as well.

From the shoreline, the battle cry of the MacDougall echoed across the water. "*Buaidh no bàs, Buaidh no bàs!*" *Victory or Death.* Swords clashing together broke into the dark silence. Under it, men cried out in pain and yelled during the attack.

The sounds blended, and the war cry came again. "*Buaidh no bàs.*" Colin hadn't heard it in so long. It sent shivers down his spine and resolution to his heart. He took a deep breath and closed his eyes. The battle had begun.

Colin whispered, "Bree, I'm coming, my love. Death is coming for Tony."

****

Bree sat next to Ainslie huddled on the rocks, the cold breeze biting. Almost numb, Bree could nearly slip back into nowhere and not be here. Tony might touch her, but she could go to a place where he couldn't reach her. She needed that now, needed to go away.

Ainslie cradled Bree, speaking softly in her ear, "Bree, we have a plan. Colin and Rannick are coming with many warriors. They are coming for us."

Bree took a deep breath and let it out slowly. *Colin, is he here?*

Tony peered from behind the largest rock. "Silence, ye bitch."

Ainslie glared at him over her shoulder. "Come, make me. If ye come out, ye reveal ye are here."

Tony grunted but stayed where he was. "Bree, ye call out or reveal I am here, I kill his sister before yer Scottish lover arrives. Think about that and tell her to obey me. Her blood will be on yer hands."

Bree shivered and bent her head to her knees. *Please make him go away. I don't want Ainslie to die.*

Off in the distance echoed yelling. *"Buaidh no bàs. Buaidh no bàs!"*

Ainslie whispered again, "Do ye hear that, Bree? It's our clan's war cry. The warriors, many of them, come to rescue us. Colin is coming, and he loves ye, Bree. He's coming."

Bree glanced up and saw torches along the shoreline. The sounds of metal clashing, men calling out in pain, and voices in fighting roars drifted to her. She stared at Ainslie, who smiled at her. She blinked and glanced around her. *Ainslie is here, says Colin is here. Warriors are fighting. She mentioned a rescue. Was this the end?*

She shifted a bit as she dug into her tunic. "Is Tony looking, or is he hidden?"

Ainslie glanced over her shoulder. "He can't see."

Bree pulled out her hand and held it out to Ainslie. "I stole this from Tony. He says it's The Stone of Lust." She opened her palm, and a large rectangular black stone winked in the moonlight.

Ainslie gasped. "In the Fae fable, it talked about The Stone of Faith."

Bree nodded and closed her hand over the stone. "In the eighteenth century, I wrote a quote in the MacDougall Family book. When I returned, the Fae came to me in a dream and told me I needed to remember it, that it would save me one day. It said *you must believe and have faith. The one who doubts is like a wave of the sea, blown and tossed by the wind. The one who has faith is like the rock standing solid against the wave*s."

Ainslie smiled. "My Fae's fable told me The Stone of Faith was on an island on the shore." Both women nodded together. The Stone of Faith—they needed to find it. They searched around the small island. The shoreline kept creeping up as the tide rose.

Ainslie gasped, "Follow my lead."

Bree followed her line of sight and caught a blue gem flash in the water near the edge. The Stone of Faith?

Ainslie slipped on the rocks and fell into the water.

She snatched the stone as Tony stepped out, grabbing her arm. "What the hell? Trying to escape?"

Ainslie shook free of him. "I slipped, ye idjit. The rocks are wet."

He shoved her toward Bree, and she fell, knocking

her, but they sat together.

Tony returned to his hiding place.

Ainslie opened her fist, showing Bree the bright blue gem shaped like a diamond, the sharp points leaving imprints on her hand.

Ainslie whispered, "The Stone of Faith."

Bree touched it with her finger and closed her eyes. "I haven't had faith during this entire ordeal. Ainslie, you brought it to me. Faith. I feel it now. Colin is really coming?"

Tony barked from behind the rock, "Shut up!"

Ainslie quickly closed her hand over the gem and hid her hand in her tunic.

Bree sat in the cold, faith growing in her heart. Colin had come, but dread spread in her. The Fae would demand a price be paid. Last time it was purgatory for Colin. This time, in the end, it would be her life.

Chapter 20

The streaks of dawn spread across the sky as Rannick's men rowed quietly to a rhythm only they heard. Colin felt soothed by the light rippling off the oars. Ivor's and Balor's men still fought in the distance going at full force. To Colin, getting to Selkie Island, to Bree was the only thing that mattered. He stood in the bow as it slowly creeped near the rocky shoreline. Colin prayed they quickly reached the island, but sailing in this area was dangerous, and the progress was much slower than he desired.

As the early dawn light grew, the distant shadow of the island came into view. The tide rose with each moment. Knowing the island became submerged at high tide, he saw the tip of the island was smaller than he had hoped. Colin glanced over his shoulder to Rannick at the stern of the boat, steering them through the rocky waters. He caught Rannick's eye, and they exchanged an anxious look. Would they make it to the women in time, or would the island flood, drowning both women before they could reach them? Colin turned to the front of the boat searching the shadows of the island for Bree.

He reached up to his shoulder and touched the Brooch of Lorne hidden under the folds. The Stone of Love pulsed. He came closer to his true love, Brielle.

As he held the stones, he thought of her. He

remembered the first moment he'd seen her from the castle wall walk, bossing the men who renovated the chapel. He smiled as he remembered their meeting, her speaking about his family history, the awe in her voice at his family heritage. During the rainstorm, he held her in the castle study, which became a favorite place for them to cuddle. He recalled her pulling him back from purgatory, the love he sensed when she pulled him through the realms was so strong. He closed his eyes and saw her bright expression when she gave birth to their children, Evie and Ewan. Her laugh he heard in his mind bright and vibrant, just as her personality. All these things, all wrapped into one moment, one emotion. He poured all the feelings from his heart into the stones. He wanted Bree to sense him, to know his love and that he came to save her.

Colin opened his eyes. The dawn light grew fast. He figured his longboat was likely visible by now to anyone looking their way. The Stone of Love's pulse fluttered, and he glanced at his shoulder. Under the fabric the red glow faded, and The Stone of Fear glowed a brighter purple. His own heart dropped— Bree's fear. He sensed it clawing at her resolve. The helplessness and loss of hope, such utter despair, poured into him.

He bent his head and choked with a sob. "Bree, feel my love. I'm coming."

Colin threw off the fold of his kilt, exposing the stones in the brooch. He wanted Bree to see the stones glow, to see his beacon. She needed to know he came. She had to keep faith.

****

Bree shivered and Ainslie tried to wrap her arms

around her as they sat on the island that grew smaller by the moment. They leaned against the tall thin boulder that made up the center of the island, too small to scale but just large enough for Tony to hide behind. Ainslie knew he had to be cramped like they were. Bree had her arms wrapped around her knees and her head tucked into her chest. Ainslie would hear an occasional sniffle, but she wasn't certain if that was from crying or the cold.

Either way, Ainslie kept a commentary running, hoping to keep their spirits and warmth up. The water continued to rise as the early dawn light spread across the sky. Now it lapped against their feet, making them colder. If they became submerged, it could bring a quick end to their lives as the waters were cold and hypothermia only minutes away from someone fully submerged.

She shivered and started her next tale. "Ye know, when I was young, I took a small sailboat out in the loch alone. Trying to prove to Da I could sail on my own."

Tony groaned behind the rock. "Would ye shut up! I don't think I could take another story of yer fucking childhood."

She ignored him and continued her story. "It was cold, and I shouldn't have gone out alone. But I was determined to show I knew what I was doing. A strong wind blew in, and stupid me hadn't checked the weather. I broke rule number one of sailing. Always know the weather before departing."

Bree shuddered hard and Ainslie rubbed her arm. "I was out on the loch and couldn't handle the wind. I let the tackline out too far and lost control of the boat.

Ended up on the far shore from the castle. The mountain-facing shoreline was rocky and steep, so there was no place to go ashore as it is with most of Loch Etive." She laughed lightly. "I thought for sure I was stuck forever. I had no radio and was too young to own a cell phone. Only had a light coat."

Bree shivered again, and Ainslie rubbed her arm. In the other, she still held The Stone of Faith. The points dug into her skin, but she took heart in the fact she still had feeling in her hands. The water covered their toes now, and she'd lost feeling in her feet a while ago.

"I hunched over just as ye are now, trying to stay warm, praying for rescue. And just when I thought someone would never save me, a boat bumped against mine." She sighed. "I glanced up, and it was Colin in another sailboat. We had a few back then to sail around the loch when we were younger." She blew a short laugh. "I thought for certain he would make fun of me and laugh, like he did with the sword practice. But he didn't. He came alongside and tied his to mine.

"As he jumped into the boat he asked, 'Ye having a little trouble, sis?'

"He scooped me into his arms and placed me in his boat. Wrapped me in a tartan and made sure I stayed warm. He sailed back with my boat trailing behind us."

Ainslie smiled and hugged Bree again. She'd grown concerned. Bree stopped moving and sat still. Shaking was the body's natural response to stay warm. To stop meant one step closer to hypothermia. Ainslie rocked back and forth for a moment until Bree started shaking again and continued her story.

"Not saying a word, he sailed back to the castle. I

thought for certain he'd tell Da, relish in the fact I failed. But he didn't. He told no one. Ye know what he did? He took me out sailing nearly every day that summer to make sure I knew how to sail safely."

Bree took a deep breath and exhaled.

Ainslie hugged her. "That's what Colin does. He makes sure everyone is safe. Colin's coming, Bree. Keep yer faith."

A loud snort came behind them. "What a touching story. I'm counting on Colin coming. I will kill him and have ye both."

Ainslie ignored Tony and stared off into the ocean, searching for any sign that Colin had arrived. As the glow of dawn continued to lighten the skyline, she saw the shadow of what looked like a boat. She squinted, and for sure she saw the outline of a longship headed their way.

As if she had summoned it, a reddish-purple glow flashed from the boat's bow. Ainslie gasped and quickly covered her mouth. She didn't want to alert Tony. He was on the back side of the rock and couldn't see her view.

She whispered into Bree's ear. "Don't say anything. Ye must stay quiet."

Bree nodded.

"Look straight ahead out on the water."

****

Bree raised her head and gazed out. The glowing light grew brighter and larger as it neared their island. With the dawn light brightening the sky, bringing light to the world under it, she made out the outline of a man on the bow, a glowing light coming from his shoulder. Tears gathered in her eyes. Was it? Could it be?

Ainslie breathed, "It's Colin, Bree." Her voice became stronger. "He's wearing the Brooch of Lorne. The red-purple glow is The Stone of Love and The Stone of Fear."

Bree blinked as tears fell down her face.

Ainslie hugged her, "Colin's come for ye, and he's brought hell with him. Bree, they've saved us."

Bree's heart dropped. She knew what his coming meant. She'd seen it play out in her dreams, and she feared what was to come. As Colin sailed closer, she thought of the twins, her wee bugs, and hoped they would have a fine life. She prayed Colin would find love again. She replayed her dream in her mind. It showed her what would happen.

She knew she had to save Colin. Colin robbed the Fae fable, The Stone of Love, of the maiden's death. It called for the maiden's death again. The dreams showed her that if she didn't step in front of Colin, Tony's sword would strike home in Colin's heart, and she couldn't live without him. She wasn't strong enough. Hell, even if they made it back to the portal, she would die, anyway. Balor cast that spell to end her life when she traveled to the future, ensuring she met death no matter what happened.

Colin was strong enough to live without her. He was strong enough for everyone. She sat on the hard rock, the cold water rising over her feet, and prepared herself. She prepared for death knowing she would save her true love.

****

As the longboat neared the island, Colin made out the women in the early dawn light. Rannick brought them closer, and Ainslie struggled to pull Bree to stand as the tide lapped closer, covering their feet. Bree had her head turned to Ainslie, facing down. His heart went out to his true love. He wanted her to know whatever had happened, it didn't matter. He loved her; she loved him, and together they would get through this.

Rannick tried to bring them alongside the island, but the boat's bottom scraped against rocks. The stony shore with the wave shoved the boat away from the island. Both women trembled in the cold. They were both soaked, and soon the tide would cover them in freezing water. To hell with silence. They were there, and he needed to get to Bree.

He yelled at Rannick, "Ye must get me closer! I cannot reach them!" The silence broken, the oarsmen began shouting orders between them, trying to coordinate their efforts.

Rannick shouted, "Men, push from the starboard, so we bring the longship closer to the island. I don't want to go back out and turn the boat for a different approach, wasting time!"

Rannick shouted above the men, "Colin, I'll bring ye closer! Try to grab the women!"

Colin nodded without looking back. He kept his focus on the females. The moment he was within reach, he would grab one. The boat swung into the island, and he reached out trying to grab Bree, but caught Ainslie. The boat hit the rocks again, which pushed them away.

Bree cried out as he pulled Ainslie from her grasp. She fell forward into the water but stood back up against the rock, now shivering uncontrollably. Colin pulled Ainslie into the boat, and she fell to the bottom. Colin stared back at the island to see Bree wet, shivering, and looking away from him.

Ainslie tried shouting over the oarsmen and the surf.

Colin turned and shouted back, "What?"

The boat bumped against the rocks and Colin fell forward over the bow, and Bree's legs came into his sight. Not missing an opportunity, he jumped off the boat into the surf of knee-deep water. The boat rocked away, but Colin only had eyes for Bree. He stood up and gathered her in his arms. She willingly went to him, keeping her head down.

A man roared, then he felt a piercing in his chest just below the Brooch of Lorne.

Bree's head snapped back, and she gaped into his eyes, grabbing his chest.

Colin glanced down and a sword jutted out of Bree's chest into his, the tip piercing his skin. He stared at Bree, her mouth open in a silent scream. The sword penetrated through her shoulder and stopped in his chest.

A man shrieked, and the sword ripped from her chest.

She screamed, jolting, and would have fallen if Colin hadn't held her.

He stared at her bruised face, but all he saw was his wee Bree.

She took a breath and hissed. "Hold me, Colin, hold me up."

He cried out a sob as he held her tighter. "Oh, God, Bree."

Her hands fumbled, and he watched in detached amazement. Her hands were on the Brooch of Lorne. She felt around the pin and pressed the secret compartment open. In her hand was a black stone, and when she placed it in the case, it glowed. She closed the latch and sighed. He gaped at her face in stunned astonishment.

She rasped, breathing harder, as if it took all her effort to speak. "You cheated the Fae fable of its maiden. The stones demand the maiden's death, and I must fulfill my destiny. I found The Stone of Lust, and now you have it." She breathed a deep sigh and closed her eyes. "I love you, Colin." Her body relaxed as she fainted in his arms.

The boat bumped into his legs, not knocking him over. Ready for it, he had his feet braced and quickly thrust Bree into Ainslie's arms.

She caught her and shouted. "I've got her, Colin." Colin turned back to find Tony on his knees in the rising surf, muttering over his sword.

The boat rocked away, but Colin stood firm.

Tony ranted as spittle flew from his mouth. "How could you? How could you kill her?" He grabbed at his head and shook it violently. "Get out of my head, Balor. Get the fuck out of my head!"

It was time. Colin needed to focus. As Tony kneeled, beating his head and shouting over and over, "Get out! Get out! Get out!" Colin concentrated on Balor, on his evil, and the Stones. The stones glowed brightly, and Colin thought harder.

Dagda spoke in his mind. ~*I am with ye. More, ye must concentrate more.* ~

Colin closed his eyes and turned his thoughts inward, toward his own soul. He poured all his energy into his focus on Balor, his evil and hate. Colin opened his eyes to find Tony staring at him, his mouth open in a speechless scream. Colin's left arm glowed bright white, filled with all the rage, evil, and hate for Balor churning. Spinning with it was the love, compassion, and care for his family. Good and bad, hate and love combined into one energy. Colin raised his arm, pointed at Tony, and spoke firmly.

I bathe thee in blood, I place fear in your heart.
That the truest love may ne'er depart!
Nor other women will go thy way,
Nor deal with you, be it as it may.
But all these things together thrown,
his heart and soul that he is torn,
He may perish and forever be,
only not in my company.

A force swirled hard in him, filling his body with energy. As he focused on Balor, the energy poured from his arm. Bright white light shot out of Colin's hand into Tony's chest, forcing him to throw his head back and scream so loud it reverberated across the land. A flash of wind blew out of Tony, and a man flew above him. Tony jolted and fell forward on his knees, panting.

The Fae floated in suspension. Everyone seemed to be frozen in time. Colin held his arm still but glared at Balor.

Balor glanced around him, then reached his hand toward Colin. The brooch shifted on his shoulder but didn't give way.

Balor's face flushed, then his focus swung to Ainslie and his arm rotated, his fingers curling in, then out. A blue flash flew out of Ainslie's hand into Balor's.

Ainslie cried out and gripped her hand.

Balor clutched something tight, then opened his

hand. In it sat a blue stone in the shape of a diamond that glowed brightly. As Balor faded, he looked into his hand. The blue stone disappeared as he screamed and vanished from the human realm.

Colin blinked. Balor had disappeared. He glanced around him, and the sun rose more. Dawn had arrived. From his shoulder, the stone's glow dimmed and faded. The boat bumped his legs as he stood in knee deep water.

Before him, Tony was on his knees, panting with his head down. With Balor gone, Colin's vengeance was upon him.

Colin drew his sword. The ring of it coming from his scabbard brought Tony's head up.

Tony shook his head as tears streamed down his cheeks. "God have mercy. Please have mercy on me."

Colin took the sword in both hands. "Mercy is not here for ye, Tony Stiles. Ye have plagued this earth long enough. Ye have tortured my true love for the last time. It is time, Tony. It is time for ye to get the death ye deserve and perish in hell."

Colin raised his sword, flexed his arms, and in one broad stroke cut off Tony's head. The head rolled into the surf and sank. Tony's body fell at Colin's feet. Colin stood there a moment, watching the blood drain from the corpse.

Rannick shouted loud and long the MacDougall war cry, signaling his men to repeat it. *"Buaidh no bàs. Buaidh no bàs!"* Now that Balor had left the human realm, with Rannick's rallying call, the men who Balor entranced would return to their own will and minds.

As the water lapped at his thighs, the cheers from the island answering Rannick's war cry drifted to him.

Colin sighed in relief. It was over, and he had Bree.

The boat bumped against his leg, and Ainslie grabbed his shoulder. "Come, brother, the fight is over. We are the victors."

Colin sheathed his sword. With Ainslie's help, he climbed into the boat. He didn't look or speak to anyone. He scooped up an unconscious Brielle and held her as he slowly slid down the wall of the longboat, cradling her in his arms.

Ainslie went to the back of the boat. The oarsmen and Rannick shouted commands back and forth to navigate the rocky water. Ainslie returned with a heavy blanket and a couple of pieces of cloth. She placed fabric on the wound at Bree's back and the injury at her front, tucking them into her tunic. She picked up the blanket and wrapped it around Colin and Bree.

Colin never took his gaze from Bree's face as he helped position her for Ainslie to stop the flow of blood. The wound seemed to go clean through Bree's shoulder. With the flow of blood reducing, the stab hopefully damaged nothing vital. He breathed a sigh of relief.

Ainslie patted his shoulder and returned to sit with Rannick, cradling her injured hand.

Colin examined Bree's face. The bruises pulled at his heart. He brushed her hair back, tucking it behind her ear like he had done a million times. He bent and slowly kissed her cold lips, a sob escaping at the temperature and lack of response. Colin brushed her face with his hand and held it under her nose, feeling a light breath there. *Alive, thank God.* He gathered her closer, trying to warm her with his heat, holding her close to his heart.

His stab wound went forgotten as he sat and held his true love. "Please, Bree, don't die. I have come for ye. I said I always would. I have come to rescue my true love." Colin sat, tears streaming down his face.

He held her, praying with all his might, "Please, Bree, please hold on."

Chapter 21

Rannick held Ainslie in his arms as they sailed around Colonsay to Ivor's village. The last of the men from Balor's encampment made the way on foot after they loaded a full set of oarsmen into Rannick's longship to sail them quickly, each greeting one another in gleeful victory.

Ainslie glanced at her brother in front of the longship, still cradling an unconscious Bree in his arms. He seemed to have fallen asleep holding her. Good, he needed the rest.

Rannick leaned down and whispered in her ear. "Are ye alright?" She nodded and snuggled into his embrace. Rannick took a deep breath and grunted.

She glanced at him. "What is it, Rannick?"

He gathered her closer and stared out over the ocean. "Ye left without telling me where ye had gone. Tried to save Bree on yer own. Ye are only a woman."

Ainslie shifted out of his embrace. "Only a woman? I am a woman warrior who bested ye in a fair fight."

Rannick grabbed her hand. She flinched. It was the hand Balor ripped The Stone of Faith from. He released it and ran his hand through his hair.

She backed farther away, turned, and moved to the side of the longship. Rannick called for a man to take over steering and mumbled instructions to him.

Ainslie knew he approached, knew he had more to say, but she was too angry and frustrated to want to listen.

He took a deep breath and stepped closer. "Ainslie, I worried about ye."

She spoke without turning around. "Well, ye don't have to worry. Colin and I will be gone before ye know it, and then ye can have all the females ye want to do yer bidding."

Her throat burned, and tears gathered in her eyes. The thought of leaving Rannick permanently left her empty. One tear escaped before she could stop it, and she quickly brushed it away.

Rannick stepped closer, his breath tickling her ear as he whispered, "Ainslie, I know ye are a strong warrior and able to defend yerself, but I am a man. Ye leaving to fight on yer own—ye should not have placed yerself in danger. Ye need to leave the fighting to the men."

Rannick took a deep breath and placed his hands on the railing, encircling her. She stood rigid, refusing to touch him.

He whispered in her ear, "Ainslie, allow me to protect ye."

He blew out his breath. "When I saw ye stranded on that island, with the tide coming in. I, I love ye. Do ye hear me?" He kissed her ear as he enunciated each word. "I...love...ye."

Ainslie shivered. His kisses shot straight to her heart, making it flutter in her chest. But he commanded her to be something she wasn't. She was a fighter, and to not fight was something she couldn't do. She wanted to stay in the Viking time—she fit here. But she wasn't from this time, truly didn't belong here. She now understood how her and Rannick's worlds were so different. They saved Bree, and it neared time to return. To go back to her time, where she belonged.

She turned in his embrace, her throat closed in as a tear escaped.

She spoke with a broken sob. "Rannick, I must return with Colin to our time." She turned to walk out of his embrace, but he refused to allow her to pass. A sob escaped her, and tears flowed down her cheeks.

Rannick spoke lowly, "Please, Ainslie, stay. Stay with me forever."

He stared at her and kissed her lips lightly.

Ainslie choked out a sob and broke free of his embrace to weave through the rowers and stand at the bow of the boat.

****

As the two longships approached Ivor's village, a cheer went up from the shoreline. Ainslie stayed by Colin's side as the men safely beached the longboats. He rushed off the boat and the men onboard cleared the way, seeing he held the unconscious woman that Balor kidnapped.

Colin yelled above the roar. "Ivor, yer healer. I need yer healer now!"

Ivor approached and shouted above the men, who all fell silent. They parted a path between the men, and Ivor led Colin carrying Bree in his arms. As he passed, Colin heard many offer a prayer for the woman in his arms. He gathered her tighter and prayed himself. *Please, God, let her live.*

In the healer's hut, Colin sat on the bed, still holding Bree. Ivor stepped forward with a hand on his shoulder. "Come, my man, leave her to the women. They will heal her."

Colin sat still, holding Bree. "No, I will stay with my wife." The healer glanced at Ivor then Colin but uttered something in Ivor's ear, who nodded and turned to leave.

His sister stood beside the bed wringing her hands.

Colin glanced up. "Go, Ainslie. There is nothing ye can do here."

She sighed. "I can stay and help."

Colin stared at her. "I'd prefer it if ye left. Go to Rannick."

She fisted her hands at her sides. "I don't need Rannick. I don't need anyone. I want to stay and help."

Colin roared for the first time since he had Bree in his arms. "I wish to be alone. If she dies, she dies in my arms and with me only." Colin hadn't yelled at anyone like that in many years. He knew he was being unreasonable, but this was his wee Bree, and he never would let her go again.

Tears built in Ainslie's eyes, and she kneeled beside the bed. "Colin, I know ye are in pain, but Bree will pull through. Let the healer see to her and then ye can hold her again. Come, brother. Let me tell ye what we spoke of together on that cold rock."

Colin shook his head, but the healer stepped forward and pleaded, "Please, I will come get ye as soon as we finish. Ye may hold her until I need to change the bandages. I must clean and stitch her. If she wakes, I will send for ye."

Ainslie helped Bree from Colin's arms as the healer laid her on the bed. Colin held Bree's hand until Ainslie pulled him away.

He touched the healer's shoulder.

As she glanced at him, he spoke lowly, "I'll be just outside." The healer nodded as the other women started stripping Bree.

Colin stopped and stood at the end of the bed. When he saw the marks and bruises on his wife, he sobbed. Never in his life had he seen anything like it, and he prayed he never would again. All the anger he held came surging to the surface, and he fisted his hands. As they turned Bree to her side and the bruising on her back came into his view, his heart broke into a million pieces.

She was a strong woman, bore twins with an ease that few women could. But to see her like this, battered and broken. He swore then and there nothing, absolutely nothing, would stop her from healing. He would have enough will and strength for them both. She was his true love, and they were soul mates. He'd see them through this.

He allowed Ainslie to pull him out of the hut. Ainslie stood beside Colin as he stared into the forest. His mind filled with the images of Bree's broken body, then the man who caused all this pain and suffering. They flipped through his mind, one then another, gaining speed each time, landing on Tony, then Balor hovering above Tony. He felt dizzy. The look on that Fae's face sickened him—the power, the hate. He took a few steps into the woods, bent over, and emptied his stomach.

A woman from the healer's hut approached and offered Ainslie a couple of mugs and retreated quietly. Colin stood a moment, leaning against the tree, then returned to Ainslie. She handed him a mug, and he rinsed his mouth then drank deeply from the mug, ale soothing his throat.

Ainslie went to sit on the bench outside the healer's hut. She patted the seat next to her, and Colin joined her. The wooden bench, smooth and worn, saw much use by those waiting for their loved ones to be healed. Colin stayed there for a while in silence, occasionally sipping from the mug until the brew was gone. Ainslie seemed content to allow him time to compose and contend with what all had happened. Ainslie went to get more ale and returned with two full mugs.

Handing him one she spoke. "They stitch her wounds. She is still unconscious."

Colin rubbed his face with his hand. "Was there something ye wished to tell me, or was that a ploy to get me to leave the hut?"

Ainslie sighed. "Both."

Colin snorted. *Both.* What all happened in the cold rock as they sat waiting for rescue full well knowing Balor hid in wait to bring harm to all those they both loved?

Ainslie glanced at Colin, then at the woods. She took a deep breath, then let it out in a long exhale. She nodded, seeming to gather her courage. Here it was. He was about to learn part of the hell Bree had been through, and he hoped he was strong enough to hear it.

She turned to Colin. "At first, when I saw her, she wasn't herself. She was there, but she wasn't."

Colin rubbed his neck. "Aye, she has done it once…I, I didn't know what it was, but she was there one moment, then not herself. It was as if her body was there, and her mind wasn't. I had to shake her, shake her out of it." He growled. "It's a defense she's built into herself. Something she used when that bastard hurt her. She went someplace else so she wouldn't feel the pain."

Ainslie nodded. "Aye, but she came out of it. On the island."

He turned to her. "What did she say?"

Ainslie gazed at the forest, shaking her head. Tears gathered in her eyes. Then she glanced into her mug.

Colin's voice cracked when he spoke. "Tell me, no matter how bad, please."

She glanced at him. "She thinks ye will not want her anymore. She said Tony ruined her and that ye wouldn't want her—that way."

Colin nodded. "I suspected so when she wouldn't look at me. She is so far from the truth. I will always want her. She's my soul mate. She just needs to keep faith in me, in us."

Ainslie gasped. "Faith! I had forgotten. So much has happened. It's all just catching up with me now."

Colin fully turned to his sister. "Aye, what is it?"

"The Stone of Faith. I found it. That's what helped Bree. She touched it and said it brought her faith."

She held up her bandaged hand. "But when the Fae came out of Tony, he made the stone fly to him. It cut my hand since it's the shape of a diamond. I lost it, brother. I am sorry."

Colin nodded. "I saw the flash of blue, then a stone in Balor's hand. It disappeared before he did, lost again. I assumed as much. It's yer Fae fable, but we didn't recover the stone, as the fable said." He breathed hard. " 'Tis no concern. We saved Bree, and that's what matters."

They both sat and stared at the forest, sipping the

ale. Colin thought of all the gifts of love and joy Bree brought into his life. Her love she freely gave, and he cherished. The warmth she provided him with in her expression. Then their greatest gift of their love, their kids, Evie and Ewan. He prayed Bree would live to see them grow into a man and a woman. Her strength was his rock and her love empowered him to live and return her love. He breathed, and the Brooch of Lorne shifted on his shoulder, reminding him of another of her gifts.

Colin turned to Ainslie. "She did the most amazing thing. Bree did."

Ainslie nudged him. "What was that?"

Colin looked at the forest but didn't see it.

He saw Bree standing before him on the island just after the sword came free of her. "After Tony stabbed her, she asked me to hold her, hold her up." He choked on a sob, the memory still raw and painful. "She opened the brooch and placed a stone in it."

Ainslie grabbed his arm. "The Stone of Lust. She showed it to me. Said she swiped it from Tony."

Colin shook his head. "She ensured I had what I needed, even in immense pain from her wound. She made sure I had another Iona Stone to power the brooch." He sighed. "She said the Fae fable got cheated its maiden's death. That she had to fulfill her destiny and die for the stones." He fisted his hand. "I cannot allow that to happen."

Ainslie hugged him. "We won't, Colin. We won't."

Later, Ainslie found Rannick by his three longships, still assessing the damage and going over repairs and supplies with Erik. She stood to the side, not wanting to interrupt but needing to see him. As if sensing her, Rannick turned, and their gazes locked. He spoke to Erik, who nodded.

Without taking his eyes off her, Rannick approached. "How does Bree fare?"

Ainslie exhaled. "Better. They stitched her wounds and got her to drink some ale, but she is still unconscious. At first Colin refused to leave her, insisting he hold her. But I talked him into allowing them to work on her."

Rannick picked up her injured hand. "Did a healer see to this?"

Ainslie nodded as Rannick brought the bandaged hand to his lips and kissed an exposed knuckle. "Does it pain ye?"

Ainslie shook her head. "Not much."

He kissed another knuckle as he ogled her over her hand. "Yer brother is still with her?"

Ainslie sighed. "Aye, he lies holding her, whispering in her ear, hoping she hears him. I'm worried. He's really taken this hard."

Rannick kissed another knuckle. "He will be fine. Leave him to heal her. We can check on them in the morning."

She nodded. "Aye, he promised to send someone for me if anything changed."

Rannick kissed the last knuckle and grinned. "Now how will he know where ye will be? I thought ye were done with me?"

She tried to pull her hand away, but he held on. "Ye have kissed all my knuckles. There is nothing left to kiss."

Rannick's smile grew and from his expression, she knew he thought of all the places he wanted to kiss her. He started over at the first knuckle, kissing it slowly.

She pulled her hand from his and glanced away. "Ivor has announced a feast. It seems the Vikings never miss an opportunity to party."

Rannick laughed and took both her hands in his. "Aye, but I have something else planned for us." He kissed all her knuckles and stared at her over her hands.

She blushed. "Ye do?"

He pulled her to go with him toward the hut they had shared previously. "Aye, I do."

Chapter 22

Rannick pulled Ainslie into his arms as they entered the hut, kissing her deeply. She stepped back as her eyes traveled the place. The room was much the same as before, a small room with an open fireplace and a curtained area for the bed. The same tub she washed Rannick in, sitting by the fire.

Rannick whispered in her ear. "I want to bathe ye. May I?"

Ainslie shivered. "I have never had a man bathe me before."

Rannick kissed her again. "Good. I have never bathed a woman before."

He set her aside and pulled the pot of heated water from the fire. As she stripped her clothing away, he watched her with hooded eyes as he poured the water into the tub. He set the pot outside the door and returned as Ainslie tried stepping into the tub. He halted her with his hand.

She stared at him, crossing her arms over her nakedness, and he grinned. He went to the shelf, took down a vial and some soap, and set up the drying cloth by the fire to warm. He set his items by the tub and picked Ainslie up before she could protest. As he lowered her into the water, he kissed her. She stood, returning his kisses, and he stepped back.

"Lower yerself before the water chills." The warm

water soothed her aches. He used a smaller bucket, carefully wet her hair, soaped it, and gently massaged her scalp.

Ainslie leaned back and pulled her legs out of the tub, so her calves dangled over the side. She unwrapped her hand and left it to soak in the water.

Rannick rinsed her hair and washed her legs and feet, massaging each foot, toe, and calf. She enjoyed the attention, and when he tickled her foot, she pulled her feet back into the tub, laughing. He soaped his hands, waving her to lean forward. As he washed her, he massaged her back, then her neck, and she rolled it, moaning. She was tense and sore, not realizing till now how much the event on the island affected her.

He pulled her shoulders, so she leaned against the back of the tub and kneeled behind her. He rubbed the oil in his hands and rubbed her chest. He rested his head on her shoulder and blew in her ear. She smiled, liking all his attention. He shifted and ran his hand down her abdomen to cup her while kissing her neck.

She turned her head, and he kissed her full on the mouth. He retreated and poured more of the oil on his hand, then returned to her, rubbing her as he kissed her, their tongues dancing. He inserted a finger, sliding in easily, and her knees opened as she moaned into his mouth. His other hand massaged a breast, and she arched in the small tub as far as she could.

His hand continued its play under the water as he shifted to her side. He sucked her nipple into his mouth, and she cried out, the pace of his hand in the water picking up. She gasped when he inserted a second finger, continuing his torment. He kissed her hard on the mouth, and she cried out again.

He grinned into the kiss. "I want to see ye, Ainslie. I want to watch ye enjoy my loving. Let go."

He increased his pressure and pace under the water, sloshing water out of the tub and wetting his tunic without care. Ainslie's walls clenched, and he added another finger, the pressure causing her to scream in his mouth, leaving her convulsing in the water. He slowed his pace, allowing her to ride her organism out. She huffed a few times sharply, then panted, trying to catch her breath as he continued his play with one finger but slowed, bringing her down from her high.

She exhaled as her head dropped to the back of the tub. Rannick withdrew his hand and dried it.

He bent and kissed her softly on the lips. "I hope ye enjoyed yer bath, my love."

Ainslie took a deep breath and didn't open her eyes. "God, that was heaven. I have never had one that hard before." Her eyes snapped open. "Ye have done this before?"

Rannick kissed her softly. "No, my warrior queen, ye are the only one I have bathed and the only one I want to bathe, ever." He scooped her up, set her next to the fire, gently wrapped her in the drying sheet, and dried her body. As he dried her hair, he combed it out with his fingers.

He whispered in her ear, "Sheer midnight," then kissed her neck. He wrapped the sheet around her and carried her to the bed, laying her on it. He covered her with fur, and she curled up and sighed.

His breath tickled her ear. "Rest, warrior queen. Ye have earned it."

****

The bed shifted, and she came awake with a start.

Rannick was next to her and placed his hand on her shoulder. "Ye slept some. I thought ye might be tired from yer ordeal, so I allowed ye to rest."

She snuggled into the bedding and smiled. Rannick's hair was wet. He must have bathed. He left her to return with a tray that he set at the end of the bed.

He slowly stripped naked as she watched with the same hooded eyes he had for her earlier. His shaft leaped to life under her gaze, and she grinned as he climbed into bed. He covered them both with the furs and fluffed the ones behind them. He leaned down on the bed, drawing the tray closer.

Ainslie sat up, surveying the spread. There was grilled lamb and a small baked bird. Steamed root vegetables sat beside fresh fruit, and a bowl of candied nuts finished the tray.

Her stomach loudly growled, and Rannick laughed. "Aye, I knew ye'd be hungry."

She reached for some meat, but he picked it up before her hand could. "Please let me feed ye. I wish to care for my warrior queen."

Ainslie allowed Rannick to feed her. She reveled in this very intimate act, allowing another to provide her, depending on him, trusting him. He would offer an item, and she nodded or shook her head. When she denied an item, he'd shove it in his mouth with a smile. He wouldn't allow her to reach for anything. He wanted to serve her. Between her bites, she fed him a couple, but his hunger won, and he ate with enthusiasm.

She grinned as she watched him, this hardened warrior from the twelfth century, become a caring and passionate man serving the woman he loved. It touched her heart more than anything he could ever say.

He popped a candied nut into her mouth, and she savored the flavor of candied almond. She wasn't sure if it was sugar or honey, and she must have made a face.

He ate one himself, chewing as he spoke. "Ivor has an excellent trade business. This is a grain he gets from afar. Very expensive, and it was an honor he gave to ye. These he only makes for himself."

Ainslie hummed. "It's a nut. The covering is sugar, and the taste is called sweet." She grinned as he fed her another. "I will have to thank him. Sugar is costly here but, in my time, readily available."

Rannick kissed her full on the mouth, then lifted his head as he spoke. "Ye can thank me if ye like."

Ainslie kissed Rannick and spoke between kisses. "I thank ye."

Rannick cupped her face with his hand, deepening the kiss. Ainslie shifted her body, lying down, and Rannick rose over her. His leg connected with the food tray, and he huffed a laugh. He rose, moved the tray to the floor, then returned to Ainslie, covering her with his body.

As he kissed her, Ainslie's hands roamed his back, molded his shoulders, and trailed down his stomach, her hand brushing him. Rannick sucked in a breath and kissed her harder. She pumped him as Rannick kissed her from her neck to her breast, laving the nipple. Ainslie arched in response and moaned while working him. Her free hand gripped his head as his mouth teased her nipple to a fine point. As Rannick shifted to the other breast, she kept her hand on his shaft. He sucked hard on her nipple, and she cried out but kept her hand moving. He arched as she rubbed her thumb along the top, picking up the drop of moisture and rubbing it on the tip. He growled and kissed her harder.

As he shifted between her legs, Ainslie spread hers for him, welcoming him with a smile.

He rubbed his staff against her, spreading her juices. "By the gods, I can never get enough of ye."

Ainslie moved her hips in line with his rubbing. "I know. It's never enough."

Rannick cupped her face with one hand and gazed at her. "I want all of ye, forever."

He drove into her with love in his eyes. So captured by his look, Ainslie couldn't look away. So mesmerized by the love she saw in the depth of his emotions, she returned the expression. He seated fully in her for a moment. He closed his eyes and began a pace known by man and woman for all time, a slow loving built upon the foundation of true love. He continued to rock against her, and she met each with a moan as he hit her sensitive spot deep inside. She raised her hips with each stroke, and he quickly set a faster pace as he kissed her. Ainslie arched and grabbed his rear, asking him to go deeper and faster, and Rannick took the cue. He growled as he answered her call.

She sensed energy built within her. She arched and cried out his name as he roared, his release still pumping in her with the aftereffects of his orgasm.

He shifted and rolled to her side, gathering her in his arms as they both tried to catch their breaths. Ainslie rested her head on his shoulder and trailed her finger in his chest hairs.

Using his thumb, Rannick tilted her head, so he saw into her eyes. "Ainslie, I have asked ye once. I am asking ye one last time. After tonight, the choice shall be yers. Please stay with me."

He kissed her slowly, keeping his lips connected with hers longer. She did as well, so she might always remember this sensation in her heart.

When he lifted his head, he gazed into her eyes. "Please be my wife, the mother of my children, and my warrior queen." He kissed her again. "Ye do not have to answer now. But when the time comes, I will not ask again." He closed his eyes and sighed, then opened them. "Ye will need to make a choice."

A tear escaped, and he caught it with his thumb. Another escaped, and he kissed it away. He placed her head on his shoulder and held her in silence. She shivered, and he covered them with the furs but held her tightly to him.

Every few minutes, Rannick would kiss or squeeze her but not ask anything more. Just loving her in the time they had left. Eventually, his breathing eased, and his hold on her relaxed as he fell asleep.

Ainslie lay awake most of the night, watching the pattern of the shadows from the fire's flames on the ceiling. She had much to think about. Choosing to stay in the twelfth century was a huge decision that would mean forever. If she stayed here, she could never return to the twenty-first century. It meant she would never see her family again.

She thought about each person as memories flipped through her mind. The twins, Evie and Ewan, and playing with them in the yard. Classes she taught at the school and all the special-needs kids who needed her. Who would take care of the special kids if she wasn't there? And who would explain why she left them? She thought of talking to Marie and John about the castle and the Priory they now live in. The reenactment events for Dunstaffnage castle that she loved planning so much. She thought of Mrs. Abernathy and her care of the family. She smiled at the memory of filching her cookies as a child. She thought of Bree and the day she first met her in the study as they discussed her living in Scotland if Colin never returned from purgatory. Ainslie breathed heavily. Colin, her brother. God, she would miss him the most. Could she turn her back on all that she knew and all she loved for one man?

She thought of her days here in the twelfth century. From the moment she landed here, she fit in. She thought of her obsession with the Viking life, the fighting, the way they lived. The way they sailed. All of it. She loved being here, but she loved being with her family.

Family.

Her thoughts turned to Rannick. A family. He mentioned wanting her to be a mother, something she had also dreamed of—children. She closed her eyes and imagined a day with Rannick as husband and her a wife and mother. Rannick holding a young boy, helping him with a wooden sword. She imagined a girl, sweet and small but strong, a warrior like herself.

Slowly sitting up, she turned and gazed at Rannick in the firelight, calm and relaxed in sleep. He seemed years younger without the fierce expression he always carried as a leader and warrior.

She ran her finger along his strong brow and down his angled nose, regal on his face. She cupped his cheek, and his beard brushed her hand. He shifted in his sleep and brought his hand to hers, cupping her hand against his face.

Without opening his eyes, he whispered, "Ainslie, I love ye." And kissed the inside of her hand, then placed it back on his cheek, holding it there. She laid her head back on his shoulder and kept her hand on his face, torn between two worlds.

Chapter 23

Ainslie found Colin the following day lying with Bree in the healer's hut. Nothing had changed except they both got some sleep. He was still asleep, and she didn't want to wake him. Rannick spoke with the healer. The hushed whispers were not different from anything one heard in a hospital hall in the twenty-first century. Worry for the ill not recovering well. Worry for the loved ones who had trouble coping with illness. It all sounded the same. Ainslie sighed as she observed her brother and his true love sleep. She prayed it was a healing sleep. They both needed it.

Rannick returned to her side and pulled her out of the healer's hut.

As they sat on the bench outside the hut, Rannick took both her hands in his. It was the same bench she sat on with Colin the day before. It seemed to get a lot of use.

Rannick took a deep breath. "I wish to sail with the evening tide. No, I wish to sail as soon as we finish loading."

Ainslie pulled her hands from his. "I am not leaving my brother and his wife."

Rannick grabbed her hands. "Ye misunderstand. I want to take Bree to my mother. She is the best healer in the western isles. I think Bree needs her."

Ainslie exhaled. "They are resting. That is good."

Rannick shook his head. "Bree has not regained consciousness. They worry she won't. She needs my mother's help." He sighed. "I want ye to speak to yer brother. We need to go soon, so we don't waste more time. The healer worries Bree will waste away if she doesn't wake soon."

Ainslie nodded. "I understand what ye are saying. If she doesn't wake soon, she cannot eat." It reminded Ainslie once more of the difference in the times. This wouldn't be an issue in the future, medical technology being what it was. But in the twelfth century, they didn't have IVs to maintain human nutrition. Here in this time, if a person didn't eat, they died.

"I'll speak to him now. How long till yer ships will be ready to sail?"

Rannick glanced toward the ships. "An hour, no two. I'll need two. We can load Colin and Bree right before we sail. I will outfit a tent in the bow for them. I hope to make it in one day."

Ainslie raised an eyebrow. "Half the time?"

Rannick nodded. "We can set that pace. The men would do it if I mentioned it was for the injured woman."

Ainslie sighed. "I'll speak to Colin now."

Rannick took her hand in his and kissed the back. "I'll ready the ships."

****

Almost two hours later, Colin cradled Bree in his arms as Ainslie helped them settle in the bow of the smaller longship. Rannick agreed to take it ahead of the other two, so they sailed faster to get Bree to his mother quicker. Ainslie covered her brother and Bree with furs.

He growled lowly, "I do not like this. Bree needs

rest, not to travel the western isles."

Ainslie nodded. "I know, but Rannick's mother is a talented healer, and I suspect she uses a little magic along the way."

Colin huffed. "Herbs and brews do not make the doctor. A chant only works if ye really have magic."

Ainslie patted her brother's leg as she sat near his feet. "Aye, but going to Oban puts us one sailing closer to the portal. If Bree really needs help, then the portal is where we will find it. She may need modern medicine that is not here in the twelfth century. Ye planned to take her back, so maybe we'll go sooner than later."

Colin shifted Bree in his arms. "She needs to heal first. I don't know if she can survive the portal in her state. It drains yer energy, and each trip is more taxing than the previous."

Ainslie stared at Bree's face, pale and bruised, as it rested on Colin's shoulder. The bruising had faded, but dark marks still marred her skin. Ainslie watched her for a moment and thought she saw her eyes flutter behind the lids, but maybe that was a trick of her eyes, her mind wanting to see what she hoped for, Bree waking.

She glanced at her brother, who focused on Bree's face. "Have ye tried calling for Brigid, yer Fae?"

Colin growled. "Aye. No, she hasn't come. Damn sprite. I called for Dagda, too, but nothing. They've abandoned us."

Ainslie sighed. "Well, see if ye can get some broth down her. She needs nourishment. I'll check back once we are out of the inlet and on open water."

Colin grabbed her hand before she rose. "Have ye thought more on yerself?"

Ainslie glimpsed into his eyes, looking for an answer, and only saw a brother's care for his sister.

"I don't know. This is a hard decision." Colin patted her hand. Ainslie glanced down and then back at her brother.

He let go of her hand as she settled against the ship's hull beside him.

Colin tilted his head to see her face. "Did ye want to discuss it?"

Ainslie exhaled. "I don't know. They both seem right, and they both seem wrong."

Colin grinned. "Did ye ever wonder why ye had such an obsession with the Vikings?"

Colin stared at her; he could always see through her. "Did ye ever wonder why our parents never stopped ye from this obsession? Maybe wonder why they supported it as they did?"

Ainslie picked at the furs, refusing to meet her brother's glare, and shrugged her shoulders.

Colin patted her hands. "Why was yer Fae story the Viking story?"

Ainslie glanced up, curious as well. "I always thought she did it to make me happy." She smiled. "It did make me happy. To be a Viking warrior, princess, saving the day."

Colin gazed at Bree and ran his finger down her cheek. "Did ye know our mother handpicked Bree for the chapel project?" Ainslie shook her head, and Colin's eyes never left Bree's face as he spoke. "She did. Emily MacDougall argued with the scholars over the chapel renovation repeatedly. She insisted Bree had to be the one."

He kissed Bree's forehead and continued to stare at

her face. "When Bree first came to the castle, I thought it was all a nuisance. But then I saw her for the first time and knew she was meant for me. She is my soul mate." He turned to Ainslie. "When ye first saw Rannick, what did yer heart tell ye? Was there something special that happened? Something that moved ye more than anything else in the world?"

Ainslie gasped. "I....well, I told no one."

Colin tilted his head. "Tell me."

Ainslie looked away. "Ye will think it's stupid."

Colin huffed, and Ainslie glanced at her brother. "A dream. He came to me in a dream."

Colin frowned. "Before ye came back in time?"

Ainslie nodded. "Aye, the day before, actually. And the Green Lady visited me when I woke."

Colin gasped. "Ye didn't tell anyone. Why?"

Ainslie glanced at Bree again. "I didn't want to worry anyone."

Colin leaned his head back. "What did ye see in the dream?"

Ainslie took a deep breath and released it slowly. "It flipped around. A part was him, and part was the Fae fable. But the part about him was very clear in my mind. We were in a village, in a battle. I felt the weight of my sword on my arm as I lifted it to fight. I smelled the smoke and the blood from the battle. It was *so real*. Then I sensed something in my heart and glanced to my side. He fought beside me. We battled together. He beamed like he knew I enjoyed fighting. We were equal. Equal in our task, equal in our goals, and equal in our love. I have never felt that love ye and Bree have, or the spark John and Marie talk about. When I woke, I thought it was just a dream, but when I returned in time,

I saw his eyes."

Colin nodded. "Aye, they are unique."

Ainslie smiled. "It's not only the color. It was the way he gazed at me when we first met. The way he stares at me now. No man has ever looked at me that way, and I fear no other man will."

Colin sighed. "He came to me, ye know."

Ainslie shook her head. "No, I didn't. When?"

Colin chuckled. "Back in Oban. The same day I found ye both in bed." Ainslie blushed and hid her face, making Colin laugh. "I knew he would. He is a man from the twelfth century. He naturally asked for yer hand."

Ainslie turned to Colin. "What did ye say?"

Colin smirked. "Well, I wanted to tell him to bugger off, but I'd seen the way ye look at him, with puppy eyes all lovesick."

Colin made gagging sounds as Ainslie slapped his leg. "Seriously, what did ye say?"

Colin laughed, then stared at her for a moment. "I explained that ye would want to be a mother, a wife, and a warrior—his equal. He would need to understand that and allow ye to be all those things." She grinned at Colin as he continued. "Then I told him the decision would be yers, not mine." Colin chuckled. "I shocked him. What has he said to ye about it?"

Ainslie blushed. "He has asked more than once."

Colin took a deep breath. "Have ye answered him?"

Ainslie shook her head. "I don't know. He said he would ask no more. That when the time came and I made my choice, he would accept it."

Colin snorted a laugh. "I doubt he'll let it go that

easily."

Ainslie blushed. "Well, he has been making an excellent case for staying."

Colin laughed. "No more. My ears burn. It was bad enough finding ye both naked in bed."

Colin glanced at Bree and then back at Ainslie. "Ye know, I think our parents knew much more about our futures than they ever admitted. I think they watch us now, knowing where we are is the right place." Ainslie breathed, and Colin glanced at her. "When the time comes, ye will know what to do."

The boat shifted, and Ainslie rose. "I'll go see how we progress. See if ye can get something down her?" Ainslie turned and glanced back at her brother. She prayed Bree would wake soon.

****

Colin shifted again and set Bree beside him. He fumbled for the aleskin filled with broth. Colin settled himself next to Bree, preparing a mug of broth to feed her. He needed to get some fluids down her as he filled the cup halfway. He set the mug down and lifted Bree back into his lap, cradling her in his arms. Her condition worried him. Moving her was like carrying a rag doll. She was so weak.

He whispered in her ear. "Please, Bree, please drink this. Ye need it." He set the mug to her lips and poured some. The back of his hand rubbed her throat, trying to get her to swallow, but the broth only spilled out of her mouth. She coughed, choking on some. Colin set the mug down and wiped her mouth with a cloth, concern for her growing.

He rested his forehead against hers. "Please, Bree, ye have to try." She exhaled, and Colin opened his eyes.

She opened her eyes and stared at him. "Colin?"

He placed his palm on her cheek. "Bree, speak to me. Tell me ye are all right."

She blinked, closed her eyes, and rasped, "I can't. I'm ruined."

Colin kissed her and whispered back, "Ye are my love, and ye're not ruined. I love ye. I need ye. Evie and Ewan, they need ye."

She choked out, "My wee bugs."

Colin smiled. "Aye, will ye drink the broth for them?"

Bree nodded.

Colin grabbed the mug and tipped a little into her mouth, and she swallowed. He waited and then gave her more, which she drank. She sighed and fell asleep.

Colin settled her in his arms, and he sat against the ship's hull. He wasn't giving up and would not let her doubt win. He loved her, and she—him. She only needed reminding. She needed to remember her purpose in her life, the kids' lives, and mostly his.

The ship shifted as calls from the oarsmen carried through the air. He sat and told her repeatedly how much she meant to him and the kids, how her family needed and loved her. He knew if her will wasn't strong enough, then his will would be strong enough for them all. He would not lose her, not now, not ever.

Chapter 24

Rannick sat across from Dougal MacDougall in his study in Donielle castle in Oban, giving his report from the raid at Colonsay.

Dougal rested his elbows on his desk. "I am pleased with the outcome. Ye have saved Brielle, recovered the longship and yer wayward men. Colin killed the evil Tony Stiles and sent Balor to purgatory as the Fae had requested."

Rannick nodded as Dougal continued. "I debated a penalty for Ivor for not rescuing Brielle himself. However, Colin was firm. We forgive Ivor, as an evil Fae can dupe even the best warriors or leaders." Dougal grunted as Rannick tipped his mug and studied it silently.

Dougal sat staring at him for a moment, then spoke. "Ye are my best warrior and long-time friend. Ye should be happy and celebrate. Yet ye sit here silent and brooding." Dougal barked. "Out with it, Rannick. What else is on yer mind?"

Rannick took a breath and opened his mouth, only to sigh. It was hard to reconcile all that had happened.

He spoke softly, the thoughts still rattling around his mind. "When the Fae first came to ye to keep the magic Fae stones, it seemed like such a simple task. Protect a few stones from falling into the hands of evil. But now I've witnessed their power. I know of the battle between the good and evil Fae, and it's impossible to fathom."

He stared into the flames in the fireplace. "The stones. I worry about the stones and what is to come." He glanced at Dougal, who nodded to him to continue. "Ye haven't seen what they do or are capable of. Is this something we want to be taking on?"

Dougal sighed. "Aye, I have similar feelings. These Fae fables and how the stones have affected my kin, even from the future. What will they do to us, eh?"

Rannick nodded, glad his king saw it as easily as he had.

Dougal rose to refill his mug and offered the pitcher to Rannick, who allowed Dougal to fill his cup. Dougal set the pitcher down, sipped, and gazed into the flames. "Now that we know their power, we must be cautious with the stones. We will have to be canny in their hiding. Ye will need to ensure that very few know they exist and even fewer where we've hidden them."

Rannick nodded. "Ainslie mentioned a chapel in my settlement where they house them in the future. Possibly that is where we need to begin, a worship house. She can show me the location in the woods."

Dougal nodded. "Aye, that is good." He focused on Rannick and smiled. "Ainslie, ye like this woman?"

Rannick blushed and nodded. "Aye, very much. I have asked her brother for her hand in marriage, but he stated in their time, it is her decision."

Dougal laughed. "Well, what has she said, the warrior woman?"

Rannick shrugged. "She hasn't decided. A decision to stay in this time and forgo yer entire family and existence is much. She's asked for time to decide, so I wait."

Dougal grinned. "That is generous of ye. I hope she appreciates the gesture."

His king peered into his mug. "How fares Colin's wife? Has yer mother made any progress?"

Rannick shifted in his seat and stared at Dougal. "No. Two days ago, when we arrived, I thought she did better, but she has a fever. She weakens daily, and Mother and Ainslie work day and night to save her. I fear what is coming. Colin has not left her and refuses to release his hold on her, cradling her all the time."

Dougal frowned as he gazed into his mug. "Yer mother is the best healer in my kingdom. I have seen her work wonders. At times there are rumors she is a witch, for she can heal almost anyone. Give her time."

Rannick nodded. "Ainslie pushes Colin to take her back to their time. She claims the healers there are much more advanced. But Colin fears Bree will not survive the portal. He claims it's draining."

Dougal grumbled. "Aye, and if they stay here, it gives ye and Ainslie more time to make her choice. She would make a fine bride and a perfect companion to help ye build our settlement. Ye have made a good choice. Don't lose her, Rannick. The warrior woman is yer match for life."

Rannick grinned. "Aye, that she is."

****

Rannick stepped quietly into the bedroom. His mother was at the fireplace stirring something in a pot over the flames. Even after two days of continuous care for Brielle, she still looked composed. He marveled at how she could always keep herself together. There were only a few stains on her apron, and the rest of her looked crisp and clean. She even hummed to herself.

Ainslie was asleep in a chair by the fire. She had tied her hair back but still had a disheveled look. Her clothing sat at an angle on her body. A few stains were apparent on the front. She looked like she hadn't bathed in days, a fact he already knew.

He leaned against the door and let his gaze settle on the bed. Colin sat propped against the headboard with pillows and furs supporting him. The brooch with the stones winked from his shoulder since he refused to let them out of his possession. In his arms, laid between his legs, was Brielle. She looked flushed from the fever, yet her bruises had faded to yellow. She shifted and moaned, and Colin gathered her in his arms and whispered into her ear.

Rannick's heart went out to them. He glanced at Ainslie and knew he would lose his mind if he had to face this same predicament with her. He didn't know how Colin stopped himself from going insane.

His mother turned and spotted him. She put her finger to her lips and crossed the room.

They stepped out into the hall. "Mother, how do ye progress with Bree?"

Astrid shook her head as she partially closed the door, leaving it cracked. She spoke lowly. "I work to heal what I can, son. The fever should break tonight, and her bruising fades with the help of my salve. But…" she shook her head.

Rannick touched her shoulder. "What is it, Mother? What else ails Bree?"

Astrid glanced back into the room and muttered, "I don't wish to speak it aloud. That would call it to us, but I will remind ye of another. Do ye recall the young girl ye brought back from one of yer first raids, the one who wouldn't speak?"

Rannick thought back for a moment, and then his eyebrows shot up. "The one who the enemy abused. I recall being so angry I saw red for days. She was too young for sexual play, and men took her, anyway."

Astrid nodded. "Aye, that one." She glanced back into the room and sighed.

Rannick took his mother's shoulders. "Will Bree die as she did? Is that what ye fear?"

Astrid shook her head. "Yes, and no. I can heal the cuts, the bruises, a broken bone. I can cure fever and many other ailments. But it's her heart, Rannick. I cannot heal her heart."

Rannick ran his hands through his hair. "She has Colin, Mother. I see how he is with her. No man does this. It's an obsession. He never leaves her side and constantly speaks to her."

She nodded and glanced into the room. "Aye, he is a good man. A very loving and caring husband. Bree should be thankful for a man so attentive to a woman's needs."

Astrid eyed Rannick, tapping his arm. "Ye should heed what he does, for it fairly melts my heart. Imagine if yer father had done that when I was young." She fanned herself. "Ye'd have a herd of siblings for sure."

Rannick blushed. "Mother…"

Astrid took his hand in hers. "Rannick, I can heal the body, but I cannot heal the soul. I cannot save her if she has lost her will to live. Colin believes he has enough will for them both." She breathed heavily. "And maybe he does. But I fear it will not be enough."

His mother patted his hand. "Now, speak to me of

Ainslie. We have been so busy I have not had the chance to ask. Will I have the daughter and wife I so wish for?"

Rannick blushed. "I still work on that, Mother. It's her decision."

His mother patted his cheek. "Ye're a good man, Rannick. A great warrior and a caring soul. Fortune will smile upon ye soon."

Rannick glanced in the room and saw Ainslie shift in her chair, then settle back to sleep. "Have they spoken about going back to their time again?"

Astrid dropped his hands, putting her own on her hips. "Aye, they bicker about it often. Ainslie swears that future medicine would heal Bree in hours compared to what I do here, and damn if I don't want to go see this for myself." She sighed. "Colin claims the trip would kill Bree, and I fear just the trip to yer new village would do that." She peeked into the room. "Ainslie is nearly asleep on her feet. Why don't ye take her, feed her, and allow her to sleep? I'll come to get her if there's any change."

Rannick nodded.

Astrid opened the door, and Rannick followed her in.

Colin glanced up at their entrance.

Rannick approached the bed and bent, murmuring in Colin's ear, "I will take Ainslie away to eat and rest. My mother stays with ye to tend Bree."

Rannick saw the concern in Colin's eye. "Mother says Bree's fever should break tonight. This is good news."

Colin brushed his hand down Bree's cheek.

Rannick patted his arm and went to Ainslie, still

sleeping in the chair. He bent, and when he touched her, she jolted awake. "What, is there a change? Has Bree woken?"

Rannick shushed her, picking her up. "No, they sleep, and so shall ye."

She tried to wiggle out of his arms. "No, I wish to stay. I want to help."

From the bed came Colin's stern voice. "Ainslie, ye will go with Rannick now and sleep. Astrid will come to get ye if there is any change."

Ainslie huffed a protest, and Colin spoke again. "Rannick, take my sister away. She bends my ear too much about time travel, and I need my beauty sleep."

Rannick chuckled and took Ainslie from the room.

****

Colin bent, speaking lowly in Bree's ear, "My sister is gone. She had plagued me enough today. I now have my time with ye."

Astrid glanced at him as she settled into the chair Ainslie had vacated and closed her eyes for a nap. Colin would only need to call out if he needed her.

He whispered again, "Why don't we have a date night right now? Ye and me. I will tell ye about our first date. Do ye remember? We had dinner in the dining room at the castle. That was when I started calling ye Bree. Do ye remember?"

Bree sighed. "Yer wee Bree."

Colin kissed her cheek. "Aye, my love. Ye are my wee Bree." He took a cloth from the table and squeezed it, then bathed Bree's forehead with the cold water. He placed the material back in the bowl and kissed her again. She shifted and curled into Colin.

She whispered, "Chocolate kisses."

Colin smiled. This was the most she had said since he had pulled her from the island. It was progress, a sign she was here with him. He wasn't giving up. He had enough will for them both.

****

Rannick shouldered his way into his room in the castle. He had a full bath delivered, and the water sat steaming in the wooden tub, a luxury. Ainslie wavered after he set her on her feet. He stripped her clothing down her body.

She batted him, missing his hands in her drowsy state. "Rannick, ye insatiable man. I am too tired for sex. Leave me be."

Rannick continued to strip her. "I will not bed a corpse, Ainslie. I only bathe ye."

She yawned and nodded. "Mmm, bath sounds nice. Don't let me drown in the deep end."

Rannick chuckled as he picked her up, then deposited her in the tub. She gasped when she dipped into the water, then sighed as the warm water covered her.

Ainslie fell asleep in the tub, so he quickly bathed her. He left her hair for the morning, picked her up, and laid her on the bedding. He wrapped her in the drying cloth and folded furs over her body. He stripped himself and climbed into the bedding naked, pulling Ainslie into his embrace. She snored lightly, and he smiled. Food, he guessed, could wait till morning as well.

Rannick ran his hand up and down her arm, thinking about everything he wished to tell her.

He spoke aloud without even realizing it. "I wish to tell ye of my plans for the village. Of all the great things we will build there. The busy market, the

257

stronghold filled with trained fighters and a fleet of vessels for the Lord of the Isles, a fighting group like no other. The settlement of many families in a prosperous village. It will be the most modern settlement to date."

He exhaled. "I always wanted a wife, but now I find the idea of a woman to share this with, someone who can aid me in my goals, much more appealing. The things we could accomplish together, ye, the warrior woman, and me, the right arm of the Lord of the Isles. I grow excited with what we can build for the western isles."

He glanced at her, and she was still sound asleep. He kissed her head, and she snuggled into his embrace, breathing heavily in sleep.

Rannick bent and whispered in her ear, "Ainslie, please stay. Please choose to stay and build this new land with me. Having ye by my side would bring me great honor and joy. Please choose to be my wife." Ainslie shifted in her sleep and moaned.

She uttered, "Mmm, wife."

Rannick shifted to see her face, knowing what he had heard. He gazed at her face, slacked in sleep as a light snore escaped. He chuckled and gathered her in his arms. He at least had her dream of being his wife. It was a step in the right direction.

Chapter 25

Ainslie woke to the most beautiful smells of roasted meat and fresh bread. Her stomach loudly growled as she rolled over, her hand reaching for Rannick. In their short time together, she already searched her bed for him. He wasn't there, and she buried her head in the furs, not wanting to wake. She had had a wonderful dream.

She was in the village, the one Rannick built. They both strolled through the town center with many people calling out to them, wishing them well. The warriors greeted them with equal slaps on the back, and one asked her about a fighting technique. They treated her as a peer in their talk of raids and war. She and Rannick stopped to speak to some villagers, and she turned, and her belly was round with child. Rannick spread his hand over her stomach, rubbed it, and kissed her deeply.

Her stomach growled again, louder this time, and a chuckle came across the room. "If ye can rise, ye can break yer fast. I went to the trouble to bring ye food."

Ainslie peeked from the covers and saw Rannick fully dressed, seated near the fire with a food tray. He stuffed some meat into his mouth and chewed, moaning in satisfaction.

Ainslie snorted a laugh. "From the looks of it, ye brought the entire tray for yerself and will leave barely a breadcrumb for me."

Rannick spoke between bites, "Hurry and rise, woman. If ye want something, ye will have to eat it soon. We both missed a meal last night, and I am hungry."

She rose and gathered the drying cloth around her. She shuffled to him and dropped, sitting next to him. She sleepily took a piece of bread, broke it into pieces, and began nibbling on it. He offered her a cup of ale.

She frowned in the mug. "What I wouldn't give for a hot cup of tea."

Rannick dropped his meat and moved to Ainslie. "Tea is for when ye are ill. Ye are not ailing as well?"

Ainslie laughed. "No, we drink tea in the morning where I am from. It has caffeine and helps wake ye up."

Rannick glanced at her as he continued to eat. "Caffeine? What is it?"

Ainslie mumbled under her breath. "A gift from the gods that I could use right now."

He huffed, returning to his meal. "Well, ye should rest today. Yesterday was long and ye are tired."

Ainslie yawned. "I'll be fine soon. Has yer mother sent word of Bree?"

Rannick grunted. "Eat first. Then I tell ye the news."

She dropped her bread. "Tell me now."

Rannick picked up her bread and handed it to her. "Yer health first, then we speak of others."

She sipped her ale and ate her bread. When she finished, she reached for a fruit and began eating it. Rannick sat, allowing her silence to eat in peace. She chugged the rest of her ale, belched, and looked at Rannick, who chuckled.

She raised an eyebrow. "I have eaten. Now tell me,

how does Bree fare?"

"Her fever broke last night." Ainslie gasped and rose. Rannick placed a hand on her arm. "They bathe her now. Colin refuses to leave her side, even in the bath. My mother continues to compliment his skills as a husband to the point it makes me ill."

Ainslie grinned. "Men differ from where I come. He shows her how much he loves and cares for her."

Rannick grunted. "How does a man not appear weak when he fawns over a woman that way? What do people in yer time think?"

Ainslie nibbled a raspberry. The sweet taste was smooth in her mouth. "They don't appear weak, Rannick. It takes a powerful man to admit his emotions. That he has fears and concerns above his duty to ensure he protects the woman who serves him." She barked a laugh. "Actually, the idea of a woman serving a man just due to gender in our time is offensive. We are equals."

Rannick huffed. "Yer brother said the same. Men and women are equals."

They sat silent a moment, and Ainslie glared at Rannick, curious at what he and Colin discussed, maybe about her.

Rannick glanced at her, then back to the flames. What was he not telling her?

Ainslie took his hand. "What is it ye are not telling me? Is there still something wrong with Bree? What has yer mother said?"

He sighed. "She fears Bree has lost her will to live. That no matter what Colin does, she will still waste away as she won't eat for herself, care for herself, and live as a human should. She has seen it before and sees it in Bree now."

Ainslie frowned. "Well, I doubt Colin will allow her to do that. He can be a very formidable man. She should know this. They've been married for years."

Ainslie knew Colin and Bree had a more powerful love than most relationships. It's what brought Colin back to Bree from purgatory, the power of their love. After witnessing it, she wished for something as powerful but wasn't sure she'd ever find it. That was until she had the dream before coming back in time to the Vikings and Rannick.

He cleared his throat, interrupting her thoughts. "Did ye sleep well last night?"

Ainslie looked at him and smiled. "Aye, I slept deeply. And dreamed well."

She blushed, and Rannick gathered her in his arms. "Sweet dreams?" He kissed her.

Bam! Bam! Bam! The banging on the door had Ainslie jolting.

Rannick sighed. "Enter."

A guard entered and announced. "Yer king has summoned ye."

Rannick set her aside. "Rest today. I will return when I can."

The guard spoke as Rannick rose. "He has summoned ye both and Colin MacDougall."

****

Colin paced in front of Dougal's desk. His sister sat in the chair before Dougal's desk. Rannick leaned against the fireplace.

He slashed his hand down. "I am uncertain she is well enough to travel. Aye, I wish to return to our time, but I won't do it at the risk of her life."

Dougal nodded. "Astrid has assured me in two days Bree will be well enough to sail. As for the portal, that is yer decision to make." He glanced at Rannick, then at Ainslie. "Ye can spend time at Rannick's village. Ye say it is the future location of a castle."

Colin nodded. "Aye, but ye are right. The sooner we return, the better for all. The Stones need to return so the Fae can begin the process here in this time."

Colin laughed and ran his hand through his hair. "John MacArthur, my first, would love this. The circle is complete between times. One where we find the stones, so the Fae can give ye them in the past so that we will have them in the future. This time continuum is something he studied."

Dougal scratched his chin. "Time continuum? I shall have to explore this more."

Colin eyed Ainslie. "It is time, sister. We'll have to go soon. Two days then."

She glanced at Rannick, then to the floor, and breathed deeply. This wasn't good. Ainslie always knew her mind, decisions coming easily to her. But then again, she'd never had to contemplate her entire future in one choice.

Colin glanced at Dougal, then at Rannick, who stood staring at the floor. He wondered if Ainslie had even discussed the decision before her. From the muted response to his announcement, he'd have to assume the answer was no. She'd have to decide soon. He needed to get Bree healed, and they both needed to return to their time. The time had come; they needed to leave.

He sighed and turned to Dougal. "If I may take my leave, I wish to return to my wife."

Dougal waved him away, and Ainslie rose to

follow, both leaving the room.

****

Dougal peered at Rannick. "Ye will sail tomorrow. Astrid assures me Bree has healed in body. She will be fine. Ye must return the Stones to their time and ensure Colin and Bree return."

Rannick glanced up and bowed. "Aye, my king."

He strode to the door, and Dougal spoke. "Rannick…"

Rannick turned as Dougal grinned. "Invite me to yer wedding. I want it to be the first for the village."

Rannick grinned. "The bride has to agree first, Dougal."

Dougal toasted his mug. "Of that, I have no doubt."

Chapter 26

The following day, Colin carried Bree onto the longship as Dougal stood on the dock. Rannick used the same smaller ship to transport Bree and Colin with the tent setup, as Bree was still weak. He arranged for another captain, so he and Ainslie would sail on the largest and newest of his vessels. Astrid was there to oversee her patient's loading and bid them all farewell. Astrid followed Colin onto the ship.

She took the furs from him and spoke. "She is fine for now. Go bid goodbye to yer grandfather. Ye will not see him again. Dougal has enjoyed his time with his family from the future." Colin grunted but did as Astrid asked as she followed him.

Colin stepped off the ship, and Dougal hugged him as if they had been family forever. "I shall miss ye and wish ye well."

Astrid stepped off the ship and joined them as Rannick approached.

She hugged her son and spoke lowly, but Colin still overheard. "Ye will wait to hold yer wedding till we all can come?"

Rannick's eye caught him, and Colin raised an eyebrow.

Rannick patted his mother's back and whispered in her ear, "If she says aye, then there will be a wedding."

Colin huffed as Ainslie approached the group.

Ainslie went to Astrid, hugging her. "I shall miss ye."

Astrid patted her cheek. "I'm sure, dear."

Ainslie followed Rannick into the largest longship, and Colin went to the smallest, where Bree was. He glanced in, and she was curled up in a ball, safe. He stood next to the tent as everyone said the last goodbyes.

Rannick called Gunnar, who stood next to his mother. "Come on, Gunnar, time to go."

Gunnar put his arm around Astrid. "Fortune has smiled upon me, Rannick. Astrid has agreed to be my wife!"

Cheers went up from both ships, and Rannick grinned and waved. "Aye, good fortune to ye both!"

Colin settled in with Bree, holding her in his arms. "Bree, please. Astrid says ye have healed. Please speak to me." She rolled away, but Colin held her, convinced if he showed her what she meant to him, that she had so many reasons to live.

It took two days to reach Rannick's village. During this time, Bree's condition worsened again, as she stopped eating. Colin's worry for her increased the closer they came to where Rannick's new village prospered, and Dunstaffnage castle would stand. He grew frustrated with everyone around them and more so with Bree, but he would never allow her to see it. He treated her with the utmost care the entire trip, begging her to eat and live.

By the time they landed, he was beside himself. Erik, Rannick's first, permitted Colin to unload Bree before anyone else. He sat under a tree in the afternoon sunlight holding Bree in his arms as the men unloaded the ships. They were alone beside the dock's hustle, resting under a tree in the woods.

She shifted, and he glanced down at her. She blinked at him. She made the first real eye contact since he pulled her from the island over a week ago. He smiled as he brushed her hair away from her face, a gesture he repeated often. It reminded him of the day they had met. He had a cup of water ready and offered her some, which she drank.

He took the cup away. "Not too much. It might make ye ill."

She spoke, and her voice broke and cracked. "Colin?"

He breathed. "Please repeat my name, Bree. I want to hear it on yer lips."

She took a deep breath. "Please leave me here. I don't know if I can make it in the portal."

Colin shook his head. "I can't do that, Bree. Ye will go where I go, forever."

She sighed, and a tear escaped. "Take the stones and go. You can leave me here with Ainslie. I suspect she will stay."

Colin wiped her tear with his thumb. "Aye, I have known for some time Ainslie will stay, even if she won't admit it herself. She probably will wait till the portal is open to decide." He huffed. "Women. I think she does it to torture Rannick."

He stared at her and placed his hand on her cheek. It was so good to have her looking at him. He took and moment to enjoy it.

She glanced down as he breathed. "Bree, we will get through this. I will always love ye."

She shook her head, and Colin wanted to shake her

but knew he'd hurt her.

He growled and shifted her, so she had to look at him. "I love ye. Ye are my true love. Ye will come home to yer family. We love ye and need ye."

She choked on a sob. "Colin, I will die if you take me through the portal. I know it. I fear it."

He rested his forehead against hers. "Then I will bring ye back as ye brought me back. I love ye." He nestled her in his arms again and sat staring at the longships. Bree brushed her hand on the Brooch of Lorne. Colin's eye followed her hand. The stones did not glow but winked in the sunlight.

She whispered, "The Stone of Love doesn't glow." Colin snorted as Bree's tears flowed freely. "Your true love isn't nearby."

Colin grabbed her shoulders, making her cry out, not caring if he hurt her. She had to hear him and believe in him, in them.

"I love ye, and no damned stone will say otherwise. I used all the power to send Balor to hell. 'Tis why they don't glow. I love ye."

A footfall crunched the grass, and he glanced up to see Ainslie approaching. He tucked Bree into his arms as she huffed. It was good she argued with him; it meant she was alive.

When Ainslie arrived, she glanced from Bree to Colin. Colin glanced down. Bree was awake and alert. She even had a pout.

When he shifted his gaze to Ainslie, she grinned. "Rannick has a hut for ye both. He felt ye may want a day to rest before going through the portal."

Colin gathered Bree in his arms and stood. "Tonight. We go tonight, Ainslie. I have to get Bree and the stones back. No more delays. Ye have until this evening after sunset to decide if the twelfth century or the future is yer home."

He shifted Bree roughly in his arms, causing Bree to cry out. "Show me the hut. I am hungry and tired."

****

Already? Ainslie glanced at the sky. Dusk was near. As tears gathered in her eyes, she sought Rannick. Ainslie found him overseeing the distribution and storage of supplies. He smiled, and she waved him aside.

He frowned as he approached her. "What is it, Ainslie? Is Bree okay?"

Ainslie nodded. "Aye, she is awake. I suspect she and Colin argue."

Rannick studied her. "This is good news."

Ainslie choked a sob and covered her mouth with her hand as tears threatened to spill over. "No, it is not. He announced he would go through the portal tonight. I have until sunset to decide."

Rannick glanced at the setting sun and then back at Ainslie. He grabbed her hands and moved them farther away from the men working.

He turned and took her hands in his. "Ainslie, ye know how I feel." He bent and kissed her hard. She returned the kiss in full measure. Rannick huffed as he gazed into her eyes.

She sobbed again, tears falling. "I don't know, Rannick. 'Tis so hard. I fit here and there."

He gathered her in his arms and held her tight.

She hiccupped. "I had a dream, ye know. A dream of us together here."

Rannick kissed her again. "Then make yer dream

come true. I told ye I would not ask again, but stay with me, please. I beg ye."

Ainslie shook her head, but Rannick kept speaking. "Ainslie, don't stay because ye love the Viking way of life. Don't stay because ye are a great warrior. Don't stay because this is the time ye belong. Stay because I ask it." He kissed her again. "Stay because I love ye. Stay and be my wife. Stay and be my warrior. Ainslie, stay and be my equal."

A loud clearing of a throat interrupted them, and they both turned to see Colin standing there.

"It is almost sunset. Rannick, I need ye to clear the woods, but I want ye to stay with us to see us through. No one else can witness the portal, and I need ye to know where it is and how it works. Ye may need it. I must search for it since it's hidden in this time.

Rannick nodded, and Ainslie stepped out of his embrace.

Colin approached Ainslie. "Bree is sitting by a tree, just over there. Please sit with her while I find the portal." He had Bree's book of *Poems and Sonnets* in his hand. Rannick shouted orders to clear the woods. Ainslie wiped her tears and turned to move away.

Colin grabbed her hand. "Ye should stay, Ainslie. Ye have found true love." He glanced back at Rannick, then at Ainslie. "He's a good man. I know ye would be happy."

Ainslie sobbed. "But what of ye, the kids, and our family?"

Colin embraced and held her, reminding her of her da, and her tears started anew as he spoke. "I told ye before. I love ye. Whatever ye decide is fine with me. I feel ye belong here, Ainslie, and here is where ye should stay." He released her and wiped her tears with his hand. "Even if it tears my heart out, I will miss ye so. But I want my wee warrior to be happy."

Ainslie nodded, and he patted her back. "Go to Bree. I'll come to get her when I am ready to go."

Ainslie moved toward Bree, who sat staring at the woods. She sat next to Bree and took her hand in hers. Bree patted her hand. Ainslie was a little surprised. It was the first interaction they had had since they were on the island.

Bree spoke, her voice cracked but stronger. "You should stay. You belong here, Ainslie."

Bree sighed. "I asked to stay."

Ainslie stared at her. "What the hell for?"

Bree gazed out at the woods. "I won't make it in the portal. I have seen it. Colin won't listen. Balor showed me I won't live."

Ainslie huffed a laugh. "Ye believe what that insane bastard has told ye?" Ainslie huffed a hard sigh once, then again. What the hell?

She turned on Bree and spoke firmly. "We sat on that cold damned rock together, and I will not allow ye to toss our survival away, Bree. Yer wee bugs need ye, and my brother needs ye because I won't be there. I love Rannick, and I am staying. Ye have to go back and live for Colin. I need ye there caring for my brother, yer true love. So, I know he'll be okay. That way, it will be fine that I can be here with mine." She took Bree's hands in hers. "I will make ye a promise. Ye make it back, and I will stay here and be happy, damn it."

Bree patted her arm. "If it makes you happy, Ainslie, you should stay here."

Ainslie huffed. "Well, that isn't a promise, but I'll

take it." She hugged Bree tightly. "I will miss ye, sister."

Bree exhaled. "I as well, Ainslie."

She squeezed Bree twice more. "That's for the wee bugs."

They sat there together, staring at Loch Etive. The last rays of sunlight faded, and darkness closed in quickly. Now darker, it took more work to make out Colin and Rannick searching the woods.

Soon, wind blew through the woods, swirling and gaining power. Colin had found the portal. A bright white light flashed, then shone through the woods.

Ainslie turned to Bree. "That's yer ride."

Colin and Rannick approached, and Colin stepped before them. "It's time. We must hurry. I don't know how long the portal will stay open."

Ainslie rose, and Colin bent and scooped up Bree into his arms. The three went together toward the light.

****

As the love of his life walked to the light, Rannick's heart broke. All he wanted was to take Ainslie into his arms and hold her forever.

She walked toward the portal. She would leave him forever.

He took a step toward them. "Ainslie!"

A ringing rose in his ears, and a painful pressure built in his head. He took a step back, and the tension and sound dissipated.

Ainslie stopped and turned at his call. She hugged Colin and brushed her hand on Bree's cheek. Colin kissed her cheek, said something to her, and nodded toward Rannick. She spoke to Colin and Bree, then turned to face Rannick.

His heart was in his throat. Not sure if Ainslie would say goodbye or come toward him, he stood still.

She smiled as tears ran down her cheeks. She took one step and then another. Before Rannick knew it, she ran into his arms. He twirled her and roared in joy. She cried out, sobbing.

They both settled and waved to Colin, who nodded at them, turned, and entered the light, carrying Bree. He rotated back from the other side, and tears streamed down Colin's face. He grinned at them and nodded once more. The light enclosed upon itself and disappeared. Ainslie cried out, stepping forward as Rannick clung to her.

He gazed at her as he held her. "Ye stayed. Ye stayed here with me."

Ainslie nodded between sobs. "Colin told me this was where I was meant to be and that I belonged here with ye. He said to visit him in his dreams, but I needed to be with my true love."

He cupped her face in both hands and kissed her.

Rannick ended the kiss and caressed her face. "Come, my warrior woman, my Viking queen, let me show ye yer new home."

Chapter 27

The other side of the portal, Chapel in the Woods, present-day

Colin lowered Bree to the chapel floor.

"Bree, Bree, we made it. We are finally home." They were safe. They'd finally made it back to the twenty-first century. It seemed like forever since he had been here, but that didn't matter. He had saved Bree, and Ainslie was happy with her true love.

Bree lay unmoving. Colin shook her shoulders. Maybe she had passed out from the trip through the portal. She had spoken with Ainslie, wishing her well in the twelfth century and promising to hug and kiss Evie and Ewan.

He shook her again. "Bree." Still no response. He placed his hand under her nose, and no puff of air came. He sobbed and bent to her chest, trying to hear a heartbeat—nothing. It was as if something suspended her in time. He cried out and shook her hard, hoping to jolt her awake. She was like a rag doll in his arms.

He screamed. "John!" Being in the Chapel in the Woods, no one at the castle heard him.

He gathered her in his arms, rose, and went to the chapel door, knowing he could run to the castle in minutes. An ambulance would take over thirty. Could a helicopter land in the yard? He needed to get to the castle to call emergency crews and save his wee Bree.

Thoughts ran through his mind so quickly that he didn't realize someone stood at the chapel door until he almost ran into them. Colin came up short, almost falling backward. He stopped so fast he had to adjust Bree in his arms.

His Fae, Brigid, stood at the door.

He growled. "Brigid."

She appeared to him full-sized and not the sprite he was used to seeing. She had no wings, but her ears still pointed at the ends. She seemed more like a grown woman than the playful, short, floating imp she had always appeared as. She wore long, flowing white hair and a shimmery white gown.

Colin nearly yelled when he next spoke. "Out of my way, ye goon. I have to save Bree."

Brigid hmphed. "Modern medicine cannot save her, Colin. She is not ill, and she is not dead." Colin's eyes shot to Brigid, whose sober expression returned his.

He blinked. In all these years, it was the first time Brigid had ever looked at him that way, seriously. His gaze shot to Bree in his arms. He examined her closer now that he had a moment without panic. Her color was good. Now that he stopped noticing, her body was warm beside his. She seemed—asleep.

Brigid brushed her hand along Bree's head and shivered. "It's black magic, Colin. It's evil Fae magic."

Colin choked a sob and turned with Bree still in his arms. Brigid's voice echoed in his head. *"This cannot be undone. Colin, the evil Fae, have cast their spell."*

It was what Brigid had said to him when she referred to the evil spell cast upon his parents when they went to find The Stone of Love. Evil spells cannot be undone. Bree was truly lost to him.

He moved to the center of the chapel and slowly kneeled on the floor, holding his true love. He cradled her to his chest as he sobbed into her neck. He still smelled her scent, roses coming from her warm body.

Brigid kneeled across from him.

He continued to hold Bree as he spoke. "Why are ye here, Brigid? Have ye come to tease me, mock me in my worst time? A poem to tell me how ye cannot save my true love like ye couldn't save my parents because it's evil magic. The kind ye cannot change or reverse?"

He gazed at Bree and brushed her hair off her face. He caressed her face and kissed her lips. Then he sat staring at her, for he could never let her go.

Brigid took a deep breath and spoke in a tone Colin had never heard from her—soft, sweet, and forlorn. "Colin, I am yer Fae. I am yer family's Fae. Ye are family to me as I am family to ye." She shrugged. "It seems like I am all fun and games because I love life and like to make some of the harder times lighter."

She reached out and touched his hand. "Today is not a day for fun and games. Ye are right."

She took her hand away when he growled but continued speaking. "This is black magic. Magic from Balor." She sighed. "No, I cannot undo this magic. I do not have this kind of power." She huffed a laugh. "I don't even think my da, Dagda, has this power. Black magic is twisted and evil, and for a Fae to have the power to undo it, they must be evil as well. I am not evil, Colin." She smirked. "I may be devious from time to time, but evil is not in me."

Colin snapped his face to hers and barked, "Then why are ye here? Why come to me if there is nothing ye can do but sit there and watch her die?"

Brigid touched Bree again. "She is not dying, Colin. It's a spell. She's suspended in time."

Brigid closed her eyes and placed her hand on Bree's head. "Balor told her she would die if ye brought her through the portal. 'Tis part of the reason she lost the will to live. That and her fear of what ye would think after all that has happened."

Colin yelled, "I don't give a damn what has happened! She is mine, my true love." He gathered her closer to his chest and spoke softly. "I love her. She loves me. She only needs to remember."

Brigid smiled at him, and he gaped at her, thinking she was insane for smiling at a time like this.

Her voice became brighter. "That is what I am counting on, Colin, yer memories. Yers and hers. That is what will bring her back."

Colin gasped. "Is it really so simple?"

Brigid did laugh this time, but not the tinkling laugh he usually heard from her. This was a deep, throaty laugh of a woman. "Yes and no."

She glanced around the chapel, took his hand, and placed it on Bree's heart. Brigid held it firmly with one hand. Colin's other hand, she put over his heart and held it.

She stared into Colin's eyes and smirked. "Colin, they will probably punish me. Showing ye a heart meld breaks a Fae law."

Her expression softened as she gazed at Bree. "She gave herself for ye, her life for yers. She stayed awake to ensure ye had The Stone of Lust to power the brooch and so the good Fae would have it in the end."

Brigid glanced at Colin. "We never knew The

Stone of Lust was with Balor. It could have proven very dangerous for both our realms if it had remained in his possession. Bree saved both our worlds, again."

Brigid shrugged. "I think I can justify bending a rule, connecting yer hearts to save one human who has given so much."

Colin exhaled; Brigid would help, help save his true love.

Brigid cleared her throat. "Do me a favor, Colin…"

He nodded. "Anything."

Brigid frowned. "Just in case my da sends me away as punishment. Try not to find any more stones for a while. I may not come to yer rescue till I'm released."

Colin nodded. "Aye, sprite."

Brigid spoke lowly. "Concentrate on all the memories ye have of Bree. All the happy ones, even the sad ones."

Colin bent his head and rested it on Bree's forehead. Brigid kept her hand on Bree's heart and a hand on Colin's over his heart.

Colin thought of the day he met Bree in the study. When the sunlight shone through the window, making a halo around her head. He remembered wanting so desperately to touch her, but he held back.

Brigid bent her head. His arms glowed white, creating a beacon of light from his heart to Bree's. He recalled the night of the storm in the study and how he held her while she jumped at each clap of thunder. He remembered when she first came through the portal to the eighteenth century, and he was so concerned for her, for them.

Brigid shifted her hand slightly on Colin's chest, and a light pulse flowed between Colin and Bree. Colin thought of her in the eighteenth century, all the things they did flashing through his memory faster. Images flipping like a movie. He had a clear view of her in the chapel in the eighteenth century of their wedding. She was so beautiful. He saw her holding their babies, crying at their births.

The pulsing light Brigid held between them moved faster and became brighter.

Bree was there in his mind, and he gasped. She shifted in his arms as he held her, and he hoped she was awake.

He shifted and stared into her closed eyes. A light flashed from Brigid's arms. A red light grew from his periphery, and he turned his head. The Stone of Love glowed bright red from the brooch. He glanced back at his wee Bree and willed her to open her eyes. She breathed now. The light in Brigid's arms faded, and she removed her hands, sitting back on the chapel floor. The light faded from his arms as The Stone of Love's red glow grew.

Colin caressed Bree's face and whispered, "Bree, come back to me. Please, Bree, come back." He bent and kissed her on the lips.

When he lifted his mouth, she sighed. "Colin." Bree opened her eyes and gazed into his. Her brow scrunched, and she looked at the Brooch of Lorne on Colin's shoulder. He followed her eyes. It still glowed bright red.

She gasped. "The Stone of Love. It glows."

Colin kissed her forehead. "Aye, it glows for my true love."

Bree stared at him and tried moving in his embrace. Colin held her closely.

She looked around. "We are in the Chapel on the Woods."

Colin chuckled. "Aye, that we are."

She glanced around again and tilted her head and spoke. "Brigid?"

Brigid nodded.

Bree looked back at Colin. "Last time I saw her, she was a wee sprite, a midget. This is a grown woman."

Colin laughed. "Aye, that she is."

Dagda's deep voice came from the front of the chapel. "Brigid."

Brigid jumped and stood next to Colin, appearing like Evie after getting caught doing something naughty. "Aye, Da?"

Dagda stood at the front in his white suit with white-toned skin, long flowing white hair, and eyes so white they glowed. He smiled at Colin as he approached the group.

He stopped, gazing down at Colin and Bree as he spoke. "Brigid, ye have done enough for today. Come along. Ye have to answer to the Fae Council now."

Brigid peeked at Colin as she went by. "Remember what I said? I may be gone for a while."

Her father huffed as he waved her ahead of him. He stared at Colin, then at the Brooch of Lorne. Colin's gaze followed his. The Stone of Love stopped glowing.

Dagda sighed. "Ye will put those back where they go when ye finish playing with my stones?"

Colin nodded. "Aye, I will."

Dagda shifted his focus to Bree. "Heal well, Bree. All the Fae thank ye."

Dagda and Brigid moved to the front as they faded

from sight.

Colin shivered. "I hate that when they do that. Gives me the willies."

Bree tried to sit up in Colin's arms but moaned.

Colin growled. "The least they could have done was fully heal ye." Colin gathered her in his arms and rose.

Bree placed her hand on his chest. "Wait. We are in the twenty-first century, right? The chapel looks like the one in the future. We are really back home?"

Colin stood with Bree in his arms and went to a pew, sitting with her on his lap. He bent to kiss her on the lips, and she turned away.

Colin shifted her in his arms, so she had to look at his face. "What's the matter?"

She groaned. "I am ruined."

Colin growled, "Ye aren't ruined, just bruised. Ye will heal."

A tear escaped and trailed down Bree's cheek as she glanced away again.

Colin brushed it with his thumb. "I love ye. As long as it takes for ye to heal, I will wait. I will be here for ye. The kids will be here for ye. Hell, the world will be here for ye." He tilted her face to his and kissed her lightly on the lips. He brushed them again, and she sighed.

She sat back and stared at Colin. "How am I not dead?"

Colin growled. "Balor lied. Ye should know not to trust an evil Fae. It was only a spell."

Bree blinked at Colin and gasped. "You brought me back. Like I brought you back."

Colin nodded. "Aye, and I would do it time and

time again. But ye won't be needing to be brought back anymore."

Bree smiled. "Not anymore?"

Colin kissed her again, for he could not kiss his love enough. "No, ye will stay here with me forever."

Bree breathed. "Forever sounds nice."

Chapter 28

The following day, Dunstaffnage Castle

The bed wobbled and shifted, and Bree jolted a little. She didn't want to open her eyes. The sunlight was bright, and her body was still sore. She figured Colin had risen, and she sighed, then thought of drifting back into the bliss of slumber on the modern mattress with the fluffy pillows inside a heated castle. The bed wobbled again, and whispers of young children filled the room. She smiled. They were her young children. God, she missed them so, but this was a game they played on weekend mornings.

Evie spoke first. "Shh, ye will wake her. Da said not to wake her."

Ewan huffed just like his da. "She usually wakes before us. I want to see her."

Evie shifted. She was on her left. "Look. She looks like a sleeping princess."

Ewan snorted. "She looks like a bruised peach. Her face is all brown and yellow."

Evie shushed him. "That's not nice, Ewan. Da said she was treated roughly by the bad man. We have to let her heal."

Evie shifted again, but Ewan spoke next. "Where did ye get those?"

****

Colin approached from the hallway and peeked

into the room. The twins were on the bed on either side of Bree. He wanted to walk in and scold them for waking her, but he stared and noticed Bree lay still with her eyes closed. He was concerned, then saw Bree take a deep breath, and her eye lids fluttered. So, she was awake, listening to the kids. He waited to see what would happen next, enjoying his family back together. Evie had something in her hands. He stood hidden by the door from their view.

Evie took a stone in each hand and clapped them together, the clap sounding loud in the room. Evie showed her brother the one rock in her right hand.

Ewan gasped. "Evie. Ye made two stones one."

Evie giggled. "Watch, Ewan. 'Tis a new trick." She blew on the stone and pulled them apart as two halves of one stone, the same as where they started.

Ewan clapped, then stopped.

Colin stood rooted. He could not believe his eyes. Evie had merged two white Iona stones into one, then pulled them apart again.

Ewan sat forward. "Wait, isn't that Da's stone? The one he always carries in his pocket?"

Evie held up one stone. "Aye, I swiped it off his dresser."

Ewan tilted his head. "Then what is the other stone, Evie? The one ye made whole, then pulled apart?"

Evie held up the other stone in her other hand. "It's Mother's stone. Brigid gave it to me to give to her."

Bree gasped, sat up in bed. She cried out, hunching in pain.

Colin barged into the room and barked at the twins, "Evie, Ewan, what goes on here?"

Both kids jumped at their father's stern voice.

Bree spoke softly. "Colin, not so gruff."

She slowly sat up, and Colin rushed to help her and fluffed the pillows behind her. He sat beside her on the bed and wrapped an arm around her. She put her arms out for the kids to come to her, and they cuddled next to her on each side, something they had done since they were infants. Bree wrapped her arms around her children, shifting at the discomfort, but savoring the feel of them in her arms again.

Evie sniffed, and Bree patted her arm. "Da didn't mean to be so fierce. He's just concerned about me. Now dry your tears and show me what you have." She bent and brushed a kiss on Evie's forehead.

Evie held up both stones, one in each hand.

Bree gasped as Evie spoke. "Brigid came to me in a dream."

Colin growled, and Bree glanced at him and shook her head.

Evie continued, oblivious to the exchange between her parents. "She said the bad man tossed Mother's stone in the ocean, and Brigid had to make sure Ma got her stone back. She said it was impo...impo..."

Colin spoke, knowing the kids learned new words. "Important."

Evie sighed. "Aye, Da."

As she spoke, Evie held up each stone and handed each one to her parents. "This one is Da's, and this one..."

She placed the second one in Bree's hand and closed her little hand around it. "It's Ma's. I made a promise, and I kept it."

Bree held her stone as a tear escaped.

Colin shifted and reached for Bree's stone. "Let me

see yer stone, Bree."

He held them up in the sunlight above them, so all four people saw. Each half was the perfect match for the other, making the shape of the heart.

He and Bree gasped together; they saw it at the same time. The stones, once one, now two identical halves, were in each of his hands. The same stones his parents had shared. The same they had made their wedding vows over. Bree gazed up at Colin, and he at her. He kissed her and handed hers back.

Ewan groaned as they kissed. "Ewww."

Colin laughed. "Ye should be so lucky. Ye have parents that are in love."

Evie nodded.

Bree looked at her stone. "Evie, where did you learn the trick with the stones?"

Evie sat up in her mom's embrace, elbowing her side as Bree winced. "Brigid taught it to me. She said I would need that trick one day."

Colin and Bree exchanged grimaces, but Bree shook her head.

She spoke brightly to their kids. "Well, probably not for some time. For now, I am glad to have my wee bugs with me where I can hold ye and love ye."

Ewan stared at his mother. "Da said Auntie Ainslie had to stay. She had to stay with her true love."

Bree smiled. "Yes, that is true, but she gave me something to give each of you."

Bree bent and kissed each child on the head. "For each of you from Ainslie. She said to watch for her in your dreams."

Ewan's chin wobbled. "Will we ever see her again?"

Colin spoke wanting to alleviate their fears. "Aye, someday."

The four sat together for a short time, chatting and hugging. Colin sat with his family, enjoying the warmth that spread through his heart. The love they shared and the joy of seeing them together again. Eventually, the kids got hungry and looked for Mrs. Abernathy and lunch.

Colin gathered Bree in his arms and held her.

He kissed her head and spoke. "How do ye feel?"

Bree grimaced. "Like a used punching bag." Colin grinned. If she had her humor back, she would be on the mend.

"The family's private doctor has come by to see ye. I want him to see ye now."

"Dr. Reid? I like him." Bree groaned. "The modern world returns. Will the authorities grill me endlessly?"

Colin kissed her head again and hugged her. "The doctor has told them it is too early to be bothering ye after yer ordeal. I have given a sufficient statement that will hold for now. We will get our story straight before they question ye."

He sighed. "I cannot say the same for yer brother. He has harassed John endlessly."

Bree turned. "Dom is here?"

Colin nodded. "Aye, but ye will speak with no one till ye are ready."

Bree hugged Colin. "Shower, doctor, then I can have lunch with my brother."

Colin held her and snorted. "Are ye sure ye are up to the interrogation from Dominic? It will probably be worse than the authorities. His grilling has helped us flesh out our story for the authorities."

Bree laughed. "It will be fine."

****

Later, Bree and Dominic sat in the kitchen alone. Bree nibbled on a sandwich while Dominic ate two. The rest of the household had agreed to leave them be, and Mrs. A took the twins down to the priory to see Marie and Doug.

Bree sighed. "So, you know about the stones now?"

Dominic nodded. "Not something I'd imagine in a million years when you got yourself kidnapped. But yes, I know."

She tapped his arm. "You can't speak of this. It must remain a secret."

Dominic nodded. He took her hands in his and stared at them. He glanced at Bree. "Bree, I feel awful about the kidnapping. I am sorry."

Bree shook her head. "It's not your fault. It's no one's fault."

He huffed. "I'm better than that."

Bree smirked. "Dom, trust me, no one is better than an evil Fae." Dominic started to speak, but Bree cut him off. "Not even my special-ops military adrenaline-junkie brother can beat them." Dominic nodded and held her hands.

He looked out the window. "Bree, I haven't been the best of brothers." Bree patted his hand. She in turn started to speak, but he stopped her with his hand. "No, I mean it. I should have been there for you. For you and Mom."

Bree exhaled. "After she died, you were there."

Dominic pulled his hands away and ran them over his wavy brown hair, which always seemed to fall into place perfectly. "I want to be there more, here more." He sighed. "I want to be a better brother. I want to be a better uncle for the twins." He gazed at Bree. "We almost lost you, Bree. I couldn't live with that. I should have been there for you."

Bree took his hands in hers. "Well, the important thing is you are here now."

Dominic smiled. "Yes, I'll have to go back to the base soon. But I'll make more trips, and when you are in the States, we'll spend time together."

Bree grinned. "I'd like that."

****

While Bree and Dominic had lunch, Colin sat in the chapel on the front pew, the Brooch of Lorne in his hand. He'd almost lost Bree. He tilted his head back and sniffed, trying to stay composed.

A footfall shifted behind him, but he didn't turn. He had a feeling who would show up. He set the brooch down and reached next to him for the bottle of whisky and two glasses. He uncorked the bottle, poured a healthy measure into one glass, and held it into the aisle without looking.

The man took it, and a long, noisy sip sounded in the chapel. He swished it in his mouth, swallowed, and smacked his lips. Dagda sat next to him on the pew, the Brooch of Lorne between them.

"Stop feeling so damned sorry for yerself. Bree's back and safe."

Colin moaned. "At what cost? What is the cost to Bree and all she has been through?" He sighed. "I don't even know if I have my wife back or just a shell of the woman she once was."

Dagda sipped his whisky again and exhaled. "She

will be the same woman but different. She cannot go through what she did without changing."

Colin took a deep breath and released it. "I know."

He glanced at Dagda. "What of Balor? Is he truly gone?"

Dagda held his cup out, and Colin filled it as Dagda spoke. "Not gone. Imprisoned." At Colin's raised eyebrow, Dagda grunted. "We cannot kill each other."

Colin grumbled. "Can I do the honors? And how will ye know ye can keep him? He got out before."

Dagda sipped his whisky again and nodded. "Aye, but this time we have him someplace different." Colin opened his mouth, but Dagda spoke. "Ye don't want to know, so don't ask."

Colin sipped his whisky. "What happened to Brigid?"

Dagda snorted a laugh. "She should be a solicitor, not a Fae princess. I think ye've rubbed off on her. She made such an exemplary case for her actions the council released her. She's free of all guilt."

Colin sat back and looked at Dagda. "Really? Where is she now?"

Dagda chuckled. "Ye'll like this." Dagda grinned. "Helping the dragons."

Colin coughed on his whisky. "That's right; she showed me. Ye have dragons in the Fae realm."

Dagda nodded. "Aye, really nice ones, beautiful creatures. But the ones she visits, these live among ye, in the human realm."

Colin took a long sip of whisky. "Dragons, here."

Dagda grunted. "Balor's sons, of all things. They are half human, half dragon. Shifters. It's a long story.

Brigid went to help."

Dagda held his glass out for another refill, and Colin lifted an eyebrow.

Dagda belched. "I have to finish up. Hit me one last time. No whisky in our realm. It's blue crap and not as good."

Colin laughed. "I find that hard to believe."

Dagda chuckled. "Well, it has much higher potency on humans than a Fae." Dagda drank half his glass and set it on the pew. He stood and grabbed the Brooch of Lorne. He tossed it once, then twice, catching it. The third time, it stuck in the air and floated momentarily. A bright light burst from the brooch, blinding Colin. Dagda stood unflinching. The brooch floated down, empty of its stones, into Dagda's hand.

He handed it to Colin. "For Bree's tour. It's old, a historical piece. She'd like that."

Colin held it and smiled. "Aye, she would."

Dagda grabbed his glass, chugged the rest of his whisky, and set the glass down.

He turned to go but stopped. "Almost forgot to mention the twins."

Colin's head snapped up. "My bugs, what about them?"

"Brigid blessed them without permission. They have…a few Fae powers. Might want to keep an eye out for that."

Colin yelled. "She what?"

When he turned, the chapel was empty.

Chapter 29

"And here's the dessert." Bree set the small plates with mini chocolate lava cake topped with powdered sugar and one raspberry, her favorite dessert. He, Marie, and John were in the dining room at Dunstaffnage. A fire burned brightly in the fireplace, casting a romantic glow about the formal room. The family kept a vast dining table that occupied most of the room. The four sat at the smaller table before the fireplace for more intimate dinners. Doug and the twins watched a movie together. Colin snorted. Usually, they didn't allow the television to babysit, but tonight was special, so they planned a slumber party with popcorn, soda drinks, and a movie. He hoped they fell asleep watching the movie.

Bree sat eating her cake in small spoonsful, as she always had. She always tried to make her favorite dessert last longer. It was over a week since their return from the twelfth century, and he watched over her constantly, working remotely for the law firm from the castle. Soon, he would have to return, but another few days at Dunstaffnage wouldn't hurt. He'd had a light caseload since her ordeal. Colin had not pressured her about intimacy, which drove him insane. He loved her now more than ever and promised to take things at her pace from the beginning, and he kept his word.

Colin recalled his conversation with the family's

private doctor, Dr. Reid. Colin met with him the day after they'd arrived back in the twenty-first century after his examination of Bree. Dr. Reid had been with the family for years, mainly tending to bumps and bruises. He was called to the castle occasionally as one of the few doctors still willing to make house calls. Colin figured it was because he had cared for three generations of MacDougalls.

"She's going to be fine, Colin. The sword wound closed nicely and will heal, while rough in its closure. I've offered a referral for a plastic surgeon to remove the scar. She refused…"

Colin spoke as he stared out the window. "She'll have the scar removed. I'll speak to her about it."

Dr. Reid cleared his throat. "I did a pelvic exam. She's fine and mentioned she's had her…"

Colin growled. "I know. I cared for her myself this last week before we could return to the mainland."

Dr. Reid took a deep breath. "I've left her with the prescriptions, but she refused the antidepressants and refused to accept my recommendation for a psychiatrist. I-I think under the circumstances, she should see someone."

Colin glanced over his shoulder. It was the first time he had ever seen the man concerned. His usual bedside manner was one of calm control, with a dose of humor on the side. Even when Colin broke his arm, Dr. Reid had cracked a joke about it, calling the incident "humerus" even though the broken bones were lower, being the radius and ulna.

The doctor sat in the chair before the desk, fidgeting.

Colin returned to his desk and sat. "I'll not force

her to speak about what she's been through. She will come around in her own time."

Dr. Reid rubbed his neck. "Colin, I've answered many calls to yer family over the years. I've seen some really...unique incidents." He smiled at the memory. "A wild boar gored your father during a hunting accident. I had never seen an injury like it, and I doubt I will again." He sighed. "Colin, what Brielle has been through is no mere injury. It will take time for her to recover. Some women, they never do." He fidgeted again. "Colin, she may never want to be intimate again. Ye must prepare yerself for that."

Colin stared at Dr. Reid, a trusted family friend. The man had bandaged more of his mishaps than his own ma.

"I am prepared for whatever Bree needs."

The doctor nodded. "Colin, ye have been the backbone of this family since yer father passed. I know you will do what is best."

Dr. Reid rose, and Colin moved around the desk. He shook Colin's hand. "Call if ye need anything else, Colin. I'll stop by anytime."

John cleared his throat, bringing Colin out of his memory. John and Marie exchanged a glance. Colin had a feeling of what they may announce. He wasn't a stupid man, far from it. Marie hadn't had a drop of alcohol since he and Bree returned, and she and John liked their drink. He hoped Bree would take the news well. Having a new baby around could go either way. She could be happy, or it could send her into a downward spiral after her ordeal. He hoped she would find the news joyful. Marie was her friend, after all.

Marie giggled. "We had wanted to wait to tell ye

our news, but it seems it won't wait."

Marie and John held hands and smiled widely at Colin and Bree. "We are expecting."

Bree gasped and jumped up, hugging Marie. "Oh, I had a feeling. I don't remember you passing up a glass of wine. The last time you did, you were expecting Doug."

Happy Bree took the news well, Colin clapped John on the back. "Congrats to ye both."

Marie glimpsed at Bree as she sat. "I am glad ye are happy." Marie glanced at John, who nodded. "Ye know, before ye…recently traveled in time—" Bree and Colin exchanged a glance as Marie continued. "—well, Evie said the strangest thing. She told me Brigid told her we'd have another child, a daughter. And she would be her best friend."

Bree patted Marie's hand. "Yes, well. Maybe there is something to it, and maybe not. It turns out Dagda told Colin that Brigid blessed the twins without the Fae's permission. Dagda said they may have a gift or two from the Fae."

Colin snorted. "So, if ye see anything, let us know. We need to monitor it. Don't want the kids getting into some mischief they can't handle."

Marie and John exchanged a glance. "Of course, we'll help any way we can."

Colin spoke as they resumed dessert. "Have ye heard from Morrigan?"

John shook his head.

Colin nodded. "Good." No more Fae activity for a while would be a godsend. Bree needed time to heal, and they needed a chance to get back into the routine of life.

They continued to eat their dessert as the women chatted about the baby.

Bree sat and ate her cake, smiling. She glanced at him, and he took a bite, smiling over his spoon at her. He thought of the first dinner they had together. The one where they shared the same dessert as tonight, offering each other bites between kisses. She called it chocolate kisses, and ever since she had insisted that they kiss every time she ate chocolate. To his knowledge, tonight was the first time she had eaten chocolate since her return.

When she saw Colin look over his dessert spoon, Bree froze. Her spoon was halfway to her mouth. She glanced down as she set her spoon down.

Colin sighed.

Marie smiled and took a bite of her cake while John studied his. They said nothing as if they hadn't noticed anything out of the ordinary—the rest of the dessert they spent in silence.

Bree rose to take the plates, and John beat her to it. "I'll get those." He stood and gathered all the dishes and took them to the kitchen.

Marie rose as well. "John and I will look after the twins tonight. We want the two of ye to have a special night for yerselves."

John returned to the dining room with a bottle of champagne and two glasses. He folded a white towel over his arm and pretended to be a waiter in a fancy restaurant.

Marie cleared the rest of the glasses and removed the two chairs they had occupied.

John set the two glasses on the table and opened the champagne bottle with a pop. The foam spewed out a bit. He quickly grabbed a glass and filled it.

He handed it to Bree. "For ye, madam."

She took it and smiled.

He poured another for Colin and handed it to him.

Marie returned with the champagne bucket filled with ice and set it on the table.

She giggled when John bowed with a flourish and set the white towel over the bucket. "*Au revoir*, lovebirds."

They both turned to leave, and Marie glanced over her shoulder. "I don't want to see either of ye until noon. And the twins won't bother ye." The door swung as they passed through it, then settled, letting them know they were alone.

Colin sighed and chugged half his glass.

Bree sipped hers. "It seems we are the victim of some plotting by Marie and John."

Colin tipped his glass, draining the rest, and poured another drink. "They mean well, Bree. They love us as family and are trying to help."

Bree rose and crossed to the fireplace, her glass still in her hand. "I am tired, Colin. Tired of everyone walking on eggshells around me." She sipped her champagne and fumbled with the glass. She dropped it on the rug and gasped. "God, no wonder everyone acts this way. It seems I can't do anything anymore."

Colin rose and approached her, never taking his eyes off her. He took her hands in his and escorted her back to the table. He sat her in her chair and kissed her hands. He went back to the fireplace and picked up the glass. He used the white towel to clean it and poured another glass.

She was right though, and everyone had treated her

like she would break at any moment. He was the guiltiest, but she needed care, the time to heal. But maybe now was the time to face what bothered her.

He handed it to Bree and kneeled in front of her. "Bree, ye can do so much. Ye have done so much. There is so much more to yer life."

He took his glass and raised it for a toast. "I propose we start new tonight. Here we are. It's our dinner. Like our first one, but a new one." He clinked their glasses together and waited for her, hoping she'd take the cue.

Bree sighed. "To a new start." Then took a sip.

Colin sipped his glass again and smirked. "I will tell all in the castle to stop treating ye like an eggshell. How about a hard-boiled egg?"

Bree smiled and relaxed in her chair.

Colin sat at her feet, leaning against her leg. They both stared into the fire, silent in their thoughts. Colin desperately wished Bree would come around to dealing with their intimacy. She had tried several times, and each ended in her jolting from memory and then closing in on herself. He'd never pushed or instigated any physical act. However, he had insisted that he sleep holding her. He would permit no one to come between him and his wife. She only needed time, and Colin could wait forever. He had been to purgatory and back for her. He could do this, even if it drove him to insanity. She was his wee Bree, and he would move heaven and earth for her.

****

Bree sat in the chair, staring at the flames. She wanted so desperately to have a new start. The efforts at resuming their intimacy had not gone well. Tony haunted her at each attempt. Colin was so understanding with her she figured he had the patience of Job. God, she only wanted her husband, Colin, her burly Scotsman, to take her, hold her, and love her. Like when they first met.

Colin emptied his glass and rose to refill it.

She stopped him with her hand. "Colin, please hold me. Hold me as you used to."

He took her glass and set it on the table next to his. He pulled her to stand and sat in the chair, taking her in his lap and wrapping his arms around her.

He kissed her temple and whispered, "Bree, I have always held ye the same way. With all the love in my heart."

Bree sat up, stared into his eyes, and saw his love for her. She wanted to return his affections so badly and make this right as husband and wife. She closed her eyes and kissed him. A vision of Tony leering into her face flashed through her mind, and she jolted in her seat.

Colin held her tighter. "I have ye. I won't ever hurt ye, Bree."

Gazing into his eyes, she saw his love. She bent to his face, and when she kissed him, she kept her eyes open. If she saw him, maybe the visions wouldn't come. *This is Colin, my husband, and I love him.*

Colin held her but didn't move. As they kissed, her hand slid up his arm and into his hair, jet black, not brown. He deepened the kiss, and she moaned. The same hand trailed down his neck to his shirt, and she slipped it inside and rubbed the hairs on his chest, thicker than Tony's.

Colin tightened his hold on her. She flinched, and

299

his eyes snapped open, meeting her stare. His eyebrows creased, and he loosened his embrace.

She moved to kiss him, timid at first, with her eyes open. Her tongue danced with his, and she felt him against her hip. He shifted her away, but sitting in his lap made that difficult. Bree stood and straddled him, kissing him again. He slid down in the chair, and she rubbed herself against him. He opened his eyes as she continued to kiss him as they stared at each other. She sat up and rocked against him, watching him the entire time. *This is Colin. This is my husband, and I love him.*

He slid his hands up her front and cupped both breasts. She looked at his hands on her. This was him touching her, not anyone else, and she loved it. She glanced at his face, curious to see if he enjoyed this as she did.

He kept his eyes on her face as if he gauged her reaction and wouldn't proceed without her approval. His care and concern made her fall in love with him all over again. She wanted to show him how much that meant, and she desired to share herself with him.

She unbuttoned his shirt one button at a time, watching the entire time. He cupped her face as she spread open his shirt and ran her hands over his chest. She bent down and kissed him full on the mouth. Colin growled like he always did, then stopped. Was he worried he'd ruin the moment for her?

She stopped and gazed into his eyes. "Please, Colin, take me to bed and make love to me."

Colin caressed her face. "I would love to make love to my wife. I love ye, Bree. I wish to show ye how much." Colin gathered her in his arms and rose, carrying her out of the dining room. She watched him the entire time. He tried to keep eye contact with her but had to navigate the way. When he staggered at the top of the stairs, Bree giggled. When he almost banged her head against the door frame, she laughed out loud.

Colin groaned. "I used to be better at this. I'm getting old." When he got to the bed, he lowered her, and they stood beside it. They stayed there a moment next to the bed in the firelight.

She slowly removed his shirt and rubbed her hands on his chest hair. She watched her hands as they molded to his body. She undid his pants and slowly lowered them with her hands. His boxers were still on, and she took those off as well. Colin kicked his clothes aside and stood waiting. She rubbed her hands on his firm abdomen, then went around to his muscular rear, and squeezed it fully. She glanced down as her right hand came to the front and gripped him.

He tilted his head back and groaned.

She watched her hands on his body the whole time. She pumped him, and he gripped her to his chest. She jumped at the sudden contact, and he loosened his hold.

"Bree, ye are killing me. I want to love my wife. C-can I take yer clothes off?"

She stared into his eyes and nodded. He slipped her shirt over her head. She lost sight of him momentarily, but his eyes gazed into hers when the shirt was gone. He undid her bra, and she slowly lowered it down her arms, watching it slip from her hands. She watched his hands as they cupped each breast softly. She rested her hands on his hips, and he slowly lowered his mouth to her breast and suckled it lightly. She moaned, and he looked up to see her watching him, seeming to catch on to what she needed to know. This was him doing these things to her.

He kept eye contact as he licked the other nipple. She clutched his hips. He dragged his tongue up the middle of her chest to kiss her full on the mouth, never taking his eyes off hers. His hands dropped to her pants, and he undid them. She grabbed the sides and dropped her pants, underwear and all.

Colin smiled into the kiss. He backed her to the bed, and her knees hit the mattress. She slowly climbed onto the bed and sat on her knees while she kissed him. He laved her nipples, one and then the other. She watched him the entire time. Colin climbed into the bed and lay on his back. Bree grinned and slid over him. He rubbed their bodies together, never breaking eye contact with her. She rose and slid him into her.

"Bree, I love ye. I love ye with all my heart."

Bree cupped his face. "Colin, I love you too." She slid the rest of the way, fully seating herself on him. Colin growled fully, and Bree moaned, for this was her husband, and making love to him was like no other in the world. She rode him slowly, watching him the entire time. He watched their bodies as his gaze rose to her face. She rode him a little faster, and it hit her so quickly. She threw her head back and moaned loudly. She collapsed on his chest, panting.

She kissed his ear and nibbled it lightly. "Colin?"

He moved, and they remained connected, and he was still hard. "Aye, Bree?"

She giggled. "Can you make me soar like you used to? I'd like you to take your wife, hard like you like to."

Colin took her shoulders and lifted her, so their faces were close. "Bree, are ye sure?"

She rolled to his side, dragging him on top, and

grabbed his rear end. "Colin, I swear if you do not make me scream, I will be a very disappointed wife."

Colin shifted and slid deeper inside of her.

She kissed him hard and spoke. "I am not an eggshell, Colin. I will not break."

Colin started slowly, and she knew he meant to go easy on her, but she was not having it. She grabbed his rear, pulling, begging for a faster tempo, and Colin quickly complied. She kept her eyes on him as he made mad, passionate love to her. Shortly he roared his release as she screamed in ecstasy, staring into her husband's eyes with love.

Afterward, naked in the firelight, Colin kissed each spot left marring her body. While most of the bruises had faded, he lavished love upon her and worshipped her body. He held her long into the night, caressing her face and arm. She would moan at each one, delighting that her husband still loved and cherished her.

He whispered as he held her, "I'll chase yer fears away, my wee Bree, always." He kissed her on the lips. "Brielle, no matter where we go, no matter if something separates us, ye will always and forever be my true love."

Colin hugged her, and she stirred in his arms, whispering, "Never fear that we will not come back together."

Epilogue

Twelfth century, Rannick's village settlement

The entire village, along with more guests from Dunollie castle, crowded the clearing beside Loch Etive. Viking weddings always took place on a Friday also known as Frigga's day, a day sacred to Frigg, the goddess of marriage, love, and fertility, and waiting for the day was the longest thing Ainslie had likely ever done. Fiona and Astrid threw themselves into full planning mode to host the first wedding to occur at Dunstaffnage, and they left no detail out.

But the day finally arrived and Dougal, the Lord of Lorne and Lord of the Isles, held Ainslie's hand on his arm. "I am proud of ye and this moment. Ye are the perfect choice for my best warrior."

Ainslie teared up. With Dougal giving her away, it seemed like her da stood there. Nearly an impossible dream that had come true.

"Thank ye, Dougal. It means so much to have ye here for me."

Earlier Astrid and Fiona oversaw the bathing ritual for the bride which included the cleansing of the body and soul to prepare Ainslie for Rannick. Ainslie fingered the fine lace of the over bodice as she recalled the special moment.

Fiona pulled out the finest lace overtunic Ainslie

had seen. "A gift from me to ye. I had it made for my future daughter but couldn't wait that long."

Ainslie gasped at the fine workmanship of the cream lace. "Fiona, I can't. Ye will have a daughter, I promise."

Fiona waved and her hand landed on her stomach. "Well, that may be, but as ye say, the son is the first and he's already on the way. Ye did say the boy was first?"

Ainslie nodded.

Astrid clapped. "I knew it!" She threw her arms around her longtime friend. "I am so happy for ye and Dougal."

She released Fiona and picked up a wooden box. "Now that we style yer hair, it's time for my gift."

Ainslie sat beside the brazier in Fiona's large tent wearing a day dress, her beautiful cream wedding attire spread out before her. An undertunic of cream silk, leggings to match, and now with Fiona's added lace overtunic, she felt like a queen.

A maid set to braiding her hair as she weaved glass beads and pearls through the dark tresses.

Astrid approached her and handed her the box. "Fiona and I had it made for ye."

Ainslie opened the box and inside was the most exquisite crown. Silver weaved together in an intricate pattern resembling branches, like the willows used for their ceremonial archway. Pearls and clear glass beads winked from the crown. But the most astounding feature was the teardrop pearl the size of her thumb pad.

Astrid took the crown out and placed it on Ainslie's head, shifting it till it fit where the pearl hung over her forehead. "This, my dear daughter, is a combination from Fiona's crown and mine. A symbol of the blending of our families and something ye will keep for yer own daughters' ceremony."

Ainslie blinked back tears and she adjusted the crown to ensure as she paraded before the people of the village, she would look her finest.

Later that day, Rannick stepped up to the archway made of willows decorated with wildflowers. The crowd went silent and turned to Ainslie and Dougal.

As she strolled with Dougal, her eyes were only for Rannick. He wore a tunic of similar fabric, but the design held a lion rampant embroidered in the front decorated with clear glass beads. His beard was trimmed short, his hair pulled back, and his expression appeared full of love. She loved this man and as they neared him, her heart fluttered.

Dougal stood there a moment before he gave away Ainslie. "Ye will treat her as my own daughter. I consider her as such."

Dougal passed her hand into Rannick's, and his thumb caressed the top softly. "I will honor her as my wife and love her into the afterworld."

Dougal stepped behind them and announced for all, "I pledge the wedding of these two souls. May they find love and happiness. May Frigga bless them with many bairns!" He bent to Rannick and Ainslie as he whispered, "Aye, many bairns. I'd like some grandbabies from my daughter!"

The crowd erupted in roars and cheers at their king's announcement.

Ainslie blushed deeply as Rannick replied, "Aye, my king. Already at work on that!"

Dougal huffed a laugh, and as he stood, all went

silent.

Ainslie turned to Rannick, ready to exchange their wedding vows. Rannick wrote them special for this ceremony, saying he needed it to keep his promise to her, to treat her as his equal. She'd memorized them and spoke them from her heart.

Beloved, I seek to know you.

I ask the gods and goddesses that I have the wisdom to see you as you are.

I will take joy in you and delight in your love.

You are to me the whispering of the tides, and the seduction of summer's heat.

You are my friend, my husband, my lover, my warrior and my equal.

Grow old and wise with me, as I will with you.

We have a life before us of rainbows and sunsets, with a willingness to share happiness and sadness.

Be mine forever.

She teared up and huffed at the end. *Be mine forever* meant so much to her.

Rannick squeezed her hands, and she blinked her tears away.

He took a breath and gave his vows in his rich clear voice. She teared up again, knowing what he said came from his heart as he repeated the vows.

In true Viking tradition, Ainslie and Rannick exchanged swords, symbolizing the blending of the families.

Astrid handed Rannick's sword to Ainslie, who easily took the large heavy blade with both hands and bowed as she gave it to him.

He took it from the handle and held it above his head as the crowd cheered. As he passed it to Gunnar, he smiled.

It became Rannick's turn to gift her with a sword, and Rannick was rather secretive with the present. She suspected he'd have something fashioned for her and hoped it was something she could fight well with.

Gunnar passed Rannick the sword, covered in fine burgundy cloth.

He held it between them in both hands and spoke so all could hear. "Ainslie, cousin to Dougal MacDougall, Lord of Lorne, Lord of the Isles, now his adopted daughter, it brings me great joy to gift ye with a special sword fashioned only for ye."

Gunnar reached over and removed the fabric. It slipped away with a wisp, and Rannick held the most beautiful sword Ainslie ever saw. Detailed etchings covered the blade and handle.

Rannick bent close and whispered to her only, "One side has blessings etched in runes calling for the goddess Frejya to gift ye with her strength and might while fighting."

He turned the sword and revealed the other side. Etching also covered this side. "This side has runes calling the goddess Idunn, for the special children ye care so much for."

He kneeled, offered her the sword with raised arms, and spoke loud enough for all to hear, "I offer ye yer new weapon, my warrior queen. Goddess of War and the woman for all the children." He glanced up. "My equal in life."

She took the sword by the handle and held it above her head as Rannick had and the crowd cheered.

Rannick stood and raised his sword, so the blades crossed, signaling the blend in families and conclusion of the wedding ceremony.

Ainslie couldn't have dreamed of a better wedding in her life. A Viking ceremony with the man she loved. The only thing missing was her family from the future, but in her dreams, they were there. She took heart that one day they would reunite. She, Rannick, Colin, and Bree would be a family, together.

Rannick lowered his sword, and she followed suit. "Ainslie, my warrior woman, kiss yer Viking husband." He took her in his arms and kissed her deeply as the crowd cheered again. This was right, the Viking life, and she planned to live it!

Dougal clapped and his voice boomed over everyone as they finished their kiss, "Now on to my favorite part! The *bruðhlaup*."

Fiona and Astrid warned Ainslie about this tradition, bride running, a ritual that involved a foot race. Once the ceremony ended, the bride's and groom's families would race to the mead hall. The family that lost must serve drinks for the rest of the wedding celebration to the family who got there first.

Rannick caught her eye and winked as he bent ready to take off at a run. "Ready, wife? I'd hate to have to serve Dougal all night on my wedding night. I plan to win!"

Ainslie tucked her sword under her arm and bent with him. "Ye win? Doubtful, husband. It shall be ye who must serve me all night, for I plan to win."

Dougal took off at a run and called over his shoulder. "Go!"

****

Present day, six years later, Miami, Florida. The Museum of Science

"Now that you are done with the Scottish exhibit, we need to unload the Egyptian one."

Both workers hefted a large create.

Bob lifted his end and called to George, "Damn, this one's heavy." As they moved it into the area, George's hand slipped and his end crashed to the floor. The edge broke open.

"George, watch it! These are priceless. The curator will have our heads if you break it."

Bob rested his end but lifted when George picked up his. "Let's face it to the wall. Maybe no one will notice and when they break them open, it won't matter, anyway."

They turned it to the wall. The Eye of Ra peeked from inside the opened crack. The center swirled and light broke through the crack in the crate.

George jumped back as Bob froze. The bright white light flashed, then disappeared. George leaned and peeked into the crack, not believing what he had witnessed.

Bob stared, frozen.

George glanced at Bob. "I saw nothing. Did you?"

Bob slowly shook his head.

George moved the open end to the wall, and both men turned away to bring in the next item.

Neither spoke of the incident again.

A word about the author...

Margaret Izard is an award-winning author of historical fantasy and paranormal romance novels. She spent her early years through college to adulthood dedicated to dance, theater, and performing. Over the years, she developed a love for great storytelling in different mediums. She does not waste a good story, be it movement, the spoken, or the written word. She discovered historical romance novels in middle school, which combined her passion for romance, drama, and fantasy. She writes exciting plot lines, steamy love scenes and always falls for a strong male with a soft heart. She lives in Houston, Texas, with her husband and adult triplets and loves to hear from readers.

You can email me at info@margaretizardauthor.com

www.margaretizardauthor.com

Thank you for purchasing
this publication of The Wild Rose Press, Inc.

For questions or more information
contact us at
info@thewildrosepress.com.

The Wild Rose Press, Inc.
www.thewildrosepress.com